SPEED WEEK
■ ■ ■

SPEED
WEEK

S. V. DATE

G. P. PUTNAM'S SONS
NEW YORK

G. P. Putnam's Sons
Publishers Since 1838
a member of
Penguin Putnam Inc.
375 Hudson Street
New York, NY 10014

Library of Congress Cataloging-in-Publication Data
Date, S. V. (Shirish V.)
Speed week / by S. V. Date.
p.   cm.
ISBN 0-399-14513-3
I. Title.
PS3554.A8237S64   1999   98-50629 CIP
813'.54 — dc21

Printed in the United States of America

1   3   5   7   9   10   8   6   4   2

This book is printed on acid-free paper. ∞

Book design by Ellen Cipriano

For Mary Beth

Many thanks to Craig Quintana for a critical eye,

■

Daniel Zitin for encouraging words,

■

Neil Nyren for his confidence,

■

Edee Dalke for insights into a bizarre world,

■

and as always, Mary Beth for her boundless enthusiasm.

SPEED WEEK

###

ONE

■ ■ ■

Circuit Court Judge Anthony Antoon, Civil Part, Volusia County, Florida, pushed his bifocals toward the end of a long thin nose, carefully pulled open the Ziploc bag on his desk and gingerly withdrew Plaintiff's Exhibit F from its bubble wrapping. Slowly he raised it toward the recessed lights high above in the vaulted ceiling.

With a wrinkled, liver-spotted hand, he spun it around twice clockwise, then stopped, turned it the other way. Still with the one hand, he flipped it end for end and spun it around once more.

"What in hell is this?" he growled finally.

Nolin and the other lawyers behind the railing in the brand new, faux nineteenth-century courtroom slunk even lower and buried themselves in suddenly fascinating legal briefs. No one dared a smile, let alone a laugh. Judge Antoon held a powerful sense of decorum about Judge Antoon's courtroom. Judge Antoon also held a grudge.

The lawyers on the other side of the rail weren't so fortunate. They looked at each other helplessly. Finally, the plaintiff's attorney cleared his throat. It was, there was no getting around it, his exhibit.

"An egg, Your Honor."

A couple of snickers erupted from the rear of the gallery. Antoon extinguished them with a death glare.

"Counselor, Justice may be blind, but I'm not. Why is it in my court-room?"

Nolin bit his tongue, bit hard, until he tasted blood. His case was next, his client an irredeemable weasel, but a rich irredeemable weasel. One he couldn't afford to lose. And Antoon was still mad at him from a case a month ago. If his stony mask crumbled, he was finished.

"Well, sir," the plaintiff's lawyer began again. "It's one of 1,559 eggs found this morning at thirty-six sites between the Seabreeze Boulevard and Raceway Avenue access ramps in Daytona Beach. That's the portion of the beach we maintain has suffered the most adverse impact from beach driving, sir. Where the traffic volume and the associated pollu-tants, motor oil, antifreeze—"

"I've heard it before, counselor," Antoon intoned heavily. "Automobile traffic on the sandy beach has curtailed the nesting of green, hawksbill and leatherback sea turtles on Volusia County's shore, blah, blah, blah, in contravention to the federal Endangered Species Act, yaddah, yaddah. Such is your client's position. So how do you explain thirty-six nests in the most heavily driven strip of beach?"

"I apologize, Your Honor. I was returning to the coincidence of thirty-six so-called nests, where none has been found for the last dozen years, appearing just in time for today's hearing."

"Vile subterfuge. So you allege." Antoon lifted the egg toward the light again. "And how do you know that thirty-six actual turtles didn't crawl up the sand last night and lay them?"

"They couldn't have, Your Honor. What you have in your hand is a *chicken* egg. Actual turtle eggs are smaller, like Ping-Pong balls, and have a leathery shell. In addition, sir, whoever planted the eggs didn't know that turtles drag themselves along the sand and leave a long trench. These nests all had prints leading to and from the water, sir. My biologist exam-ined them and determined they came from the front paws of a five- to six-foot male alligator."

Antoon's brow visibly darkened, a gathering storm. "They brought an alligator to the beach?"

"No, Your Honor. Just its paws. Just its front paws."

Nolin looked up. This was a new one, even by Daytona standards. He allowed himself a smile.

"It appears that the perpetrators of this hoax didn't do their homework, sir," the plaintiff's lawyer said, more confident now. "I guess they figured eggs were eggs."

Antoon stared down the plaintiff's lawyer until he had stopped beaming and dropped his eyes to the floor. "I find no humor in perpetrating a hoax on this court, counselor. Do you?"

"No, Your Honor." The plaintiff's lawyer retreated to the safety of his table where he shuffled some papers.

Antoon turned toward the defendant's table. "And I assume Volusia County has no knowledge of any of this? That the county attorney, working *hand in glove* with the Hotel-Motel Association, the Tourism Board, the Chamber of Commerce and Daytona Raceway, has no *earthly* idea how a thousand chicken eggs showed up on the beach?"

Nolin heard a muffled gasp behind him, saw a pale, bearded man in dark glasses slouch into the collar of a plaid sportcoat. He turned back to watch the county attorney shift his weight from one foot to the other.

"For the record, Your Honor, it's more like sixteen hundred eggs," the plaintiff's lawyer offered helpfully before catching Antoon's glare again.

Within a few seconds, though, Antoon's eyes had returned to the defense table. The county attorney could stall no longer. "Your Honor makes an excellent point," he began cautiously in a thick, north Florida drawl. A purposeful effort to subvert the will of this court would indeed be a terrible and dishonorable thing. Something that my office, indeed, the entire county would condemn in the strongest possible terms. But might I suggest, Your Honor, that there is a perfectly plausible explanation for the, ah, seemingly implausible situation with the eggs. To wit, sir, upon information and belief, there may have been, and in an abundance of caution, I want to emphasize 'may have been.' We're still working to confirm this: There *may have been* a group of poultry farmers traveling from a convention in Fort Lauderdale back to their homes in

Georgia, and at least some of the hens *may have escaped* and, confronted with unfamiliar . . ."

This time Nolin bit his lip, but couldn't keep his stomach muscles from convulsing. On the bench, Antoon hadn't blinked, but his tongue started moving inside his mouth, as if trying to escape a foul taste.

The county attorney glanced up, recognized the look and scrambled for an escape. "But of course, Your Honor doesn't want to deal in conjecture, but in hard, cold facts. Let me assure you that my office and I will work hand in glove with the Beach Patrol, with plaintiff's counsel and Save Our Turtles, and with any and all appropriate authorities to make certain that something like this never—"

"Counselor."

"Yes, Your Honor."

"Shut up."

"Of course, Your Honor."

Nolin wiped the smirk away and sat up straight. His case, he reminded himself, was next.

"We've already wasted more time on this . . . chickenshit than we should have." Antoon leaned over the desk toward his stenographer. "Strike 'chickenshit' from the record, would you, Sandy dear?"

Sandy nodded, tapped at her keypad.

"The next time I see you two, you *will* be prepared to pick a jury and proceed. I've blocked out two days for this trial. It won't go a minute longer. Is that clear?"

Both tables nodded enthusiastically.

"Good. Now, as to the chicken and egg question." Antoon chuckled to himself. The lawyers looked at each other, nervously began grins.

"The matter will be noted in the record without prejudice to either side. But let me add here for the county attorney's benefit: Yes, it's true I've grown up right here in Daytona Beach. I've raced hot rods on this beach. I've screwed girls in the backseat of my car on this beach. I happen to like driving on the beach. But if someone fucks with my court again, I'll rule this beach a state conservation area and clear all cars *and* all humans, and that includes tourists foolish enough to come here instead of a decent beach, from every inch of shoreline between Cape Canaveral and the Flagler line. I hope I make myself clear."

He banged his gavel on his desk, then leaned over it again. "Sandy, strike 'screw' and 'fuck' from the record, if you would, please. Next case."

Both tables hurriedly packed up their papers as the bailiff called out "Emerson versus Emerson." Nolin stood, heard the courtroom door slam shut behind him. He glanced back, noticed idly that the man in the plaid jacket was gone.

The diver kicked his feet slowly, giving a slight boost to the propulsion pack he held before him. As usual the visibility was lousy, about twenty feet, tops, and he suppressed a wave of panic that he'd missed it.

Steady, steady; anxiety sped up the heart. That would increase respiration and therefore cut bottom time. He looked over the compass on the console and kept kicking. He'd measured it all out: With the pack on low speed and a slow kick, he moved at three knots. He'd entered the water exactly one nautical mile away, so it would take him twenty minutes. He had been swimming for eighteen. Unless there was a cross-current . . .

He forced himself to count breaths. Long, slow inhale. Long, slow exhale until, there: Dead ahead, out of the gloom, he saw it. He flicked off the propulsion pack and released it. Because he had balanced it that morning for a fifteen-foot depth, it stayed right where he left it, neutrally buoyant.

He glided over the slimy box, sliding his fingers over the rubber seam between sides and lid. Perfect: no leaks. He swam around to the shoreward side and gently untwisted the plastic tie he'd used to hold the coils of wire together overnight. It was gossamer thin, and he had worried it would break if subjected that long to waves and tide. Breaking wasn't an option. It had to work perfectly. Hence the long, risky underwater swim to set it.

From the pocket of his buoyancy compensator he pulled a small,

Styrofoam ball and gently pushed two feet of wire through its center. Where it emerged, he twisted the tip into a loose knot until he was satisfied it wouldn't pull back through. Then he let the ball drift upward, pulling out loops of wire as it went, until finally it was within a foot of the surface. It undulated with the waves, but never broke through. The wire itself would be invisible from shore. He had tested that himself, using high-powered binoculars.

Satisfied with the placement, he retied the remaining coils of wire, checked dive watch and pressure gauge. Twenty-six minutes and more than half a tank remaining. Right on the money. He patted the box once and swam over to the propulsion pack. He flicked it on, checked his heading and began kicking.

All that was left was to stow his gear on the bottom, swim back to shore, change and then hang around the beach for a few hours. That would be distasteful, what with the cars and the music and the butt-thong-clad groupies and the crowd . . .

Still it would be worth it, in the end. He noticed a shadow, turned to see a pair of blacktips swimming in formation. Mouths slightly agape, tails swishing silently through the water. Simple perfection. With luck they'd be around in a few hours. The more the merrier.

Sweat beaded Madame Rosa Castilla Murdo as she hunched over her glass ball, peering intently through at the black "antiqued" table beneath. Once again the air conditioning was on the fritz, and, though only February, the fans were no match for the heat.

"Maybe you should take off your shawl, Rosa," Barbie offered.

Rosa looked up with a glare before letting loose a Spanish-tinged tirade. "Meesez Van Horne, thees is how my mother taught me, and her mother before her taught her. Thees is how we do it in Andalusia. Maybe you like somebody else? Maybe someone with the incense and the music and the leetle crystals? Maybe you like that?"

Barbie sighed. Rosa had long ago copped an attitude about the New Age psychics at Cassadaga. Dilettantes, they were. Unschooled. Ill-mannered. Crooks. "No, Rosa, of course not. It's just that, well, it's hot."

She pulled at her green tank top. "Even I'm hot, and I'm only wearing this."

Rosa leaned back. A woolen shawl covered jet-black hair. Another draped over her shoulders. Beneath it she wore a long, sequined red gown. From Sevilla, she had told her. Like all her clothes.

"Pardon me for saying, but where I come from, Meesez Van Horne, ladies do not go out in public wearing"—she waved a long, red-nailed finger at Barbie's chest—"that. It is indecent. But, your ways are deef-erent. So. Tell me again your troubles. Today, I have the deeficulty see-ing into your eyes."

Barbie studied Rosa's eyes. They were a bright blue, all the more stunning because of the dark skin and black, black hair. She looked around at the dingy walls, decorated with the trappings of classical Spain, or at least the sort of kitschy Spain that sold for inflated prices at Epcot. Scarves, castanets, a matador's cloak, a bullfighter's killing sword.

Someday she'd travel to Spain, travel the back roads, visit the quaint fishing villages, climb the rugged Pyrenees. Someday. Someday when she had her act together, figured out who she was, where she was going and how she was getting there. Yet thoughts of the indeterminate future invariably brought up the recent past, replete with foolish choices and wasted time. How many years had she lost? Four? Five? Six, depending on how you counted? And for what: to change him? Make him grow up?

Against her better instincts, she wished again now as she frequently did that she'd taken the money and run. She had, after all, earned every penny. He'd been a jerk, but a rich jerk, and she could have taken what she needed and left him with enough that he'd never have thought to complain.

Instead she'd sworn to make it on her own. To prove to him, to *all* of them, what she was made of. Well, here she was: on the edge of depres-sion, with nothing left but an unpopular, costly crusade that she could no longer afford but didn't have the heart to abandon. Even her morn-ing in court, her best shot at victory, her lawyer had promised, had with-ered to nothing when the judge decided the other side would not be punished.

"Tell me about the turtles again, Rosa," she asked finally.

"Ah, *las tortugas, sí.*" Rosa leaned back suddenly in her straight-backed chair, her extra chins shuddering from the jolt. Her eyes fell closed. "It is as I told you, Meesez Van Horne. You, and the turtles, you are *familia.* Many years ago, in many previous memories, you swim in the deep, blue sea. And every other spring, you climb up on the beach and lay your babies in the sand, and crawl back to Mother Ocean. Thees is you, Meesez Van Horne. Thees is your soul. As free and wonderful as the mother turtle. And also as full of love and duty. Why, Meesez Van Horne? Why do you ask Rosa?"

Barbie sighed again. "Because, Rosa. I tried to help them. But it wasn't enough."

"You help them plenty, Meesez Van Horne," Rosa said quickly, wondering what the hell Barbie was talking about. "You help them plenty. And they know, and they love you."

"But it's not going to be enough, is it? And now that they really need my help, I'm going to have to give up." Barbie lay her long, bony hands on the table. "So tell me, Rosa. What happens to them? And what happens to me?"

Rosa swallowed softly, cupped her hands over the crystal ball and closed her eyes. "I see hardship, Meesez Van Horne. Much hardship and much sorrow. But, in the end, I see much joy. And in the end, you will prevail."

Barbie looked at Rosa hopefully. "So I'll find another lawyer?"

"Another lawyer?" Rosa blinked slowly, then stared straight into Barbie's pale green eyes for a long minute. "*Sí!* A *very* good lawyer. He will be everything you need."

J. Robert "Nick" Van Horne III leaned back against the wall, hands thrust in his trouser pockets, chin on chest. It was his usual pose of excruciating boredom as he waited for Joanna's attention to fall, eventually, finally, his way.

"J.R., does this midnight blue work?" She held a slinky, full-length evening gown against a no-longer-slinky figure. "Or is this better?"

It was a curse, being born a Van Horne. The richest family in stock car racing, the apex of the Daytona Beach social pyramid, yet still snubbed by the old money in Long Island, Charleston, even Palm Beach. Sure, they owned cottages in all three places. But they couldn't make the "A" list. Not even, frankly, the "B" list, and it made his stepmother crazy.

He smiled to himself, remembering the previous summer when Joanna had decided to crash the Worthingtons' ball in East Hampton. Because it was a charity affair, no one had thrown them out. But no one had talked to them either. He had cheered inwardly when they finally left after an hour of standing by themselves next to a Greek statue.

She had replaced the blue gown with a shorter, strapless black dress. She turned her back to Nick and alternated dresses before the three-part ceiling-to-floor mirror. "Black gets so tiresome. Don't you think? Perhaps I have time for a quickie down to Palm Beach. Oh, I do get tired of living in a town without a Lord and Taylor's."

Nick groaned. It had become her favorite complaint: the trials of holding a formal in a town so gauche that men actually wore rented tuxedos. He had come to dread talking to her. A lecture or a scolding—it was always one or the other, and that only after a prolonged recounting of her latest tribulation. He wondered again what it might've been like to have been born a normal guy with a normal job—timeshare salesman, or maybe a strip-joint manager. He'd have done great at either, he knew. And then he remembered the little Lotus coupe in the garage and the way the expensive, high-class debs fawned over him. Being the grandson of James Van Horne, née Jim Bob Horn, he had to admit, did have its advantages.

"You haven't heard a word I've said, have you?" he whined finally.

She kept her attention on the mirrors. "Of course I have, dear. The judge was very upset about the chicken eggs. Explain again, dear, why you used them? I'm still having a little trouble with that."

He swallowed hard. It was a subject he'd hoped to avoid. He decided to go on the offensive. "Chrissakes, Joanna, how the hell were we supposed to know? I mean, did you know turtle eggs don't look like chicken eggs? Gimme a break!" He spoke to the back of her neck. "What were we supposed to do? You said make turtle nests. You didn't tell us where to get turtle eggs."

"Do you read at all? Ever? It's in the paper just about every day. There are thousands of sea-turtle nests south of the Brevard County line, thousands of sea-turtle nests north of the Flagler line. That's why your slut wife is suing *our* county, remember?" Joanna peeled the straps of her sundress off her shoulders and pushed the black gown up to her chest, draping strands of bleached blond hair down over the fabric. "Now. If there were thousands of sea-turtle eggs a few miles north, thousands more a few miles south, explain why it seemed a good idea to use chicken eggs. Is my hair too light for this dress?"

"You didn't tell me any of that yesterday," Nick complained. He continued addressing the back of her head. "The judge knows we did it, Joanna! He's gonna rule against us!"

She hung both gowns on the rack, smoothed the yellow sundress and walked to the edge of her bed. The pink sheets crinkled as she sat down and crossed her legs, pointing a perfectly pedicured big toe at her stepson.

"How many times, Robert, have I told you never to call me Joanna?"

Nick groaned. "Come on, Joanna, I feel stupid calling you Mom. You're younger than me."

She nodded. "A technicality. It's also a technicality that I control your father's trust fund, and the foundation, and the business. So, technically, if I wanted you to call me the Queen of Sheba, it technically would be in your interest to do so." She smiled brightly. "Don't you agree?"

Nick dropped his head and sighed. "Yes . . . Mom."

Joanna wagged her bare foot, admiring the bright red nail polish. "So explain. Tell me *why* you picked chicken eggs, although I suppose I should count my blessings you didn't use ostrich eggs or robin eggs or Egg McMuffins. After all, I didn't tell you not to use any of those, either."

More than anything, he loathed the smug sarcasm. "Me and the Ramseys got way behind schedule when that turtle bit off Tony's little finger."

Joanna didn't even flinch. "Of course. What turtle would that be?"

"We needed to make tracks. You know, from the nests down to the water? So we needed a turtle. So Tony and Toby and me drove up to

Reptile Kingdom in Saint Augustine." Nick lowered his eyes. "I *told* them not to take a snapper. Anyway, by the time we got out of the emergency room, it was almost light. It was too late to find a turtle, so we figured we could make do with gator tracks, seeing as how we already had those gator-claw back scratchers in the office."

Joanna continued wagging her foot. "Of course. Gator back scratchers."

"*You* remember," he sniffed. "The Chamber sent them out as publicity for Crother's airboat rides?"

Joanna cocked her head forty-five degrees, as if a fresh angle might clarify everything. "And you made alligator tracks leading to sea-turtle nests because . . ."

"*Jeez*, Joanna, how the hell were we supposed to know they'd have such different feet? The Ramseys saw this sign at Reptile Kingdom that said gators and turtles were cousins." Nick pouted. "Sure, it's easy to criticize now, in hindsight. *You* weren't there . . ."

"We keep coming back to the Ramseys. The Ramseys this. The Ramseys that. Perhaps you've forgotten? The Ramseys are half-wits? We employ them to stack heavy things on top of other heavy things? And even *then* they need close direction? Yet now they're reptile experts?" She sighed, shook her head sadly. "Go on."

"So they figured out they weren't real turtle nests when some kids got into an egg fight this morning. Some smart-ass tourist looked at one and called the lifeguard. The lifeguard called the Beach Patrol, the Beach Patrol called Barbie."

Joanna stared icily, and Nick shuddered. For a short, on-the-dumpy-side, middle-aged lady with rounded cheeks, too much makeup and platinum hair, Joanna had a terrible stare. It gave him the willies.

"This isn't what I had in mind."

Nick snorted. "No shit, Jo—"

She lunged forward with an open hand. "You watch your mouth. A gentleman doesn't use that kind of language."

Nick opened his mouth to argue, saw her glare, shut it again. She stood and walked back to continue her inspection of her closet. "Do you have any idea what I had to go through to take us public? Do you know what's involved in lining up state funding for a project this size? We won't see a penny of it if this turtle nonsense continues. John Robert, I've devoted too much time and energy to this to let Barbie screw it up."

Nick swallowed. "Yes, Mom."

"We need to move to the next level, Robert."

"Yes, Mom," he said automatically while wondering: *What next level?*

Joanna slid gown after gown down the rack, stopped at a spaghetti-strapped creation of purple crepe. "We need to stop this lawsuit at the source."

"We already tried the lawyer, Mom. There was nothing there. The bastard pays his taxes, cuts his lawn, doesn't cheat on his wife or beat his dog."

Joanna passed on the purple and flipped more rapidly. "I said at the *source*, Robert."

Nick's eyes brightened. "You mean I can divorce her?"

She turned, aghast. "At the start of the spring season? How would that look? And with the public offering next month. No, I said the *source*."

He looked at her helplessly. "I don't follow . . ."

Joanna picked out a shimmering, semi-sheer, ankle-length gown. "You remember that lunch with the Teasdales, a couple of months ago? It was right after they took Floyd away?"

He thought back to the lunch, a three-hour ordeal with all of Joanna's gossipy friends to leak word about Raceway Enterprises' coming public offering. Their news had been overshadowed by the arrest of Floyd Chappel, of Chappel Chevrolet Buick, for hiring his gardener to kill his wife. A dimmer switch slowly turned inside Nick's head.

"You mean I should . . . kill her?" he whispered.

"Gentlemen don't kill their wives," Joanna said, untying the strap to her sundress and stepping out of it. She lifted the shimmering gown over her head and tugged it downward over various bulges. "Gentlemen have them killed. Quietly."

She turned back to the mirror. "Can you see my underthings through this?" She pulled the fabric tight over her breasts. "I might have to wear it without them."

Amee Mosher sipped her drink and watched the cue ball bounce off the cushion and roll across the table before coming to a stop. Perfect, right in front of her Joe. She put down her drink, picked up the chalk and, though she still had no idea why, rubbed it purposefully onto the end of her cuestick.

She sashayed around to the cue ball, squeezed between the table and the T-shirted tourist who held the other stick. He had pressed himself flat against the wall, but she made sure to brush heavily against him as she passed.

"Excuse me." She smiled, then leaned over the table, unnaturally and unnecessarily lifting one leg to knock the cue ball against the solid blue while simultaneously providing her opponent an opportunity to inspect the strip of swimsuit that ran between her thighs.

The blue fell into the corner pocket and the cue ball came to a stop directly across the table from her Joe: her other favorite position. She wandered around the table, sipped her drink and bent over, leisurely lining up her shot while giving her customer a nice, long view down her cleavage. She jiggled a little to swing in unison, then shot her opponent a smile and the eight ball into the side pocket. Game.

The T-shirted tourist laid down the cuestick and rooted through his Day-Glo orange fanny pack for a five-dollar bill. "You shoot a nice game of pool," he said with a strong midwestern accent.

Amee took the five and stuck it in her own fanny pack, cherry red to match the triangles of Lycra covering her nipples and groin. In the back were just thin red strings. "You shoot a good game yourself, Fred. Maybe you'll come back for another before you head home to Akron?"

"How about right now?" He dug a pudgy hand back into the fanny pack. "I'm goin' to the time trials tomorrow, and the wife wants to do Disney on Wednesday."

Amee smiled broadly, big white teeth gleaming despite the pool hall's dingy fluorescent tubes. "Can't right now, sport. Gotta take a break. But I'll be here all afternoon." She smiled at him again, studied his sunburned features. Oh, what the hell. He'd dropped $25 on her in just over twenty minutes. She stood on tiptoe to kiss him on the cheek.

"You come back to say 'bye before you leave Daytona," she warned as he stumbled through the door. "And bring your wife, next time." She walked through the passageway into the bar, where another rumrunner awaited in a big plastic tumbler.

"Thanks, Rick," she called out as she popped herself onto a stool, leaned forward to take a big slug from the tumbler. It was a Chamber of Commerce giveaway with drawings of large-bosomed women playing beach volleyball on one side and stock cars on the other. The slogan "Daytona Is *My* Beach" ran all the way around it.

"Havin' a good day, Cherry?" Rick had returned from the back room and was clearing empties off the bar.

"Same old, same old," Amee said between gulps of the bubblegum-colored drink. She unzipped her fanny pack, pulled out a fistful of bills and began sorting: two twenties, one ten and three fives. And it was barely noon. She would do even better come evening, when passersby on the Boardwalk could see in through the plate-glass windows and watch her dance around the pool table wearing only a thong, a wisp of a top, an ankle bracelet and a navel ring. She usually took in $100 to $150 a night, more during the prime tourist season of Speed Week, Bike Week and Spring Break, though the college students were notoriously tight with tips.

Her game had actually gotten pretty good, and she could usually polish off a Joe within five minutes. She would always break: Ladies first, she would tell them. Sometimes she would run the table without the customer ever getting a shot. At $5 a game—she was always a player; the rare win by the customer only earned him the right to an immediate rematch—it was pretty easy money. A hell of a lot easier than the street stuff she'd done in her younger years, back when she still called herself "Cherry on Top," back before that November five years earlier when she'd finally hitched her way down from Erie.

Now, at age nineteen, with chest and hips fully filled in, Amee Mosher had hit her prime in a town that fully appreciated her talents. She struck a match from one of the cardboard books at the end of the bar and lit a crumpled cigarette from her fanny pack. "Gimme another, Ricky-Boy," she called.

Rick poured a pink mixture into the blender, splashed in some Bacardi and flipped the switch. "You'd better watch yourself with all that cash," he warned, nodding at the pile of bills on the bar. "People here kill for less."

She nodded and smiled. "I know. Isn't this a great town?"

It was the lunch hour, the most likely time for customers until the true tourist season began, yet not even a single window-shopper roamed the street.

Barbie Baxter laid the library book on the migratory patterns of green and leatherback turtles on the counter, wedged open the front door and moved onto the sidewalk to smile at passersby. With her runway-model legs and exotic bone structure, she was Harmonic Age's best advertisement, and she certainly wasn't bringing in any customers sitting on a stool behind the cash register.

She stood with the model's permanent half-smile, but continued worrying about finances. Without $50,000 to pay her lawyer, he would drop the case just as it was going to trial. Not that she could blame him. His business had suffered already for taking on such an unpopular cause. Daytona was known the world over as the place you could drive on the beach, and here she was trying to get rid of it.

But she was right and she knew it. Ancient species that scientists knew almost nothing about were becoming extinct before her eyes. How many hatchlings had been crushed under the wheels of cars cruising the sand? How many more had been poisoned by motor oil and antifreeze drippings? The county didn't know. Because they were in Joanna Van Horne's pocket, they didn't care, either.

She sighed, wished again she'd cleaned out half the joint account when she'd had the chance. That would have paid the legal fees and then some. But no, she'd had her pride, and had wanted to walk away with no more than she'd brought in.

The decision had cost her dearly. The store that had done so well when New Age was the latest fad now barely held its own. She'd been late a couple of times on the mortgage, and the bank had threatened to call the note, which, if they'd followed through, would have finished her. And all of *that* was before she founded Save Our Turtles and took on the city, the county, the Van Hornes and pretty much everybody else who mattered in northeast Florida.

She sighed again and crossed the sidewalk to lean against the lamp-post. The unseasonably warm February sun was generating a sea breeze off the cool Atlantic four blocks away, and Barbie rubbed her upper arms to smooth away the goose bumps. She'd always been sensitive to the cold, and two decades in Florida had thinned her blood even further. She would have preferred a sweater over the white cotton minidress, and sneakers instead of the white leather sandals, but she didn't sell sweaters and she didn't sell sneakers.

If customers liked what they saw on her, and they almost always did, then she wanted to be sure they could find it on her racks. Today she had chosen a white coral necklace and matching bracelets and earrings to complete the ensemble. With her golden complexion and long brown hair, the effect was, as intended, stunning.

She turned west toward the river and noticed a bohemian couple strolling hand in hand. Both were decked out in the latest salute to the seventies: tie-dyed shirts, neckerchiefs, Birkenstocks. Barbie flashed them her best smile and smoothed out her dress. The long-haired boy grinned back sheepishly, while the short-haired girl dragged him to the window display of amethyst jewelry.

Barbie always put out that month's birthstone in a prominent location, and the display usually brought in more than its share of customers. She was about to ask if she could help them find anything when the girl tugged the boy's hand and started down the street again, telling him they had to hurry or they wouldn't get a good spot for the race. The boy raised his eyebrows and smiled at Barbie—you know how women are!—and let himself be dragged away.

Bewildered, Barbie could only shake her head. Since when did kids who dressed like hippies care about Jet Skis, for God's sake? She watched them as they walked away and noticed the glint of gold around the girl's ankle. She examined her own unadorned feet and wondered whether she should finally give in and start wearing an ankle bracelet. She'd always considered them the mark of wild teenagers and horny divorcees, the sign of a true slut, willing to do just about anything with just about anyone.

Lately, though, she'd noticed them on all kinds of women: lawyers, dental assistants and bank officers as well as the waitresses, hotel managers and salesclerks who had worn them for years. Maybe they were more respectable now. Or maybe they were only respectable in Daytona. Maybe, she sighed, it was time she learned to go along to get along.

She stepped back through the doorway and noticed the crystal wall clock was almost at one, almost time for the races. With no customers in sight, and as much as she hated to, she realized she might as well head down to the beach. She needed to keep current, and in a town that lived and breathed racing, that meant knowing who won and why.

She grabbed her book and keys, flipped the OPEN sign to CLOSED and stepped back outside to lock up.

The radio blasted out "Fun, fun, fun" and Nick snapped his fingers to the beat. Ordinarily he would have switched stations on subject matter alone, but nothing could dampen his day now. Not even the fact that he was driving the hideous green Monte Carlo he hated but had to pretend to love because Chevrolet had given it to him and Chevrolet was a major sponsor. It had bugged him for years. Why the hell couldn't Ferrari be a NASCAR sponsor? Or Aston Martin? James Bond didn't have to drive a Monte Carlo; why the hell did he?

Yet even that chronic complaint was set aside for the moment as he savored his good fortune: He would be free! And no long, drawn-out divorce, no papers, no *alimony*! Just a quick, one-time payment and that was that. Joanna had simply cut him a $50,000 check and told him to take care of it!

He came to a stop and returned the wave from the car beside him. He had no idea who the man was. A banker maybe. Or insurance agent. One of the many smarmy hangers-on who made their living off his inheritance. Someday, it occurred to him, when he was running things, he might have to pay attention to names and faces and the like. He glanced back at the vaguely familiar face and decided: no, he wouldn't. No, he was going to be *so* damn rich that he'd be as rude and inconsiderate as he wanted and people would *still* have to be nice to him.

The light turned green, Nick pushed the accelerator and the Monte Carlo surged forward as Nick held the wheel steady. Big, dumb, American muscle car. Wanted to go anywhere but straight. Ah, the hell with it. When he was boss, he would end the stupid charade and buy himself a Beemer. If GM and Ford didn't like it, well, they could go piss up a tree. They could go find some other car-racing circuit with NASCAR's numbers.

Come to think of it, he might even sell the whole works and live off the proceeds. *That* would be nice: no more pre-dawn Rotary breakfasts, no more interminable Halifax Club lunches, no more mind-numbing trips to Talladega or Bristol or Darlington. Best of all, no more races! Ever! No more obligatory visits to the grimy pits, no more ringing in his ears for hours afterward, no more inane conversations with backwoods drivers.

Nick sighed in anticipation. Patience. All that would have to wait. First things first: find someone to do Barbie. He smiled again at the $50,000 in his pocket, equal to half his yearly allowance. In fact, he'd never had so much money on him in his life. The thought made him dizzy, and without warning the light in his head came on, full and dazzlingly bright: Why did he have to spend it *all* on Barbie? Surely it wouldn't require the entire fifty grand! Whatever was left could go straight into his pocket, and Joanna would never be the wiser. He smiled to himself, wondering how to spend a $25,000 windfall. Or $35,000. Or $45,000.

God, he wished now he'd paid more attention when Floyd Chappel had been arrested for hiring his gardener. How much had Floyd paid? Surely not more than $10,000. And was that all up front? Or half now, half on delivery? What if the guy failed? Was there a refund? And what about weapons? Was that the responsibility of the customer? Or the contractor?

So many questions . . . He wished he could talk to Floyd. Well, maybe he could! Maybe he could run down to the county jail and visit him, ask him about how he'd gone about looking for someone, how he'd settled on his gardener, if he had any advice . . .

In a flash, Nick's smile vanished. Floyd was in *jail*! He had killed his wife, and now he would fry in the electric chair! Christ, what the hell was he thinking? *Visiting* him?

He slowed down, took a deep breath and calmed himself. Lots of guys had their wives killed. It was on the news all the time. Only the dumb ones got caught. He wouldn't be dumb, that's all. And on second thought, he didn't *care* what Floyd did. Floyd got caught. Floyd was dumb. *Floyd* was not a good person to emulate. He would be careful, Nick decided. He would wear his disguise when he met with prospects. He would never use his real name.

Besides. Most guys who had their wives killed didn't have the local police chief in their pocket. The smile returned. Nick turned up the radio and stepped on the gas.

Out on the river a flotilla of sailboats headed south, foresails flying in the afternoon breeze. The lead boat was a classic old yawl with a long, graceful sheer, with a middle-aged woman moving forward to remove the mainsail cover. Long black hair shimmered in the bright sun as she peeled off the blue canvas and walked barefoot back to the cockpit.

Norm sighed and pulled himself from the window. The view only depressed him, and too many briefs lay piled on his desk awaiting his attention. He locked his eyes onto the top page of the top folder, but his mind wandered back to the yawl and her crew. Middle-aged, he'd thought when he saw her. Middle-aged, with long thin legs, a terrific tan and able to wear shorts and a T-shirt every day.

Middle-aged. But then what the hell was he? A year away from forty, never married, no children. In another few years or two or one, he'd be middle-aged, too, and what would he have accomplished? A struggling law practice in a tawdry little town, that's what. A tawdry little town he'd sworn he'd leave as soon as his old man died, when there would be nothing left tying him down. That had been three years ago and, wonder of wonders, here he was still.

He stood and returned back to the big, wood-framed window looking out on the river. There had been a time when the house itself kept his attention. Big and old, with enough space for a two-room office in front and three bedrooms, kitchen and den around and above. He'd loved restoring it, replacing rotten timbers, installing new wiring, painting, staining, polishing. And then it was done, and he'd spent an ever increasing amount of time gazing at his dock that jutted out into the Halifax, with the little Boston Whaler that sat tied to the end.

He'd thought perhaps it was the location that was driving him antsy, and he'd sunk a good year's profits into a ramshackle beach house not far north of the inlet. The energy had returned as he went back to work with hammer and crowbar. He'd come to realize, though, that the only thing that would change was his view. Instead of looking out across the river at the other shore, he would look out across the ocean and think of Africa.

The last of the boats disappeared beyond the bend in the channel and he returned to his chair, once more picking up the brief at the top of the pile and throwing his long legs over the corner of the desk, the only patch remaining uncluttered by paper. Oh, what the hell. He had most of the drywall up and had already bought the tile; he might as well finish. It was grunt work, but he enjoyed it. And he knew he could sell the finished product for at least twice what he'd paid. It really wasn't a bad gig: one house to live in, one to fix up. Meanwhile, the occasional divorce case paid the bills.

Behind him he heard the car pull into the driveway that connected Riverside with 10th. He dropped the file back on top of the pile, waited for the doorbell and rose to answer it.

A soft, doughy face peered through the glass panels beside the door. Short arms rose to adjust a tie. Nolin pulled the door open, and the visitor quickly stepped past him into the foyer.

"Big fancy lawyer answering his own door now?"

Nolin remembered the face, but couldn't attach the name. "I'm between receptionists," he answered pleasantly. He glanced at the necktie, noticed the red-and-white stock cars and it came to him. "What can I help you with, Mr. Van Horne?"

Nick looked out from under lazy eyelids. "You find anything yet?"

The details came to Nolin as he ushered Nick into his reading room, stacked on three walls with the usual, floor-to-ceiling shelves of law books. "Your estranged wife, correct? The one you're thinking of divorcing?"

Nick spread himself unceremoniously into the easy chair. "You were gonna find out if she's spending my money. Is she?"

Nolin snapped his fingers and moved to the oak filing cabinet on the fourth wall. He pulled out a file and leafed through it for a moment before sitting on the couch. "You understand, Mr. Van Horne, that I have no power of subpoena, not until there is an actual petition filed and we are in the discovery process. And as you know, bank records are not public. We were only able to make some discreet inquiries. We don't know, for example, where exactly she's spending her money."

Nick crossed and uncrossed his legs, spun his fingers in circles. "Yeah, yeah, yeah. Whatever. So what do you got?"

"Barbara Baxter Van Horne. Age thirty-four. Married. Owns a single-family residential dwelling on State Road A1A, assessed value $177,000. Claims a homestead exemption. Current on her taxes. One car registered in her name, a 1989 Volkswagen, fully paid. Seems to be using a single account at Barnett Bank for all her expenses."

"That's it? The Barnett account?"

"So it seems."

"She's not getting anything out of First Volusia?"

"Apparently not. Isn't the account at First Volusia in your name?"

"Yeah. But we're still married, so doesn't she get access or anything?"

"No, sir. It has to be a joint account for her to have access. And you closed the only joint account you had, correct?"

Nick hung his head, dejected. "So where's she getting all the money?"

Nolin flipped a page in the thin folder. "As far as I can tell, Mr. Van Horne, there doesn't seem to *be* that much money. Besides, she does have the boutique on Seabreeze."

"No way." Nick shook his head. "No way that stupid place pays for everything."

Nolin closed the folder and dropped it on the coffee table. "I don't know what else to tell you."

Nick stood, stuck his hands in his pockets to jingle his coins. "You don't have to tell me nothing. All you lawyers; you're all the same. Well, I gotta get going. I'm already late for the Jet Skis. I don't need any more information, all right? So I don't want you spending any more of my money on this."

Nolin lifted an eyebrow. "You're telling me, then, that you don't need representation in a matrimonial?"

Nick scowled. "Matri . . ."

"A divorce."

"Oh." Nick considered the question a moment. "Uh, not at the moment, no. But I'm not ruling it out in the future, you understand." He thought that over, liked the sound of it. "In fact, yeah. I *do* want a divorce, just not right now. Okay?"

Nolin shrugged. "Whatever you say."

"In the meantime, I hope you realize how sensitive a situation this is."

Nolin didn't have the foggiest. "Absolutely."

"With my family's standing in town and all, you know how damaging any publicity would be."

Now Nolin understood, and suppressed a smile. "I can appreciate your concern, Mr. Van Horne. As you know, an attorney-client relationship is strictly confidential. Our dealings are absolutely private."

Nick's eyes opened a fraction. "Yeah." He nodded. "And don't you forget it. Unless you want the bar association to yank your license. And don't think I can't have it done. I have some, shall we say, *influential* friends in Tallahassee."

Nick opened the door for himself and got into his brand-new green

Monte Carlo. Nolin waited for it to turn the corner before he started laughing.

Jamie Hotchkiss stuck his grimy feet into a pair of Nike sandals, strung the credentials around his neck and grabbed the camera off the passenger seat. The beach was already getting crowded, and he needed to hurry. He walked toward the water's edge, crossed two lanes of traffic at the high-water mark and weaved through a menagerie of tourists in bright shorts, businessmen in loafers and housewives with toddlers to find the racers, their machines and, most important, their fans.

Yessir, the babes were flocking, just like he figured. Despite the chilly breeze off the greenish-brown water, the Jet Ski groupies bravely sported their thong bikinis. By the dozens, firm young buttocks faced shoreward, tanned and goose bumped.

Jamie adjusted his press badges. He'd spent hours smudging the date so no one would realize he'd dug them from the trash following the last race three months earlier. Then he adjusted the zoom lens of the Nikon he'd found on some tourist's blanket two days earlier. Carefully, he half-pressed the shutter until, with a sudden whir, a trio of bare bottoms came into stark focus. He snapped off a couple of frames, put on his best salesman's smile and walked up behind the girls.

"Beautiful day, ain't it?" he asked after a while.

At just under six feet, with dirty blond hair and a dimple, he would have drawn their attention anyway. With the credentials and camera, they were as good as his.

"Nice enough," said the shortest of the three, a long haired brunette. "You a photographer?"

Jamie affected a blush. It was a trick he'd lived off of for years. "Well, I shoot freelance for *Personal Watercraft* magazine." They looked at him blankly. "You know. Jet Skis. Wave Runners."

"Oh yeah." The tallest girl nodded. "I get that once in a while. You know, just to see what's new."

"Sure," Jamie agreed. "You've probably seen some of my work.

Remember the issue with the South Beach race? I shot most of that." He smiled broadly and extended his hand. "Jamie Hotchkiss."

One by one, the girls shook his hand and introduced themselves: Tiffany, Monica and Kristin. It was Monica, the tall one, who asked him what he'd been waiting to hear.

"So, Jamie, you ever take pictures of other things? Or just Jet Skis?"

Jamie smiled again and went to work.

No matter how he adjusted them, the blasted headphones chafed his ears. He had no idea how teenagers spent blissful hours in them, whole days in them. Within minutes of donning them, he wanted to tear them off, fling them into the surf.

Outwardly he maintained a Zen-like calm, sitting cross-legged on his towel, invisible in the dark shades, headphones and Walkman clipped to his shorts. Casually he checked his watch for the fiftieth time and, for the fiftieth time, cursed inwardly. Those damn Van Hornes! Where the hell were they? They didn't even have the courtesy to be on time for their own stupid party!

He looked again out at the racecourse: three orange buoys set in a large triangle, with two of the markers forming a line parallel to the beach. If he'd done his homework properly, the tank was just about halfway between the southern mark and the eastern one. But if they didn't start soon, it would all be for naught.

The race had been scheduled for low tide, to maximize spectator room on the beach, and that's what he'd set his float for. It was already an hour past low and rising quickly.

True, there were always at least a few people in the water even before the race. He *could* set it off now. . . . But then the only targets would be the acolytes tuning their masters' machines and a few of the bikini set who were wading in and out of water to their knees.

He had no particular love for the bikini bimbos, and the racers' helpers were certainly Jet Ski operators themselves and therefore fair game. But the statement he wanted was best made with some actual wet-suited racers. Live on ESPN, for the entire world to witness via satellite. No, he would wait. It would be worth it.

He scanned the crowd again. The miserable matriarch, Joanna Van Horne, had finally arrived on the VIP platform in a bright yellow miniskirt, white blouse and a white jacket. She was only about twenty years too old for that look, but that had never stopped her before, he remembered. Even she was looking anxiously toward the street. Obviously it was the moron son holding things up now.

He turned quickly as a high-pitched whine cut through the buzz of the crowd and the rumble of the surf. One of the racers sped straight out to sea, turned around and sped back. Who knew why? Perhaps to impress the girls, who were starting to look bored as they stood in groups and gossiped. Three of them lounged unnaturally on a Jet Ski for a photographer, who darted like a puppy from side to side, taking pictures of as much upturned and thrust-out flesh as he could manage.

From behind him a cheer went up, and he turned to see the pudgy form of J. Robert Van Horne climb the platform steps and lamely hug his stepmother. A high-pitched squeal from the loudspeakers preceded her voice, welcoming everyone to the World's Most Famous Beach for the First Annual Daytona Offshore 100.

He smiled to himself and adjusted his Walkman. It was going to work out after all.

Nick grimaced, wished yet again he'd remembered to bring what he never went to the raceway without: earplugs. Because yet again the pack rounded the far marker and streaked back toward the beach.

What the hell was he doing here, anyway? The turtle trial was supposed to start the following week. He had only seven days to work with. He should be out interviewing killers, not standing around watching a bunch of dumb Jet Skis.

Murder-for-hire was among Daytona's favorite pastimes, with at least one arrest every other month. Still, he had no idea where to begin. He tried to remember the newspaper headlines, the TV reports from the county jail or the scene of the crime. In almost every one, it seemed, the hit man was someone known to both customer and victim. Who did he know who could pull off something like that? Certainly not the twins. They'd be lucky not to kill each other by accident. Besides, having somebody you knew do it seemed almost as bad as doing it yourself. That's the first place the cops would start asking questions. There was probably a limit to how much friends in high places could do if it was obvious even to the greenest rookie that your pool guy had knocked off your wife.

No, there had to be a better way. . . . He'd taken the last gulp from his glass when the old light bulb came shining through again. He smiled as he confirmed to himself once more that he'd always go far because he was always one step ahead, always one notch smarter than the crowd.

The fact that every murder-for-hire he'd seen on the news had been committed by a friend of the family proved absolutely that that was the wrong way to go. Hah! Every single one of those cases was a *failure*, with the murderer going to prison or worse.

No, thank you. He would find an outsider. Somebody with no ties to either him or Barbie. Preferably someone with no ties even to Daytona. Someone who visited town but rarely, didn't know anybody here and was prone to violence and easy money. Someone, he smiled again, like a biker. And he knew just where to look. And as soon as this blasted race was over, that's just what he'd do.

Once again, the horde of banshees rounded the mark and headed away from the beach. Once again, he pushed the play button on his Walkman. And once again, nothing happened.

God damn it, he swore to himself. *God damn it all*. He'd waited too long. The water was too high now. The aerial was completely submerged, and it wasn't going to happen. All that time and money and planning. Wasted. All because of that lard-ass Van Horne showing up an hour late. Damn him to hell.

He bit back his anger and thought. There was still a chance. He'd have to time it with a trough of a wave, when a bit of wire was most likely to stick out above the surface. It was a long shot, but at this point, it was better than nothing. All he could do was try.

Nick winced again. It wasn't that they were particularly loud. They weren't, at least not compared to stock cars. They were just *annoying*, with a ridiculous high-pitched whine that lessened only for a blissful moment as the riders slowed to round a buoy. A swarm of mosquitoes. That's what they were. Just as persistent, just as irritating.

He swigged the rest of his vodka martini and turned to the table to make another, glancing sideways to see if his stepmother would notice. As usual, she was feigning total absorption in the race: standing upright in white pumps and miniskirt, eyes straight ahead, hands cupped around her wineglass. He had to admit, grudgingly, that she still cut a decent figure, for a woman of forty-six. Back when his dad had taken up with her, she'd been downright spectacular. He'd had trouble sleeping at night, thinking about her swimming in the pool or sitting in the kitchen in her purple kimono.

Much of that unnerving attraction was gone, thankfully, now that he'd learned to parlay his name and bank account into an active social life. The Daytona Debs hung on his every word, breaking dates and re-arranging vacations to accompany him somewhere. Alas, they weren't much fun. Plus they were *so* expensive. With money of their own at home, it took real gold and real diamonds to impress. And, eventually, they wanted the whole thing: a ring, a big wedding, the name.

Not like his little Cherry, whose heart he'd won with a $24.99 ankle bracelet. She wore it all the time, he'd noticed, and usually not much else. That was the nice thing about Boardwalk babes: they never expected much. A decent $15 meal and a couple of six-packs of beer would get you everything you wanted. He recalled again the previous week, when she'd invited one of her girlfriends along. The three of them had split a magnum of champagne when the girlfriend and Cherry started getting friendly. It had rattled him, and he'd remembered an important appointment and escaped. He'd been able to think of little else since.

Next time, he swore, he wasn't going to freak out. Next time, he'd do them both, and have plenty left to spare. In fact, he wondered if she wasn't there now, on the beach. He picked up the binoculars and started scanning Bimbo Row along the water's edge. Quickly he settled on two possible sets of butt cheeks. Both were darkly tanned, firm and perky. Both were bisected by a bright red strip of fabric. Now as soon as they turned a little bit . . .

But they didn't turn, and instead kept their eyes locked on the racers. *Damn them*! What the hell was so interesting about a bunch of cretins riding Jet Skis that they couldn't look away even for a minute? Hell, he'd met some of the racers. They weren't even rich! He couldn't understand the fascination with drivers, either, but at least some of them took home hundreds of thousands of dollars every race.

He darted the binoculars between the red-thonged girls for a while longer. Neither turned around, and out of sheer boredom he lifted the glasses toward the Jet Skis. Rounding the southern mark, they were, bouncing through the small chop out toward the seaward mark. A guy in a yellow wetsuit and blue helmet was in the lead, followed closely by a guy in a green wetsuit and red helmet. Or maybe Green Wetsuit was about to lap Yellow Wetsuit. Who knew? Who cared?

He followed Yellow Wetsuit up to the far mark. . . . Well, that was odd. The water around the orange buoy seemed darker than everywhere else, almost purple instead of green. Yellow Wetsuit slowed to take the turn, leaning toward the beach and sticking his left leg out to pivot around. . . . And he was gone.

Nick blinked, dropped the binoculars to see the whole picture. Sure enough, Yellow Wetsuit's Jet Ski sat in the water next to the buoy, but Yellow Wetsuit himself had disappeared. Within moments, Green Wetsuit was right on top of the idle Jet Ski, turning around it, trailing his leg when the water exploded in front of him, fell over him, swallowed him. And he was gone, too.

But he wasn't, completely. The crowd saw it the same moment Nick did, and as a group stepped back from the water's edge. A woman screamed, then another, as the phalanx of mechanics and gofers stood motionless by their trailers and corporate tents. Because still attached to the throttle of the little fuchsia water scooter, still driving it in ever widening manic circles, was Green Wetsuit's forearm, the thin spiral kill-switch cord still strapped to the wrist.

Nick watched with dropped jaw as the single-handed Jet Ski bounced off one boat, then another, knocking their riders into the now frenzied water before ramming a third racer head on. Both boats stopped dead for a moment before erupting in an orange ball of flame.

The remaining racers slowed to an idle, then saw why the water around the buoy was so turbulent: dark fins, more than a dozen, surrounding the riderless Jet Skis, slicing through the purple murk. Without warning, another wave exploded over Green Wetsuit's Jet Ski, shook the big plastic machine, then, amazingly, dragged it underwater.

The crowd screamed as one when, a few moments later, the boat popped back through the surface and settled low in the water. Green Wetsuit's forearm was gone.

Nick watched in stunned rapture. Five abandoned Jet Skis sat near the far buoy in various states of disrepair. The remaining dozen were back on the beach, their riders gesturing wildly at the water. The crowd of spectators murmured uncertainly, not knowing exactly what to expect next or even exactly what had happened. And everywhere, Jet Ski bimbos clung to boyfriends, strangers, one another.

Slowly it dawned on Nick what a wonderful, beautiful thing had just occurred. There would be no yellow caution flag, no prolonged delay as crews cleared wreckage and soaked up spilled oil from the track. That was it. The race was finished. He could go home.

TWO

■ ■ ■

"You know what those bastards down at Beach Patrol told me?"

Joanna sucked down a cigarette in anger. She only smoked now in anger, or in the presence of Winston officials, to demonstrate her loyalty to her biggest sponsor.

"They told me they couldn't kill them. That they didn't have the boats or the equipment. And even if they did, they wouldn't know which ones were responsible and that some kinds are protected or endangered or some such nonsense."

She took another powerful drag. Nick watched in awe as the glowing orange tip moved visibly down the paper.

"It's a crazy world," he mumbled.

"I should have them all fired. I should pick up the phone and get every last one of those cocksuckers fired."

Nick cringed. The C word was second only to the M word in implied carnage among Joanna's pantheon of traditionally male epithets. It wouldn't pay to be a smartass right now. Instead he stared down at the elaborate cardboard-and-foam model of RaceWorld, the $120 million theme park Joanna had dreamed up two years earlier. It would feature exhibits, restaurants, Jet Ski rentals, a water slide and, most important, a strip of beach where visitors could race actual replica, turn-of-the-century cars on the sand.

She had planned to unveil it that afternoon, after the Jet Ski race, but decided to postpone in light of the day's events. She wanted her announcement to lead the newscast, not play second to "Sharks Eat Jet Skiers." They had quietly loaded the model and charts and artists' renderings back into the van and taken them home.

"Well, never mind. We'll have a quick memorial service for them tomorrow and be done with it. We still have the Offshore Challenge on Wednesday. We'll announce RaceWorld there." She stubbed out her cigarette, pulled another from the pack and lit it. "How are you coming with your project?"

Nick prepared to whine that she'd only given it to him that morning, then saw how fast her new cigarette was disappearing. "I'm, uh, meeting a prospect tonight," he gulped.

"Good. Don't screw this up. If that motherfucker judge rules in her favor, we may as well kiss RaceWorld goodbye. And you know what that means?"

Nick gulped again. The M word. He nodded weakly.

"Right. No inheritance." She kicked off her pumps and started pulling the blouse over her head. "Now get out of my sight."

Amee leaned over the table, lined up her cuestick and heard the sharp crack of a ball bouncing on linoleum. She lifted her eyes to see her new assistant chase it down, bend over awkwardly to grab it and scamper back to her table, mouthing the word "sorry" to Amee on her way.

Amee dropped her head in disgust for a moment, took a breath and nailed the eight ball into the far corner. Game.

She collected her money from her Joe and glanced around the room. Only two other customers were waiting. Both had eyes glued to the new girl, Lori. Amee had hired her to help out at night during the busy season, and paid her a flat rate of $3 a game. Lori was an abysmal pool player, but she was a big girl with long blonde hair, and none of the customers was complaining. In fact, Amee was making more money than she ever had on her own.

"I'm taking a break, Peaches," she shouted, snapping her cuestick into the rack on the wall. "I'll be back in a few."

She unzipped her fanny pack, found her box of Marlboro Lights, pulled one out with her lips and kicked the door to her "office" shut behind her. It had been a long day, but a good one. More than $150 so far, not counting her share of Lori's take, and the night was still young. She threw her legs and bare feet up on the metal desk and blew smoke toward the yellowed poster stuck to the ceiling.

It was of a thin girl with a model's face and long dark hair, taken in black and white. She was nude, but sat sideways to the camera with her knees drawn toward her chest. The only thing you could see was her left breast, a slight swelling capped with a long, dark nipple. She'd only noticed the poster several months after she'd taken over the pool hall, and could only imagine what the previous tenant had done while staring up at it. The door echoed with three quick knocks and she took another long drag. Never a moment's rest. There was a brief pause and then three more knocks.

"What now?" she shouted.

The door swung inward followed by a round head. "Are you Cherry?"

He had medium-length blond hair, bright blues and a permanent dimple. He'd stood by the wall for the last hour nursing a beer, staring down Lori's bikini top, but hadn't bought a single game. She blew a stream of smoke at his face. "Who wants to know?"

"Well, I guess I do," he replied politely. "Jamie Hotchkiss. A couple of friends suggested you and I could do some business."

Ah, so the middle-class looks were only a front. He was just another Boardwalk hustler. That, she could deal with. She nodded him in, and he stepped through the door and shut it behind him. He wore a soiled T-shirt, surfer shorts and a pair of yuppie sandals a size or two too small.

"Couldn't find any tourists with your shoe size?" she asked.

His eyes widened as he glanced down at his dirty feet. "No," he said quickly. "I, ah, bought these. They were on special. Real cheap. So I got 'em even though they're kinda small."

He had the trace of a hillbilly accent. Kentucky. Or Tennessee, maybe. "So what business are you in, exactly?"

"Well, ma'am, I'm actually a driver. You know. A race car driver?" He nodded solemnly. "I've done the dirt tracks where I grew up and I thought I'd come down here to break into the big time."

He stood so earnestly, waiting for her approval. She laughed out loud. "What, you want me to sponsor you? Drive a Top Shots Billiards car?"

The blue eyes moistened into a puppy-dog softness. "Oh, no, ma'am. I guess I've realized that getting into NASCAR might take a little longer than I thought. It might be weeks, maybe even months before I get my own car. In the meantime, I'm just trying to make a living, you know? A buck here, a buck there."

She finished one cigarette and lit another. "Well, there ain't much for you to do around here. I mean, you're cute, but not so cute that some guy from Buffalo's gonna pay five bucks a pop to see you in a thong, if you see what I'm saying."

"Oh, no." He dug an envelope out of his pocket. "See, I have pictures. I, uh, heard you know some people who can use these."

She held out her hand and he passed her the envelope. Who the hell had told him she bought pictures? She hadn't done that in almost a year, not since she left the House of Babes. Amee opened the drugstore envelope and pulled out a stack of color prints. Jet Ski bimbos. Three of them, sitting on top of, next to and around a bright orange Wave Runner. She flipped through them one by one. The girls were licking their lips, flaring their nostrils, sticking their butts at the lens, everything, in fact, except the one thing she was looking for: taking off their bikinis.

She threw the photos on the desk. "You ain't got dick. You only got one or two in there where you can even see anything. Who do you think's gonna buy that?"

He quickly straightened the pile into a neat stack, bent to retrieve two that had slid off the desk. "But what about all these?" he protested. "You can see their asses in every single one!"

She took a final drag from the bit of tobacco left above the filter and stubbed it out. "Okay, Einstein, I'm gonna explain a business principle to you: Nobody pays for something they can get for free. Nobody. Not you. Not me. Not girlie magazines. In Daytona, bare asses ain't even a dime a dozen. Now get out of here. I gotta get back to work."

"But what about this one?" He flipped through till he found the shot in which the tall girl's top had, in her exertions, migrated south. "See?"

She stood, realized she only came up to his chin. He wasn't half bad-looking. Not long on brains, though. "Where, Jamie, do you think I can sell a picture of some chick sitting on a Jet Ski with one boob hanging out?"

He looked puzzled. *"Playboy?"*

She nodded. *"Playboy."* She pointed up to the ceiling. "You see that? That's the kind of girl, that's the kind of picture that's *almost* good enough to get into *Playboy.*"

Jamie stared upward, slack-mouthed. "Whoa. Who is *she?*"

Amee glanced up at the dog-eared poster again, annoyed. "The fuck should I know who she is? My point is, *you're* never gonna shoot anything like it."

He hadn't taken his eyes off the ceiling. "She's hot. I mean totally hot."

Amee grabbed the photos and shoved them back into his envelope. "Okay. Time to go. Here." She unzipped her fanny pack, pulled out a $5 bill, stuck money and envelope in his hand. "Here's five bucks. Go to the store and buy a copy of *Hustler.* You get your girlfriends to do some of the things the chicks in *there* do, and we'll talk. Until then, get the fuck out."

She grabbed his waist and spun him around. Reluctantly, he pulled his eyes away from the ceiling and reached for the doorknob. "It was nice meeting you."

Amee shut the door after him and looked into the mirror to adjust her bikini. She tilted her head upward to look at the poster. What the hell did that girl have that she didn't? She pulled one bright-red triangle down, looked in the mirror to see the effect, looked back up at the poster. She snorted, pulled her top back on and went out into the pool hall.

He looked back down at his notebook, checked his math and then, with gloved hands, put another small lump of the heavy putty on the scales. Getting hold of it was easier now than it ever had been, what with all the unemployed arms dealers in Czechoslovakia and Russia. Thank God for the end of the Cold War.

He removed the final lump from the scales, piled it onto the others and gently kneaded the mass into a half globe. The exact shape wasn't crucial. It wouldn't be cutting through metal or propelling a spray of shrapnel. No, the correct amount was much more important than the configuration, and he double- and triple-checked his calculations.

Carefully he inserted the thin detonators, ran the wires to a junction box. He'd already laid a sheet of plastic underneath, and he folded it over, forming a doubled seam to act as the first barrier against the water. Four hours for the epoxy to set, another four for the silicone sealant around the wire leads. Two hours for final assembly and then six to swim it out to the site.

And the race wasn't for another two days. Plenty of time.

Amee slid deeper into the tub, lifted her toes up onto Nick's chest. He tried to ignore the dirt ground into her soles from running around barefoot on the filthy Boardwalk all day, just as he tried to ignore the forests of mildew on the tiled walls. When he got home, he'd need a shower to wash away this bath. No matter. Now wasn't a time to nitpick. Now was a time to celebrate. He sipped at his champagne.

"Nicky baby? I had this idea for the business. You tell me what you think. Right now I'm making five bucks a game, about six games an hour during the busy time. What if I raised my rates to twenty bucks a game? Then I could make four times as much."

Nick closed his eyes and, momentarily forgetting the mildew, leaned his head back against the tile. She was in the throes of one of her brainstorms again.

"Or I could make twice as much, and only work half as many hours."

He snorted. "Maybe you could set your rate at two hundred a game. Then you'd only have to shoot one game a day."

She pinched a fold of flesh on his chest with her toes, making him yelp and spill some of his champagne. "I'm *serious*! Don't make fun of my ideas or I'll kick your fat ass out of my tub!"

Nick poured himself some more champagne, set the bottle back on the toilet-seat lid. For a moment he considered reminding her whose money was paying for the tub, but then thought better of it. He was in too good a mood. "Sorry, baby. Please tell me more about your idea."

Amee smiled. "That's better. Okay. Right now, guys pay five bucks to shoot a game of pool with me in my bikini. Don't you think they'd pay twenty a game if I was topless?"

He blinked, realized she was serious. "Cherry, you can't go topless."

"Why not?" She sat up straight, lifting her breasts clear of the bubbles, and arched her back. "Don't you think they're good enough?"

Nick felt himself tingle. He imagined her dancing around the pool hall, rubbing up against the various sleazeballs and bozos, her boobs hanging free, and he felt himself awaken. "Sure, baby, they're great. That ain't the problem. Your outfit's already barely legal. You drop the top, then the pool hall becomes a strip joint. No way is the city gonna permit you for that on the Boardwalk."

Amee was speechless with anger. "Why the hell not? They got a shampoo parlor in the back of the pizza place. Hookers sell blowjobs in the photo booths at the arcade. All the gay pimps are out on Ocean Drive, but I can't take my top off to play a game of pool, for Chrissake?"

He wondered if she'd let him videotape her shooting pool topless. She probably would. "I know," he agreed. "It's not a fair world."

She slipped back in the tub, chugged the rest of her champagne and pouted. He was always a sucker for that. Besides, he was dying for an excuse to tell her.

"Anyway, you won't have to worry about shooting pool much longer," he said, reaching for the bottle to refill her glass.

"Why not?"

"Let's just say my financial worries are about to become history. And *you* won't have to worry about working another day of your life."

Amee smiled, scooted forward to sit on his lap. "Why? What's happening?"

He shouldn't tell her. He shouldn't tell anyone. That's how these things fell apart. Oh, what the hell. "My estranged wife is about to become my former wife."

She clapped her hands. "You're getting a divorce!"

He grinned, took another sip. "I'm gonna be a widower," he whispered.

Amee's eyes grew wide with amazement and, he saw with satisfaction, genuine awe. "Nicky, I'm so proud of you!" She clapped her hands together, squeezing gobs of Mr. Bubble into the air and onto the tiled floor. "When, Nicky? When you gonna do it?"

Nick glanced at his wrist, remembered he'd taken off the Rolex in the first moments of pawing and grabbing at the front door to their love nest. "Within a couple of hours, I should be a free man."

"Oh, Nick!" She slid farther forward, bent down for a long, wet kiss. "I can't tell you how much you turn me on," she whispered. "This is the end of all our problems, isn't it? You'll get all the money now, right?"

One hand reached up to grab from below, the other stretched around to grab from behind. Fondle as much as you can, whenever you can, was his rule. You never knew when it would be gone. "Not exactly," he explained. "It's not like she's got the money. That's Joanna. But this puts me in a better position."

She slapped at his hand. "Don't pinch! How many fuckin' times do I gotta tell you? I don't like to be pinched."

He cautiously moved his hand back onto her chest. "Sorry."

"Now explain 'not exactly,' " she demanded. "What does killing her do, if it doesn't get us more money?"

Women, he thought angrily. They were the same. All of them, all of the time. Still, he couldn't piss her off. She'd promised that Lori would come over later. "Barbie's damn turtle lawsuit is wrecking Joanna's plans for the company. In other words, she's screwing with my inheritance."

Amee sat still for a moment. "I thought you told me once that Joanna was actually younger than you."

For a Boardwalk bimbo, she was sharp, he thought. "She is. By a year."

"So she's probably gonna live as long as you. Probably longer."

Nick paused. He hadn't thought of it that way. "Yeah. I guess."

"You guess." She laughed, pushed off his lap and slid back to her end of the tub. She reached over to the toilet lid for her cigarettes, lit one and blew smoke at him. "Great. Basically, Joanna's got you doin' her dirty work. You make her richer, she gives you diddly squat. Good thinking, Einstein."

He hated when she called him that. Where did she get off making fun of him? At least he'd seen the inside of a college, which was a hell of a lot better than dropping out of some bum-fuck high school near Cleveland. God damn it, though, she was right. Joanna *was* using him, and what would he get out of it? Nothing more than he was getting now. A stupid little eight grand a month. Anything more, he had to beg Joanna for.

Joanna. He sounded it out again. *Joanna.* God, he hated that name. What was his old man thinking? He didn't have to marry her. He could have kept her in a condo somewhere, gone over whenever he needed some, and nobody would have been the wiser. Joanna. Now *there* was his real problem. If he had any balls, he'd have her dealt with, too. Hell, he had plenty of money. All he'd have to do was . . .

He blinked twice, allowed himself a confident smile, refilled his champagne glass and took a sip. "What makes you think Barbie's the only one I'm taking care of?" He waited till she looked up, took a slow, casual sip.

The look of wonder returned. "You're gonna . . . ?"

He shrugged carelessly. "As soon as he's done with Barbie, he does Joanna."

Amee was speechless.

"The order's important, you know. 'Cause the old man had a soft spot for Barbie. If she outlives Joanna, she gets a chunk. This way, see, everything comes my way."

She shook her head and smiled. "Nicky, I'm sorry I got mad. I shoulda trusted your business sense."

She leaned forward, took a deep breath and plunged her face into the bubbles over his lap. He started in alarm, jerking his head back against the tiled wall with a sharp *crack*. Waves of pain drowned out all else, and he groaned in agony.

Amee finally came up for air, licked her way up his chest to his mouth. "I planned a special treat tonight," she whispered, biting his lip. "But I better let you get home."

Nick winced back tears. "Why?" he managed finally.

"For your alibi, silly. The cops are gonna come to you right off the bat. You gotta prove you weren't there."

Gingerly he pushed on the back of his skull. Pain stabbed through him again. "Oh, yeah. That."

She studied him in silence. "Nicky, maybe you better let me help you. I think maybe I got a little more experience with this sort of thing."

"With what? Having people knocked off?"

"With doing business with, you know, this type of people."

"This type?" He wondered whether he was bleeding.

"Bums. Like you shouldn't meet this guy again, in case the cops are watching."

He decided he wasn't bleeding. A skull fracture, maybe. A concussion, definitely. But not bleeding. "What guy?"

"The shooter, for Chrissake! Who you think we been talkin' about all this time? The Pope?"

He had no idea who she was talking about. She didn't even realize how much pain he was in, or that she'd caused it. The selfish bitch. "Why would I want to meet him again?"

She pushed herself off his chest, sat up straight. "To pay him the rest of the money. You know: half before, half after?" Her shoulders suddenly sagged. "Tell me you didn't give him everything up front."

A jolt of fear hit his stomach, twisted it. He'd never even stopped to worry about this. "Why wouldn't I pay up front?" he asked defensively. "This way, I don't *have* to meet him afterward."

She shook her head sadly. "You know, it's a good thing you were born rich, 'cause otherwise you'd be in the gutter drinkin' paint thinner by now." She took a deep breath. "Okay. Let's go get it back. How much?"

He gulped. "Ten."

Amee thought she would cry. "You gave him ten grand. And he told you he'd kill your wife. And that was good enough for you."

"He seemed honest."

She shook her head again. "So who is he?"

"His name's Lance. I don't know his last name. And I didn't tell him *my* real name," Nick said proudly. "I wore a disguise."

"Brilliant. So who is he?"

"A biker. Found him in a bar."

She scrunched up her nose. "A biker named *Lance*? What bar?"

"That place on Main Street. Across from the cemetery. You know: the Iron Spike."

Amee held her breath for a long moment, then screamed, slapped his ear. "Nick! You're *so* fuckin' stupid! Do you have any idea *how* fuckin' stupid you are?" She stood, stepped out of the tub. "The Iron Spike is a *fag* bar. *Fag* bikers go there. You want your house redecorated, you go to the Iron Spike. You want your wife *killed*, you go to Mike's Tap!"

He held his ear with one hand, the back of his head with the other, shut his eyes against the pain. "Jesus Christ . . . The fuck was *I* supposed to know? They were all wearing leather and chains and shit!" He opened his eyes, saw her standing over him, soap suds sliding off her body. God, she was beautiful. "It's all right! Tomorrow I'll go back there and get my money back."

She grabbed a towel and started drying off. "Forget it. You're never going to find Lance again. He's down in South Beach by now, bragging to his boyfriends how some complete *moron* gave him ten grand!"

She finished with the towel and threw it at him. "Now get the fuck out of my bathtub."

·   ·   ·

Mathematics was never her strongest suit, so she added all the numbers in both halves of the ledger again. And, once again, she came up with the same depressing result. Her assets were tens of thousands less than her liabilities. What's more, she had nothing left to borrow against. What little equity she had in her house had been mortgaged first. Next came the credit cards, and she had wisely stopped after maxing out two.

She sipped a glass of wine and looked around the dining room, assessing value. An old, scratched table, a garage-sale sideboard she'd never gotten around to refinishing, rickety chairs. The lot would get her maybe $50. A *Southern Living* home and college-student furniture. Such was her life.

Barbie sighed deeply, refilled her glass and grabbed the towel off the countertop. She returned to the living room, pulled open the sliding glass door and padded softly onto the deck. It was her favorite part of the house: weathered, light-gray wood, bordered by sea oats and a matching gray privacy fence.

She bent beside the Jacuzzi and flicked a switch on the side. The pump began a gentle rumbling, and a few feet away, bubbles gurgled to the surface of the sunken hot tub. It was a beautiful night: cool but not cold, a fresh ocean breeze. Only a thin layer of clouds off the water marred perfection. She set her wineglass on the deck, pulled off her long-sleeve T-shirt and sweatpants and climbed down the steps, nestling the small of her back against a stream of bubbles.

With another sip from her glass, she started running through the possibilities again. Income from the store barely paid the rent and utilities, so there wasn't much she could do there. The old Volkswagen wasn't costing her much but also wasn't worth much. It was the house that was killing her, pure and simple. The mortgage payment was just over $1,900 a month, which was $1,900 a month she no longer had.

She needed a roommate. That was it. Someone to take one of the bedrooms and pay $950 rent. Yeah, sure. Who in Daytona Beach well off enough to pay $950 a month was going to *want* a roommate? Only students didn't mind roommates, and Daytona wasn't exactly a college town. She wouldn't mind sharing with a professional woman who lived normal hours and kept to herself. But students, with their angst and weird ideas and weirder schedules, they were something else entirely.

No, the answer was plain. She would have to bite the bullet and sell the place. It was the only way. She could probably get enough to pay off the credit cards and get square with the lawyer. Enough, at least, to make him start the trial. And if he started the trial, he would finish the trial. He was too afraid of the judge not to. That way, the turtles would at least get a fighting chance.

Yes, tomorrow she'd talk to a realtor. It was the only way.

After three hours of drywalling, the vinyl chaise lounge seemed as comfortable as the deepest, most luxurious divan. Nolin spread himself on it, with one hand popped open a longneck Bud, flipped the cap onto the concrete with the bent nails, chipped plaster and other accumulated trash.

The first swig was cold, ice cold, and he let it slide down his throat slowly. He let out a long, satisfying burp and turned to survey his work by the light from the lone, dim bulb hanging from the ceiling. His second "project" house, it was. Just like the one on the river in Holly Hill, only better. He'd finished the outside first, pulling off all the old siding, replacing it with stained wood, re-shingling the roof, replacing the crumbled concrete driveway with brick.

He'd started on the interior about a month earlier: ripping up shag carpet and dirty linoleum to get down to bare floor, tearing down flimsy paneling, adding a skylight, nailing up new Sheetrock. He studied his calloused hands, still slightly warm and swollen from the evening's exertions, and took another swig of beer.

Whatever had possessed him to waste years of nights and weekends becoming a lawyer, he wondered for the two- or three-millionth time, when what he truly loved was working with his hands, building things? Or perhaps now building things was fun, a hobby, while writing briefs and filing motions was work. Maybe if he built houses for a living and lawyered in his free time, maybe then he would trade his loves for his hates. He took another long swig from his bottle. Maybe not.

He turned back toward the sea, which lay dark and still beyond two-by-fours that framed what would become a sun room, with ceiling fans and huge hurricane-vulnerable glass windows. It would be the only room, save the bathrooms, with tile floors instead of hardwood, his grudging acknowledgment that it would, eventually, flood. Because it was a good two feet lower than the rest of the house, he hoped that maybe the natural disaster gods would spare him, and never let the storm surge rise above the threshold into his living room.

Outside, he heard a rustling in the dune. He put down his beer and clapped twice.

"Pedro! Come!"

The dune became still. After a moment, the rustling resumed.

"Pedro!" he shouted this time. "Don't *make* me come in there and kick your butt!"

The creeping ivy and sea oats parted, and a small tan-and-brown dog stepped out, stopped and stared at him sheepishly.

"Pedro? How many times have I told you not to go in the dune at night, huh? Now come here and sit!"

The dog stared at him silently, finally walked between two studs and sat before Nolin. He bent down and squeezed his head, scratching under his chin and behind his ears. "Good boy. That's a good boy."

He'd adopted Pedro that New Year's Eve. He'd seen him almost every day he worked on the house, wandering up and down A1A. Then one day he realized he hadn't seen him in more than a week. On a hunch he went to the Humane Society and, sure enough, in Cage 14 was the familiar pointed snout, the dark eyes. The lady said he had labrador, shepherd, collie and about five other species in him, and had another two days before his stay of execution expired. He'd paid her the $50 on the spot. Even a month later it still made him nervous not to have him on his leash. Pedro had had a tendency to run into the street his first couple of weeks with him, and it had scared Nolin to death.

"There. That's a good boy." The watch on his wrist beeped twice, and Nolin stared out the framing to the north. It was almost time. "Sit, Pedro. Stay."

He stood, walked up the two stairs, grabbed another beer from the cooler, pulled the chain on the bulb and returned to the sun room. From a nail in a stud he removed a pair of rubberized binoculars and draped the strap around his neck, lifted them to his eyes, adjusted the focus. The optics were excellent, and the huge lenses picked up what little light was available and magnified it, so that every detail on the wooden dune crossover stood out clearly despite the gloom.

Rarely did he have to wait more than five minutes. On that night, he waited less than two. A wooden gate swung open and a tall woman strode onto the crossover, down the ramp and skipped down the steps to the beach. Long, graceful legs and arms, a slim waist, long dark hair; *God*, she was beautiful. She ran down the sand and waded into the water, waited for a wave, dove under it, swam five, ten, twenty strokes through the dark water and stood to walk back out.

He tweaked the focus knob a touch and held his breath. It had become a nightly ritual: knock off by nine and wait in the shadows for his uninhibited neighbor. He loved it. Someday, eventually, maybe, he'd work up the nerve to meet her. After he'd moved in. After he had the place put together. Maybe then. Bump into her one day as she went to check her mail. Someday.

Suddenly she bent over, dropped to her knees. He lowered the glasses a hair and saw her smiling broadly, petting a pointy-snouted dog as it tried to lick her face. And then his breath caught in his throat. It was Pedro, licking her hands, wagging his tail like he'd never been petted before.

Nolin dropped the binoculars and stared out into the dark in horror. The son of a bitch must have snuck off! *Now* what was he going to do? He put the glasses to his eyes again, saw her checking his collar for a name tag.

Damn it all! He hadn't bought one yet. She was liable to take him for a stray, call Animal Control . . .

"Pedro!" He slipped through the wooden studs, started running down the short crossover to the sand. "Pedro! Come!"

Yeah. Right. Like *that* had ever worked. He slowed, began wondering what in God's name he would say once he got there: Hi, I'm Nolin. That's my dog and you've got a great ass? He should go back.

Right now. He could still slip back to his porch; Pedro would come home on his own.

He froze in his steps. She had glanced up, smiled. He gulped, started walking again.

She looked up again. "Cute dog. Is he yours?"

"Pedro," he stammered. "Pedro."

She stood, nipples erect in the cool breeze. She stuck a hand out. "It's nice to meet you. I'm Barbie."

He dropped her hand. Her nipples were *so* long. Longer than he'd ever seen. Almost an inch, it seemed. Why did nipples need to be so long?

"Are you an astronomer?"

A moment of sheer panic: She'd been talking to him . . . And he'd been staring at her chest. Shamefully he jerked his eyes upward, wondered what she'd said, tried to think of something clever, something urbane.

"Huh?" he managed finally.

She pointed at the binoculars around his chest. "Were you looking at the stars?"

"Yeah. I was looking at the stars." He'd finished before he even knew what he was saying.

Together they lifted their heads to the sky, to the clouds that had been rolling in off the ocean all evening. "But I couldn't find any," he added weakly.

Barbie searched the sky in vain. "Yeah. Too bad. I love looking at the stars, and the planets." She smiled. "I'm kind of into astrology, you know? How the heavenly bodies affect our lives?"

He smiled back, kept his eyes locked on hers.

She crossed her arms, rubbing them with open palms. "Well, I'd love to chat, but I'm getting kind of cold." She bent to pet the dog, then waved a hand at him. "It was nice meeting you, Pedro."

She turned and scampered up the steps, along the walkway and through the open wooden gate to her patio. Nolin waited on the beach, silent, his eyes fixed on the closed gate. Ten minutes later she still hadn't come back out. He grabbed Pedro's collar and dragged him back to the house.

THREE

■ ■ ■

Tylenol 3, Nick decided, was a hoax. A placebo for those too stupid to figure out they'd been had. That's what the Raceway doctor had given him for his concussion. Codeine, he'd said. Take two every four hours, he'd said. Nick had taken six, and it hadn't done a bit of good.

The interminable memorial service for the "Fallen Jet Skiers," as the city had taken to calling them, hadn't helped either. What a total fraud. The mayor, the City Commission, the County Council and every weasel politician in between had made a speech, going on about the morons like they were war heroes. All they'd done was ride around in circles on water bikes, for Christ's sake, and been unlucky enough to fall off near some hungry sharks.

They'd filled First Baptist, the biggest church in town. Probably the only time they'd seen the inside of a church, what was left of them, anyway. Served the bastards right. He snorted, recalling all the little groupies in their black spandex minidresses, bawling into their hankies as they walked past the five coffins, empty except for a forearm in one, a bit of leg in another. That was all the Marine Patrol had been able to salvage.

The mayor, meanwhile, had yammered about having called in the best shark experts in the world, who'd all assured him that it had been a freak incident, an isolated event, and that there was no reason to close the beaches. Nick wondered if the tourists would be dumb enough to buy it. Couldn't they remember what happened in *Jaws*?

The car behind him honked impatiently. Nick scowled, noticed the green light and stepped on the gas. He flipped a middle finger at the rearview mirror for good measure and squeezed his throbbing head. The doctor had said the pain would last at least a couple of days. Then he'd dug some mildewy grout out of his scalp, asked if he'd fallen down in a public shower.

That bitch Amee. She'd get hers. He'd take care of Barbie, then Joanna, then he'd get Amee, too. There were plenty of women in Daytona who'd die for the chance to put out for J. Robert Van Horne, plenty of *fine* women. James Bond would never have taken any lip from some Boardwalk tramp. Neither would he, and she'd best not forget it.

Who did she think she was? Kicking him out of the apartment *he* was paying for? And all that crap about him being stupid: It wasn't *his* goddamned fault the Iron Spike was a gay bar. How the hell was he supposed to know? Sure, it was easy to look back and criticize. But where the hell had she been when he was putting out feelers, asking the hard questions, interviewing his candidate?

Gay bar. Gay *biker* bar, for Christ's sake. Who ever heard of such a thing? And of course *no* one there that morning had heard of any Lance. Couldn't remember seeing him there last night. No, come to think of it, they couldn't remember *Nick* having been there, either. And then they'd snicker and turn away.

Damn homos. They all stuck together. Well, he'd get the last laugh. Once he had his money, he'd find somebody to take care of old Lance. And maybe he'd talk to a couple of the city code inspectors about checking into the Iron Spike. Make sure they had their sneeze guards properly installed around the salad bar. Or maybe he'd just have the place torched.

On a last, desperate hope that maybe he had indeed found the one, honest, man-of-his-word gay biker, he'd cruised down Seabreeze Boulevard, peered in through the window as he passed the Harmonic

Age. Sure enough, there she was. No bullet holes, garrote scars or knife wounds.

Well, he'd fix that. This time he'd get a real biker, not some candy-ass mama's boy.

He was the essence of grace: long, tapered body, streamlined snout, smooth, scythelike tail. A million years of evolution hadn't brought even the tiniest change. He hadn't needed any. Lightning fast, agile, awesomely powerful. Not a bump or an appendage wasted. Perfection.

He sliced through the murky waters, homing in on the signal he'd known since birth. A slow pinging that triggered electrical impulses along the long, thin vibration sensors buried on either side of his great head.

Quickly he found the source, and slowed to bump the familiar figure: a dark, four-limbed creature standing on the sandy bottom. Slowly he nuzzled up against it, with one dark eye saw the stream of bubbles escaping from near the creature's top. He relaxed, enjoyed the stimulation of the limbs rubbing either side of his snout, flipped over to have his belly stroked.

And then, on cue, a limb reached into a side pocket and pulled out the little food, slid it carefully into his jaws. There were two more little foods, which he swallowed whole, even though he wasn't particularly hungry. He had eaten well the day before. He had eaten big food. Three of them, and pieces of two more, pieces he had stolen away from smaller, weaker competitors.

Eating, though, wasn't a question of hunger. It was what he did, especially when he heard the signal. He had to eat. The slow sound meant little food, and a visit with the limbed creature. The fast sound meant big food. Today was little food. And strokes.

He nuzzled his enormous head upward for more.

Joanna paged through the album as she waited. The photos had faded somewhat through the years, but not badly. She was glad she'd opted for the acid-free paper, even though it had cost five dollars more at a time in her life when five dollars meant something.

"He's still in there, Mrs. Van Horne," the perky young voice on the phone told her. "I can have him call you as soon as he's free."

"I'll hold," Joanna insisted.

The Muzak came back on and Joanna cradled the handset between ear and shoulder. It was always best to hold for the Honorable Marvin Julius Weathers, for he was a busy man, what with his twin roles of Speaker of the Florida House and chairman of the Coalition for Decency. Even busier now, on the brink of the new Legislative session: meetings all day; deals to cut; arms to twist; fresh, young college interns to screw.

Joanna smiled to herself. She couldn't complain. He'd always done right by her, even before that afternoon a decade earlier when he'd seen the pictures and come to understand that it wasn't just her husband he needed to respect. She turned the page in the album and gasped. No matter how many times she saw that one, it still amazed her. First that it had happened at all, and second that she had allowed it to be photographed.

Like the other photos, it was a Polaroid, and showed the backside, from the waist down, of a strapping young black man, the starting tailback of the Florida State Seminoles. Kneeling before him was a naked, nineteen-year-old Joanna Montgomery. She wore no makeup, but her face was unlined, fresh and smiling. And behind her, grabbing her generous bosom with both hands, was a drunken but clearly recognizable M.J. Weathers, then the 'Noles' second-string wide receiver.

Joanna shook her head at the photo, wondering again how they'd all managed to get in the picture. The camera must have had an auto-timer, no doubt. Her memories of the event were sketchy and faded, obscured by the fog of alcohol and pot that had precipitated their little party. She had been the jock fraternity's "little sister," terrified to tell her parents that she had flunked out. The frat brothers had graciously put her up in their house, passing her from room to room as their outside social lives demanded.

She had been assigned to Weathers' room for about a week, and had actually grown to like him, when his buddy Troy had stopped by one evening with a bottle of Wild Turkey and a dime bag. One thing led to another, and before she knew it, they were all three naked, in and out of the twin bed, pawing each other like the porn movie they'd just got done watching. Somewhere a Polaroid camera appeared, and they shot the whole cartridge.

Joanna decided later it must have been Troy's camera, because that's who blackmailed her with the photos just a few months before she was to marry racing magnate Bobby Horn in Daytona's Wedding of the Century. By then, Troy had long since suffered his career-ending knee injury, blown what money he'd earned in his brief NFL stint and had been in and out of jail on cocaine charges. In retrospect, he had done her a favor. The photos, after all, were a much more powerful tool in her hands, and worth a whole lot more than the $2,500 Troy had bargained for. And with his overdose a year later, there was no telling where they might have wound up if she hadn't bought them.

At one time she had considered incinerating all the photos save for the one useful shot. But as the years passed, she was glad she hadn't. She had come to enjoy reminiscing about how she once looked naturally, before the series of tucks and lifts and suctions. And, truth be told, looking at herself in the various porn-star poses still made her hot, made her wonder if she could still manage . . .

The Muzak clicked off in Joanna's ear.

"Speaker Weathers."

Joanna smiled. Not M.J., or just Weathers, but Speaker Weathers.

"Good afternoon, M.J. It's your favorite multimillionaire."

The line clicked again, as M.J. switched off the speakerphone. "Hullo, Joanna," he drawled. "What can I do you for today?"

"How are things?" she teased. "How are your buddies in the God Squad?"

A brief pause. M.J. had heard this bit before. "What is it you need, Joanna?"

She wasn't through teasing yet. "Don't you want to know what I'm looking at?"

She heard the line become muffled, heard M.J. call his secretary "sweetheart," ask her to close the door on her way out. "You know, Joanna," his voice returned clearly, "I'm sure you could find plenty of guys in Daytona to re-create that night for you. You seem awful hung up on it. What's it been, twenty-seven, twenty-eight years?"

Joanna laughed pleasantly. "Now M.J., you *know* that's not my favorite." She flipped the page on the album. "You know which one I'm looking at right now, don't you?"

M.J. knew. She had shown it to him once. Not the original, of course, but a snapshot of the photo. It had been fuzzy, but clear enough to show M.J. Weathers and Troy Jefferson, their arms around each other's shoulders, huge grins on their stoned faces as they proudly displayed the evidence of Joanna's handiwork. Of course, Joanna had snapped the picture herself, so that one photo, taken out of context, implied something else entirely. Something a God-fearing, race-baiting, gay-bashing, Bible-thumping public servant would be hard pressed to explain.

"I don't even remember it," he said calmly. "Neither do you, I bet. Besides, I was a kid. It was three decades ago."

"Save it. You were already president of the student senate, Campus Crusade and College Republicans. And if I remember right, your election campaign called for firing all homosexuals from the state colleges." She snapped the album shut, shifted into business mode. "Anyway. That's not why I called. I want to know what's happening with my RaceWorld bill."

"I shouldda known. Now Joanna, why can't you just come to the point? How many times do I have to tell you that you don't need to blackmail me? Have I *ever* turned down one of your bribes?" M.J. sighed. "Okay. RaceWorld. Like I told you last week, it ain't a bill. Bills gotta be filed, and then pesky freshman members ask dumb questions about them. I'm doin' it as two amendments on two separate bills. The first one grants a waiver to the coastal construction set-back line along the Daytona Beach–Ponce Inlet Corridor. The second allocates eighty million dollars for redevelopment projects east of the set-back line between Sebastian Inlet and the Georgia border. The restrictions are written so that only RaceWorld qualifies."

Joanna doodled on her desk pad, drew a giant, three-dimensional dollar sign, wrote out an eight followed by seven zeros. "So when are you planning on introducing them?"

"I already told you. They'll be inserted as technical amendments by the staff. It's no big deal. But I've got something for *you*: What the hell's going on with that lawsuit? I thought you were gettin' that dismissed?"

She squirmed in her chair. "We've hit kind of a snag with that."

"I read about your snag. Your idiot son plants piles of chicken eggs on the beach. And now the judge can't wait to rule against the county. Nice going. You realize, don't you, that if the judge finds in her favor, it could take years of appeals to get it overturned? And all that time, not a shovel gets turned on RaceWorld? Not to mention the possibility it might not *get* overturned?"

"He's not my son," Joanna corrected. "He's my stepson. In fact, he's older than me."

"Whatever. Point is: You don't get things in order down there, it don't make a lick of difference what I do up here. I could set aside eight hundred million, and it would just sit in the Treasury collecting dust."

Joanna wondered about his sudden enthusiasm. He'd never sounded so interested before. Perhaps she'd been overly generous with her carrot: ten percent of RaceWorld's net for as long as he lived. She did, after all, still have a pretty persuasive stick. Perhaps she'd modify the agreement—after he'd slipped the language into law.

"Don't worry yourself about it," she said. "RaceWorld will make you a millionaire."

"I'm already a millionaire."

"You can never be too rich, or too thin. I'll talk to you soon."

Joanna paged backward through the album. It was amazing how far M.J. had moved in the world since that night. He'd never actually started a game until his senior year, and even then he hadn't been very good. Now, having taken over the right wing of the state Republican Party, M.J. had a great shot at Congress. Or even governor.

She smiled, wishing M. J. Weathers a long and prosperous career.

She shut the album, walked to the wall safe behind the giant aerial photo of the racetrack and tucked it away.

Amee stood on tiptoe to wave bye to Dave from Charlotte, the night's first customer, as he walked off down the Boardwalk, $40 poorer than when he'd walked in.

She smiled, satisfied. She'd played him well, letting him win the first two games, and then beating him, barely, with what looked like a lucky shot. Then she beat him consistently and handily, figuring his ego would keep buying games until he'd won again.

Eight games from one Joe wasn't bad for the early evening lull when customers were scarce. She turned and headed for the bar, where Rick already had two rumrunners poured and waiting. She pulled a Marlboro Light from her fanny pack *en route* and had already sucked down two lungsful by the time she sat down.

A few gulps of bubble-gum pink drink later, though, the exhilaration of earning $40 in less than an hour wore off, and she fell back into the dumps she'd awakened in. She'd fucked up last night. Big time. She'd pushed that schmuck too far, and had the uneasy feeling she wouldn't be able to reel him back.

The fool needed her help, not her insults. She berated herself for not biting her tongue; it was something she'd never been good at, and this time it had cost her. This guy was rich: not owned-a-hardware-store-or-gas-station rich, but *real* rich. Millionaire rich. A chick didn't get many shots at guys like that, especially guys that rich who were also that dumb.

If she played Nick right, she'd have more money than she'd ever dreamed of, a hell of a lot more than she'd ever make scamming pool games. She had to be smarter, and treat him like any other Joe whom she needed to play for a while. She had to stroke him, make him feel important, smart, powerful, until she had him where she could finish him. With Nick, that could take months. She had to ease into a position where he'd trust her, tell her things, like where he kept the cash in his house, how much money he had in his checking account, what the code was for his

ATM card. And, if he was serious about doing his wife and stepmom, he would be in line for some serious dough. Like enough even to try to marry the fool, get in his will . . .

She had a daydream she hadn't had since she was nine—herself in a white, flowing gown, a veil over her face, walking down the aisle— when she noticed the heavy smell behind her, a thick combination of sweat, mildew and sex.

"Don't you ever wear any other clothes?"

She turned to find Jamie, the wanna-be race-car-driving pornographer. He had another day's growth of erratic facial hair and wore the same grungy T-shirt and shorts he had the day before. "Don't *you?*"

He smiled, showing off the deep dimple in his left cheek. "I had a busy night *and* a busy morning." He pulled another packet of photos from his shorts and set them on the bar. "Didn't have time for a shower."

Amee blew a stream of smoke into the air, set down her cigarette in an ashtray. "More chicks in bathing suits?" she asked, opening the packet from the one-hour lab and pulling out the inner envelope.

"I did what you told me. I bought a copy of *Hustler* to study, and I saw right away what you were talking about. Can I have your other drink?"

Amee pushed the second glass toward him and stared at the first photo. It was one of the girls from the day before, except she was in bed on all fours, looking down through her spread legs at the camera. She wore only a gold ankle bracelet and a hungry sneer.

"That's Monica," Jamie added helpfully. "She was the best. I got a real good one of her further down, holding a rolling pin."

She slipped through the stack, each new picture more explicit than the last. One had Tiffany lying back, legs open, back arched, face screwed up in feigned ecstasy.

"That's a good one, huh?" He smiled proudly. "You can see right up inside."

By the middle of the roll, Jamie had gotten the girls to start playing with assorted props: a hairbrush, kitchen implements, various pieces of fruit, stuffed animals. A few shots further, he'd gotten them to start playing with each other.

"And you met these chicks for the first time yesterday?" The pictures were amateurishly shot, with bad lighting and worse composition. But the girls were all pretty and all young. Not a dimple of cellulite among them. She could get $200 or $300 for the stack without even trying. "Who are they?"

Jamie knocked back half his drink. "They're roommates, here in town. Two of 'em wait tables at the Quarterdeck. The third one, Monica, sells timeshares." He picked up the pile Amee had finished with. "You know, they're just the sweetest gals I ever met. They really want to help me out. I don't have a place to stay, so they took me in. They made me dinner last night." He nodded sincerely. "They're like sisters to me."

Amee got to the last picture, a family portrait of the three surrounding their new brother. Jamie sat on a tattered couch, drunk and naked, each arm around a bare girl, each hand cupping a bare breast. All three girls lent a hand to cover his privates.

"These are your sisters? Where are *you* from, Kentucky?"

He grabbed the photo and shoved it into his pocket. "West Virginia. This one ain't for publication. It's just a souvenir."

Amee shook her head, drew a long puff from her cigarette, crushed the butt in the ashtray. "What did you promise them?"

"I didn't *promise* nothing. I told them I'd try to get them shoots with *Playboy* and *Penthouse*, and that could get 'em into modeling and acting. But before the big boys would even look at 'em, they had to be in smaller magazines first, like *Hustler*. So what do you think, can you sell 'em?"

"Maybe." She lit another cigarette. "I might be able to get a hundred or a hundred fifty for the set."

His eyebrows narrowed. "And how much is your take?"

"For this?" She shrugged. "I'd do it for fifteen percent."

Jamie took a deep breath. "Okay. So if you sold 'em for a hundred, that means you'd keep . . ." He added figures, mouthed out calculations, closed his eyes. "No, wait . . ."

"Fifteen dollars." She sighed. "Which means you'd get eighty-five."

"Right. And if it was one fifty, then . . ."

"Twenty-two fifty for me, a hundred twenty-two fifty for you."

She eyed him carefully. He was a total cretin, but had a certain charm. What he'd done with those girls was impressive, if he was telling the truth: met them in the afternoon, had them modeling porn for him that night.

"You're pretty good with girls, huh?"

He smiled modestly. "I'm okay, I guess. My friends tell me I do all right with the women."

She nodded. "You can pretty much talk them into anything, huh?"

"Well, not *anything*. But women listen to what I have to say. I'd say I have that ability. You want I should go back and get some more pictures?"

"No, no. These are fine. But how would you like to start doing some driving sooner instead of later?"

He tilted his head skeptically. "What kind of driving?"

"NASCAR driving."

His face melted in awe. "You serious?" he whispered.

"You'll never guess who my boyfriend is." She popped down off her stool. "Follow me to my office."

Nolin laid the two-by-four across the sawhorses, rummaged for his tape measure and pulled it the length of the stud. *Pedro*. Just friggin' brilliant. And then to make sure she noticed his blazing intellect, he'd repeated it: *Pedro*. He turned to the corner where he'd banished the mutt. "See where your shenanigans got us? Bad dog!"

Pedro perked up his ears, then laid them flat when he realized he was still being scolded. Nolin marked the wood, rewound the tape and drew it back out on the other side. Measure twice, cut once. *God*, she was beautiful. Long, lean, perfect skin. Just like she'd looked through the binoculars. And now, thanks to his traitor dog, his beautiful, long, lean neighbor knew that he was a friggin' pervert. Spied on naked women from the safety of his porch. One hand for the binoculars, one hand for himself, no doubt.

He bent for the circular saw, pushed the guide against the wood and pulled the trigger. The machine screamed to life and he slid it forward, slicing through the pine like butter. He grabbed the trimmed piece and held it to the nearly complete frame for what would be one of five picture windows along the seaward wall.

I was looking at the stars. Yeah. *I was looking at your breasts. Could I call you sometime?*

Any hope of trying to see her socially was pretty much shot to hell. He hadn't been able to stop thinking about her all day, through the routine motions in divorce court, through the lunch meeting with the cuckolded husband and new client, through the afternoon of staring out the window while pretending to read briefs. He bet she even knew how to sail. Probably owned her own boat. Of course. Why not? Probably an Ivy League grad from a moneyed family, now that he'd totally blown his chance with her.

He'd already spent hours dreaming up scenarios to salvage a second chance: Follow her to see where she did her grocery shopping, and then happen to run into her in the produce section. Or wait until she checked her mail one evening, then go out to pull his own rusting relic of a mailbox from the ground. Sure, he'd tie the wrought-iron pole to the tow hitch on his truck and yank it clean out. That would impress her.

And then, when he'd caught her eye, he'd walk over, introduce himself and pretend like the other night had never happened. In the off chance she remembered him and asked if she hadn't seen him on the beach that other night, he'd play dumb. No. That wouldn't work because of that damned Pedro. Eventually she'd see him. Unless he could hide him away somewhere . . . No, he'd just start barking. And anyway, what were the odds that she wouldn't remember his face? He certainly had gotten a good, long look at hers.

He sighed, reached for the drill. She would have been perfect: the woman he'd been waiting for since his dad died. Someone to fill that enormous void, and he'd finally found her. The only sailboat-owning, independently wealthy, well-educated woman in greater Daytona Beach. And he'd blown it. Or rather, Pedro had blown it for him.

"Bad dog," he called over to the corner again before plunging the whirring bit into the stud. It was only when the drill stopped its whine that he heard the knock. Pedro leapt to his feet, tail wagging furiously, and Nolin turned around. She was smiling shyly, wearing a blue sundress and holding a six-pack of Bud longnecks.

"Hi. I didn't mean to barge in, but you didn't answer the doorbell. And the door *was* open . . ."

Nolin gulped, tried to remember the script he'd worked out for this meeting. "Not hooked up. The doorbell."

Her dress clung to her thin figure, slid gracefully down long legs. A thin, white coral strand decorated her left ankle above white sandals. She was absolutely stunning. He stared, speechless.

She grinned nervously. "Well, I'm sorry if I disturbed you. But I thought that since we're neighbors and all." She lifted the six-pack of beer. "This *is* what you were drinking last night?"

Oh, God. Not only had she remembered he had a beer in his hand, she remembered *which* beer. He nodded weakly.

"Well, I saw you come in a couple of hours ago and decided to drop by and get your opinion on something. If you're busy, I can come back some other time—"

"No!" Nolin startled himself. "I mean, now is great. I was just . . ." He dropped the drill and wiped the sawdust on his hands onto his jeans. "Finishing up. Please, have a seat."

"Tell me." She lifted her left foot onto a stack of wood like a hunter above a kill and put her hands on her hips. "Do I look like a slut?"

Nick huddled uncomfortably in his leather jacket. The joint either didn't have air conditioning or didn't have it turned on, and between the heavy jacket and the full beard pasted onto his face, he was hot, sweaty and itchy.

Over his beer mug he again surveyed the establishment, which was either a bar doing a side business in tattoos or a tattoo parlor serving alcohol. Either way, he wondered how it had gotten a license. Probably by threatening to beat the living crap out of the health inspector, he decided.

He turned from the bar, shuffling peanut shells underfoot, and out of the corner of his eye checked out the clientele. Big, bearded, smelly.

Wearing denim, leather, both or, among those in the tattoo chairs, pretty much nothing at all. Yelling and laughing, guzzling huge mugs of beer. He understood now what Amee had meant about the Iron Spike. That place had potted plants hanging in the windows and over the bar, while any foliage brought into Mike's Tap would almost certainly expire within minutes. If the thick gray air didn't get it, one of the patrons would probably piss in it. A particularly foul-smelling man had already urinated out the front window, banging himself dry against the frame.

Which one was it? he wondered again. Which of the guys looked most like a Crawdad? The newspaper article didn't have a picture. It just described the man acquitted of aggravated assault and attempted murder after the witness disappeared. He didn't dare ask. It would probably be the window pisser, who looked to be the meanest son of a bitch in there.

On the other hand, a mean son of a bitch was just the sort of man he was looking for. He'd already seen what a polite, well-mannered biker would do with his money. He finished his beer, turned back to the bar and waited for the long-haired barkeep to wander over.

"I'll have another. And I'm looking for Crawdad." He slipped a twenty onto the bar.

The barkeep set the foaming mug onto the cigarette-burned wood and nodded his head at the near corner, where a half dozen bikers and their molls sat in various states of undress while grungy tattoo artists poked their flesh with needles and ink-filled guns.

One man lay on a couch completely naked except for his boots, while a gap-toothed woman applied the finishing touches to a green-and-purple snake that began on his shoulder, slithered over rolls of chest and belly fat, through a patch of dark hair and onto his shaft. He winced and growled as the woman poked the outlines of a pair of black snake eyes. She had already finished the fangs and nostrils.

Nick gulped, hoped desperately that wasn't his man. He averted his eyes quickly and lit upon a voluptuous young blonde in a black bikini getting something done on her back. He looked again at the bikini top. It seemed painted on, the way it hugged every contour. He blinked and realized it *was* painted on. No, worse: It was *tattooed* on.

"Nice tits, huh?"

Nick looked up, saw that a heavyset man in dirty jeans and a faded black leather jacket had walked up beside him. He carried a beer mug and grinned maliciously, reached out to pinch a matte-black nipple. She smiled at him, then at Nick.

"See, last year, they busted my old lady 'cause I had her ridin' nekkid, so she wouldn't have to keep pulling off her clothes," the biker explained to Nick, who nodded quickly.

It was a Daytona Bike Week tradition. Guys lined Main Street, chanting "Show us your tits" at the women and cheering as the women on the bikes would lift their shirts obligingly.

"This time next week, she won't even have to wear her bottoms and no one'll know the difference." He reached down to pinch her left cheek through the leather bikini. "So long as she shaves."

The girl smiled at Nick again, and he looked away quickly, noticed the faded red lobster on the back of a giant hand, over the letters L-O-N. Lon. As in Lon Stanko. As in Crawdad.

"Did you do that yourself?" Nick pointed at his hand.

"My first tattoo," he said proudly. "I did it with a needle and some paints. That's all you get in a maximum security facility like Union Correctional. Whatever you can steal with your own two hands."

"It's very nice," Nick said sincerely.

"Damn right." Crawdad stretched an arm around Nick's shoulders, positioned it gently so the crook of his elbow squeezed Nick's neck. "Mister, you didn't come here to look at my skin art, and you didn't come here to look at my old lady's titties, either."

Nick glanced back at the bar, saw the bartender drawing two drafts.

"That's right. Johnnie told me you was lookin' for me. He's my friend, see? Like everybody in here is my friend. Nobody's gonna say a word if you never leave here." He spun Nick around to look into his face and belched violently. "Now. You here for business? Or pleasure?"

It had been too long since he'd done a night dive. Even a short one, on a bare sand bottom like he was doing, was better than a lot of daytime dives on coral. All the critters came out at night, and even though he only saw the ones that swam within the beam of his headlamp, it was still a whole lot more interesting than in the day, when most of the baitfish, rays, crabs, sharks and eels hid from predators.

He kicked gently, holding the metal box out in front, stopping every now and again when a blacktip or a sand shark cruised by, passing close to examine the strange creature in their domain. It wouldn't do to antagonize them. No telling how they'd react, not at night: feeding time.

Quickly he came to the marker he'd placed that afternoon. He dove a few feet to the bottom, buried a small anchor in the sand, and let the box rise upward until it was about six feet from the surface and its attached wire just broke through, then clamped the nylon cable tie into place. It wasn't as elaborate as last time but would, if it worked right, be even more spectacular.

Finished, he turned and started back toward the dinghy, switching off his light and flipping over to swim on his back. Every once in a while a graceful black shadow passed in silhouette against the starlit dark blue.

God, he loved night dives.

Nolin realized after an awkward half minute that her question wasn't rhetorical. She would stand there until he answered. Which explained everything. She had appeared, unbeckoned, like a Venus on the halfshell, but only to chew him out for gawking at her like the hopeless reprobate that he was.

"Well," he began uncertainly. I don't think there's anything to be ashamed of about the human body. I go skinny-dipping myself, every now and then. . . ."

She frowned, set the six-pack on the ground and climbed onto a plank lying across the sawhorses. She bent her left knee, twisting first left, then right, like a fashion model.

He blinked, puzzled for a moment before realizing he was off the hook. She wasn't talking about last night after all! She wanted to know what he thought about her dress. Hmmm . . . Should he compliment her on how it clung to every goose bump? How it was obvious to the planet that she wasn't wearing a bra?

"It's very nice," he said politely. "And you really can't tell whether you're wearing underwear or not." *Aarrrrgh!* He shook his head quickly. "What I mean is, and it's certainly not a reflection on your sensibilities whether you do or you don't—"

"I'm *talking* about this." She pointed at the coral anklet. "Do you think the ankle bracelet makes me look like a slut?"

He looked down at her ankle, bewildered. "Do *you* think it makes you look like a slut?" he asked cautiously.

She jumped down off the plank, grabbed two beers and handed him one. "As a matter of fact, I do. See, I think it would help my business if I wore one, but I don't want to look cheap. It's such a small step, you know, between looking cheap and being cheap."

Nolin watched as she sat down across from him on an overturned milk crate, crossed her long legs. He studied the string of coral beads draped across her foot. "I guess I never thought of it that way. But you know? Now that I think of it, it seems like half the women in Daytona are wearing them nowadays."

"So you *do* think it makes me look like a slut." She took a sip of her beer. "Not that it matters. Even if it brings in more business, I don't think it would happen fast enough. I'm in a lawsuit, you see, and I'm way behind on my bills. My attorney told me he'd drop me if I can't pay by next week. And then the judge will rule against me."

"Not necessarily," Nolin said, sensing an opportunity to redeem himself. "Just tell the judge you have to switch lawyers and he'll postpone everything for a while."

"Not this judge."

"Sounds like Antoon." He took a swig of beer. "You're right. He never grants continuances. I've tried. You pretty much have to die to get one. Which case?"

She smiled shyly. "So you're an attorney, too. But you don't recognize me? You've never seen me on TV?"

"Never watch it."

"Well, I think the official name is Save Our Turtles, Inc., versus Volusia—"

"The Turtle Lady! Sure, I know who you are. You're the one trying to get cars off the beach because they run over baby sea turtles."

She nodded. "The way this town's reacting, you'd think I was trying to make them give up sex."

Nolin grinned. "No, in this town, you'd have an easier time banning sex than banning cars from the beach. A lot of them think it's *better* than sex."

She laughed out loud. He studied her face, the sculpted features, the smoky eyes. He remembered it from someplace, but couldn't recall where.

"This *is* a strange place," she agreed. "Bikers, race car rednecks, drunk college students, bums, escaped cons. And everybody pretends like it's all perfectly normal." She took another sip. "Sometimes I wonder why I stay. I mean, if I lose the turtle suit, I guess there's nothing keeping me."

"You don't have family here?"

"Not anymore. My mom died a few years ago. My dad is"—she waved an arm out toward the ocean—"who knows. He ran away when I was an infant."

"No boyfriend, fiancé?" He smiled. "No one who's gonna come barging in here any minute to kick my butt?"

She smiled sadly. "No. No boyfriend, no fiancé. Although, technically, I guess I still have a husband. We've been separated almost two years. It's just a matter of signing the papers."

Nick's heart sank. "Oh. I see. Well, sometimes, you know, couples realize how much they miss each other after they've been apart for a while. They find they can't bring themselves to go through with a divorce and end up back together, more in love than ever."

Barbie looked at him quizzically and laughed aloud. "It's nothing like that. It has nothing to do with love. It never did. That was the problem." She thought a moment. "All the years I was growing up, Mom groomed me to marry well. That was all that mattered. To make up, I guess, for the fact that she didn't. Anyway, so when the most eligible bachelor in town gave me a ring, I pretty much figured I'd died and gone to heaven. My mom acted like I was getting away with grand larceny. That I was marrying way over my head, that I couldn't possibly deserve everything I was getting. I guess I bought into it. I didn't stop to ask myself whether I loved him, or he loved me. Anyway. The reason we haven't signed the papers is his family image. His father got divorced to marry a much younger woman, and he and his stepmom are afraid it'll look bad if he got a divorce, too."

He snorted. "That's crazy! And what are *you* supposed to do, meanwhile? Never get married again just so this guy won't look bad at the country club?"

She shrugged. "I didn't mind. What did it matter? I've been using my maiden name, my own money, I have my own business. As far as getting married again, I haven't met anyone I've even been remotely interested in." She sipped her beer and grinned. "Until maybe now."

Jamie sat in the straight-backed chair, staring at Amee's navel. It was an outie, pierced with a tiny golden ring. Funny, but he hadn't noticed, and he'd always considered himself fairly observant about that sort of thing. Maybe it was only an outie some of the time, and an innie the rest.

"You're not paying attention," she scolded.

"I am so. I walk into her store, hang around till no one else is there, get her to go in the back, shoot her, make it—"

"Shoot her in the head," Amee corrected. "You gotta shoot her in the head."

"Shoot her in the head, make it look like a robbery and get out the back door."

"Good." Amee smiled. She sat on the edge of her desk, lifted her feet onto Jamie's chair and tucked her toes under his thighs. "I think you've got it."

"And where do I get the gun?"

"I'll get it for you."

"And what do I do with the gun?"

"Take it with you. We dump it in the ocean afterwards."

Jamie thought about it, shook his head. "I dunno. It don't *sound* that easy."

"What part?" she asked patiently. "What part doesn't sound easy?"

"Like how do I get her in the back?"

Amee smiled. "If you can charm the panties off three babes you just met, get 'em to spread their legs for your camera, don't you think you can talk *one* into getting something from the back office for you? Tell her you're buying an outfit for your girlfriend, and you need the phone to call her to get the right size. I don't know. You tell me. What sort of shit does a chick like that fall for?"

"I dunno," he repeated, looking up shyly. "I never killed anybody before."

"Nothing to be ashamed of." She shook her head with conviction. "There's gotta be a first time for everything, right? Besides, I promise not to tell Nick that you don't got any experience. And when you get this done, he won't even care. He'll be so grateful you can't imagine."

"And you're sure I'll get to drive in the Crown Cola 400?"

"You have my word. Your own car, your own pit crew and whatever else you need to give those rednecks a run for their money. Besides"— she moved her feet out from under his thighs to rest them gently on his crotch—"a fringe benefit of partnering with Cherry is you get to hang out with Cherry socially, if you know what I mean."

His eyes scanned her from brown toes all the way up to dark brown eyes. "I've never needed to kill anybody to get girls."

"Really?" With one hand she swept her hair out of the way, with the other she untied the knot behind her neck. Her breasts swung free. "You wouldn't just be getting girls, you'd be getting Cherry. For example: How many orifices do your new girlfriends let you use?"

His eyes were now glued to her chest; she felt a tremor beneath her toes.

"I told you. They give me the run of the house."

Amee rolled her eyes. "How many different *holes* do your girlfriends let you into?"

He blushed. "Oh, that. Well, one of them only does sex, but the other two give me blowjobs, too."

"Oh yeah? Well, with Cherry, you get a three-orifice woman. And if you're really good, Peaches out there can join us, and that's another three. So between the two of us, we've already got your girlfriends beat, six to five."

"Oh." He thought for a moment, then blushed even deeper. "*Oh!* Well, I ain't never done *that.*"

"Like I said, there's gotta be a first time for everything." She squeezed him between her toes. "So what do you say? You with me?"

"I dunno, Cherry. Shootin' somebody like that. It don't seem right, somehow." He thought a moment longer, glanced up at her nipples again. "How about a shot in the Crown Cola *and* ten grand?"

With a sigh, she found the strands to her top, reached behind her neck to retie them. "A shot in the Crown Cola and five grand."

He smiled happily and stuck out his hand. "Deal."

Nick understood now why the guy had urinated out the window instead of in the men's room. The first thing he'd have to do when he left would be to stop at a decent establishment and wash his hands, which at the moment were spread against the tiled wall—a wall stained with grime, mildew, urine and God only knew what else.

The girl's hands moved firmly down his chest, his sides, his groin, his legs and finally his ankles. She was barefoot, and didn't mind kneeling on the sticky floor, just as she didn't mind traipsing around in only a leather bikini bottom in the nastiest biker bar in town.

"He's not carrying," she said in a sweet young voice.

Crawdad grunted. "See if he's wired."

She began patting him down again, this time more probingly. He felt himself awaken. Perfect. That's all he needed was to get a hard-on for the psycho's girlfriend. Give him just the excuse to gut him like an animal. Like he needed an excuse.

"I can't tell through his clothes," she said.

"Then take his goddamned clothes off," Crawdad growled.

Nick turned his head in alarm, saw the biker flick a cigarette butt in the general direction of the urinal.

"Don't get excited. Just makin' sure you ain't a cop." He reached in his jacket for a pack of Camels and pulled one out with his teeth. "You *ain't* a cop, are you?"

Nick turned back to the wall. The girl had taken off his jacket and was unbuttoning his shirt. "No, sir."

"Good. 'Cause if you are, and you lie and say you ain't, then that's entrapment. You know that, dontcha?"

She pulled off his shirt, squeezed between him and the wall to undo his belt. "If you say so, sir," Nick said in a shaky voice, wondering for a moment what James Bond might have done in this situation before realizing the absurdity of the thought. Bond would already have killed the biker, bedded his woman and have been on his second martini. The notion of bedding Crawdad's woman aroused him even further, just as she unzipped his pants and yanked down both trousers and shorts, pulling the elastic outward to let him pop free. He didn't know what was worse: her seeing it, or her not even noticing. It didn't matter. If Crawdad saw, he was a dead man.

"No wires," she reported.

"Good. One more place to check."

Nick wondered what he meant when suddenly he felt her wiggling in, probing, searching. He winced back tears, but realized he was growing even harder. Just as suddenly she was gone.

"Nothing."

"Good," Crawdad said. Now go wash your hands. You don't know where that asshole's been, if you know what I mean. And *you* can turn around."

Nick reached for his pants.

"I said *turn around!*"

Nick dropped his pants, closed his eyes and turned to face Crawdad.

"Well, ain't you somethin'," Crawdad said. "Fake beard, pants down at your knees and a raging hard-on for my old lady. Put that thing away."

Nick complied, zipping up his pants, stuffing his arms back into his shirt and buttoning and buckling as fast as he could. The girl walked back from the sink and returned to Crawdad's side.

"Now tell me, mister." Crawdad reached an arm behind her, slid his hand inside her bikini bottom. "So who is it you want killed?"

Nick gulped. "Who said I want anyone killed?"

"Well, I'm just guessin' you ain't here for financial advice." Crawdad removed his hand, held it beneath wide, grimy nostrils and inhaled deeply. "Who am I supposed to do? Business partner? Mother-in-law? Girlfriend's husband?"

"Wife," Nick said softly.

Crawdad nodded, like he should have known. "Obvious choice. Never fails. You can't live with 'em, you can't chop 'em into little pieces and stick 'em in a storage unit. What, she cheat on you?"

"No." Did he have to tell him why? "It's a long story."

"Just went bad, eh?" Crawdad said understandingly. "It happens. When?"

"Soon. It has to be before next Monday. But the sooner the better."

Crawdad twisted and untwisted strands of his beard. "Rush job. Don't like 'em. Too easy to screw something up." He grinned, baring a row of skewed teeth. "I think I can fit her in. If the price is right."

Nick lowered his eyes. "Well, I don't have a lot."

Crawdad shrugged. "You can't afford it, you can't afford it. I got plenty of work."

Nick gulped. "How much?"

"Normally it's twenty bills. For a rush job, thirty."

His mind sped. He did the math twice and tried to hide his surprise. "So that's, what, three grand?"

Crawdad snorted. "*Thirty* grand."

"I thought a bill was a hundred dollars," Nick whined. He was sure of it. Every mobster movie he'd ever seen: a bill was a $100 bill.

A sneer spread across the biker's lips. "You thought wrong. For three grand, I wouldn't even bust her legs. Now this ain't some flea market. The price is thirty grand."

Nick frowned in dismay. He'd already blown $10,000 on Lance the

Gay Biker, now this guy wanted most of what he had left. So much for his own big bonus. And how the hell was he going to pay for Joanna?

"I just can't afford thirty thousand," he said quietly.

Crawdad turned for the door. "Fine. Kill her yourself."

"Wait." Nick sighed in defeat. "Okay. Thirty thousand."

Crawdad smiled. "Name, address, work address if she's got one and a picture."

Nick pulled out his wallet, removed a photo and scribbled on the back. "This is about three years old but she pretty much looks the same. Only her hair is longer."

Crawdad studied the snapshot. "Whoa. You sure you want to be gettin' rid of somethin' like this?" He bent closer to the photo. "Wait a minute. I seen this lady before."

"You and half the planet," Nick said impatiently.

Crawdad snapped his fingers. "Now I remember! She's the naked chick from that poster. I *got* that poster at home. The Nipple Girl." He showed the picture to his girlfriend. "See? Ain't that her?"

Nick sighed. "You're right. That's her. The Nipple Girl."

"Why you want to go killin' a lady like this for? You got any idea what you can get for her? Especially with titties like that?"

Nick blinked. "*Get* for her?"

"Fifty, sixty grand, easy. Tell you what, you let me take care of her. I'll do it for free. She'll be out of your hair." He thrust his girlfriend at Nick. "I'll even give you this one."

Nick looked at the girl, who smiled back shyly. He imagined taking her home to show Joanna, shook his head. "Look, let's just keep it simple, okay? Just kill her. No white slavery. No wife swapping. Just kill her."

Crawdad looked at the photo again. "Damn shame, wastin' a prime piece of ass like that. *C'est la vie.*"

Nick blinked uncomprehendingly. "You'll do it, then?"

"My friend, go start pickin' out a tombstone." He shoved the photo in his jacket pocket. "That'll be fifteen now, fifteen after. You can leave it for me at the bar. You seem like an honest guy, so I don't gotta tell you what I'll do to you if you don't pay up afterward."

Nick reached for his wallet, remembered again what his last hire had done. And here he was about to give this guy $5,000 more than he'd given Lance. "Mr. Stanko, I hate to ask you this, but you're not by any chance gay, are you?"

Barbie knelt down, lifted her hair out of the way and pressed her ear against the mound of sand. "Sometimes I think I can really hear them in there." She sat back up and smiled. "I know it's just my imagination."

Nolin ran his hand over the mound. "You know, I've lived in Daytona fifteen years, but this is the first time I've been this close to a turtle nest. How many eggs are inside?"

"A hundred. More or less." She turned toward the sea, sat up straight, cross-legged. "They've come here for thousands of years, you know. Long before any people were even here. The Indians used to catch them, eat their eggs. But they never ate enough to kill them off."

He brushed the sand off his hand. "I guess you do know your turtles."

She shrugged. "I've read up. They're found in every ocean. They thrive in warm water. They haven't changed in aeons. The females lay eggs every other year. Of those hundred hatchlings, maybe fifty will avoid the seagulls and other critters and make it across the beach and into the water. Of those, most get eaten by fishes and crabs. Maybe one or two will grow to adulthood."

He studied her in profile, the pale eyes, the line of her nose, and knew again he'd seen her somewhere. "How'd you get so interested in them?"

Barbie laughed, flicked a small shell at the white surf line. "You'll think I'm a ditz if I tell you."

"You don't know that."

"You will. I can tell from the way you talk. You're very linear. You go straight from point A to point B. There's never any question, never any mystery."

Nolin smiled. "I don't know whether to be insulted or flattered."

"I didn't mean it in a bad way. I'm just saying I'm not like that, and that's why you'll laugh."

"I promise not to laugh. At least not until later, when I'm by my-self."

She sighed. "My fortune-teller told me I was a sea turtle in a past life."

"Ah." He nodded effusively. "Fortune-teller."

"You know. Psychic. Seer. Medium. Whatever you want to call it. Anyway, I have one in Cassadaga I go to a couple of times a week."

"Sure. Cassadaga." He'd never been there, but had read the news-paper's annual Halloween story about the strange little town populated by mystics and spiritual advisers. He thought it all a crock.

"You think it's all a crock, don't you?" She turned to him seriously. "Okay, so it probably is. I know most of 'em are just con artists, but I thought Madame Rosa was different. For a while I did, anyway. Lately I haven't been too sure. Anyhow, the one time she told me I lived in the sea in a past life, I just *knew*, right away, that she was right. Even now, when I close my eyes, I can still see coral reefs, and fish, and when I look up, the surface of the sea."

"Maybe you're just remembering a nice dive you've done."

"I've never been diving in my life. I'd *like* to, but I can never get past the first class. It's something to do with my ears. Anyway, I think she's right about the turtles. There's something sort of mystical about them. The way they coincide their trips to the beach with the phase of the moon. Did you know"—she put a hand on his knee—"that a female tur-tle swims hundreds, even thousands of miles but still returns to the exact same beach to lay her eggs? Now, when scientists can explain *that*, maybe I'll put more faith in them and less in Madame Rosa."

Nolin glanced nervously at her hand, still on his knee. He tried to keep from shaking, looked out at the starlit water. A soft breeze drove gentle waves onto the sand. "So how come they're still disappearing? The turtles I mean. I thought they're protected now."

"They are. From hunters. But not from condos that undercut the beach. Or from streetlights that confuse the babies and lure them onto the road. Here in Daytona, they're not even protected from cars running over their nests. Not to mention all the pollution."

Nolin nodded. "That's right. That's one of your main points in the lawsuit, isn't it? About the pollution destroying the habitat of an endangered species."

"Ever notice how much oil and antifreeze and God knows what else drips onto a supermarket parking lot?" She lifted a handful of sand, let it slip between her fingers. "Well, that's exactly what cars leave on the beach, too."

To his chagrin, she removed her hand from his knee to stroke the turtle nest again. "That's the whole reason I got a house way down here near the inlet. The sand's so soft that most drivers don't want to risk getting stuck." She brushed the damp grains off her hands. "Tomorrow will be different, though. Tomorrow every idiot between Jacksonville and Miami will be parked right here."

"Oh yeah." Nolin remembered hearing an ad on the radio. "Some speedboat race, right?"

"*The* offshore speedboat series of the year, if you believe the hype. Four hours of the biggest, noisiest, dirtiest boats in the world, tearing up the water, spewing unburned gas, leaking oil. The whole shebang."

"I can't wait. Why here?"

Barbie shrugged. "Probably something to do with the Van Hornes' RaceWorld scheme." She sat up straight. "Did you see that?"

He sat up also and stared out at the water. "Where?"

She pointed. "Out where they have those buoys set up."

He squinted, shook his head. "I don't see a thing."

"It's gone, now. I'm pretty sure I saw something, though. Something dark, just out beyond that marker. It looked like, I don't know, one of those little inflatable boats." She peered a bit longer. "Maybe it was nothing. Just a dolphin or something."

"Or a shark." He grinned. "Maybe the same one that ate the Jet Skiers is coming back for more."

"I was there that day." She shivered at the memory. "It was amazing. One moment everything was fine. The next, a feeding frenzy. It was like they were teaching us a lesson. We can poison the land all we want, but we better leave the sea alone. Or else."

"Maybe they just hate Jet Skiers." Nolin shrugged. "Can you blame them?"

"They *are* pretty annoying. And smelly, and noisy, and rude. No, I guess I can't."

He lay down on the cool sand, stared into the clear sky. This night, *all* the stars were out. "So what's RaceWorld? I've never heard of it."

She turned toward him. "Oh, it's this monstrosity the Van Hornes want to build. Sort of a racing theme park. There'll be Jet Ski rentals, boat racing, exhibits, three-dollar Cokes. But the biggest attraction's supposed to be a quarter-mile strip where tourists can race old-time cars up and down the beach. It was going to cost like a hundred million or something, but Joanna figured a way to scam the state into paying for most of it."

"Down here?" Nolin asked in alarm. "They want to build that *here?*"

"Uh-huh." She nodded. "Land's cheaper than in Daytona proper. They've already bought off whoever they need to buy off to get it done."

He shook his head in wonder. "I haven't seen a word about this in the paper."

"That's because they *own* half the paper, or just about. The paper will write about it when the Van Hornes are good and ready to have it written about."

A series of previously random thoughts coalesced in his head. His breath caught in his throat as he tried to remember the address listed for Barbara Van Horne, née Baxter. "How come *you* know so much about it then?" he asked as nonchalantly as he could manage.

She laughed. "Because when you marry into the family, you learn a lot of stuff, even when they don't want you to."

Nolin sat silently for a minute. Shock slowly became anger. The one woman he'd met in years who seemed like she could be The One, and that asshole Van Horne had made her unavailable. His client's estranged wife, and here he was. On the beach, drinking beers. Working up his courage to reach out, casually touch her forearm. Perfect.

Well, to hell with it, he thought bitterly. He'd see her if he wanted to, and that was that.

And then J. R. Van Horne would file a complaint with the Bar, and they would process it, and a judge—with his luck Antoon—would hear it, and he would be disbarred. He shook his head in disbelief.

"Is something wrong?"

"I just can't believe"—he turned to face her, saw the earnest eyes, the full lips he suddenly needed so badly against his own. To hell with J. R. Van Horne. He'd tell him he wasn't going to represent him anymore—"that they're going to ruin the last piece of undeveloped beach in the county."

Barbie sat glumly. "Me neither. Or actually, I *can* believe it. I can believe it pretty easily. And they'll do it, too, unless by some miracle I win this lawsuit."

Nolin grinned. "That's right. If you get cars off the beach, I guess that goes for race car rides on the beach, as well. I bet they're worried sick about how Antoon's gonna rule, especially after that stunt with the chicken eggs."

"Yeah. That's got Nick all over it. He's such a loser. I must have been out of my mind to marry him. You know he goes to all the hearings? Except he doesn't want anyone to know that the family has an interest in the outcome, so he wears glasses and a fake beard."

"Aha." Nolin recalled the odd figure behind him at the chicken-egg hearing. "Things become clearer."

Barbie stood, brushed sand off her dress. "Well, I don't mean to be a party pooper, but I've got to wake up early. The curse of running your own business, I guess."

Nolin picked up her sandals, handed them to her. "Can I walk you the rest of the way home?"

She smiled. "I would be honored."

They began walking, occasionally touching at the shoulders and elbows. Nolin's nerves crackled at every contact. "I'm glad you came by."

"I'm glad I did, too."

"Thanks for the beer."

"You're welcome. Next time you can bring it."

Yes! There would be a next time! "Maybe later this week? Or this weekend?"

"I would love that." They reached her dune crossover. She reached for the weathered two-by-six that served as a handrail. "Well, this is where I get off."

Nolin stood awkwardly, toeing the sand. He couldn't remember the last time he'd been in this situation. Was he supposed to put his arm around her? Or would that be too forward? Before he could react, she had pressed against him, reached up onto tiptoes and kissed him lightly.

"Good night, Pedro."

His dog's name rattled around his head as, once again, he watched her climb the stairs and slip through her gate before he turned away to walk home.

FOUR
...

The sun was out again, and for the fourth straight day it was unseasonably warm. Amee ached to take off the T-shirt and shorts and take advantage of the sunshine to maintain her tan. She turned an olive green when she didn't get enough sun, and olive green just didn't bring in the Joes like nut brown did. Still, the little red thong would turn too many heads out on the street, and this was one morning she didn't want attention.

She glanced again at the clock on the lamppost. It was almost quarter after. He was already a half hour late. Served her right for picking a moron. She glanced back up at the clock and reached for the handlebars on her bike when a dirty orange Datsun pulled up alongside the curb.

Jamie gave her a big grin. "Hey, Cherry! Sorry I'm running a little late." He leaned over to push the passenger door open for her. "My room-mates didn't wake me up early enough, and when they did, they were all getting ready for work. So I jumped in the shower with one of them, you know, to save a little time? But I think it actually slowed things down instead." He smiled again. "You know how *that* goes."

Amee swung herself into the seat and slammed the door. "I've been standing here for a half hour, asshole. If you ain't up to this, just tell me, okay? I could get a hundred other guys"—she snapped her fingers—"like that."

Jamie lifted his hands defensively. "Okay. All right. I'm sorry. Keep your shirt on. I'm here now, ain't I?"

Amee shook her head, reached to open her knapsack, pulled out a towel. "Here."

"What do I need that for?"

"Inside, numbnuts," she hissed. "I got it for you last night. It's only a .22, so remember what I said about shooting her—"

"In the head, I know. I'm not a *complete* moron." He took the towel, reached inside and removed the pistol. It was a tiny automatic, barely the size of his hand. "This? I'm supposed to kill somebody with this? I had a bigger gun back home to shoot squirrels with."

"Fine. You think of a way to sneak a rifle into her store, go for it. Until then, shut the fuck up."

Jamie examined the gun unhappily. "I don't like it. But you're the boss, I guess." He squinted through his window at the store across the street. "Is that it? The Harmonic Age? What's that, like a music store?"

"She sells crystals and shit. You know, New Age stuff."

He watched three women standing around a dress rack. "Which one's her?"

"See? That's why you were supposed to get here a half hour ago. To see who opened up. Lucky for you, I was here to save your ass." She pointed through the window. "The skinny one in the yellow dress. Now let's go through this once more."

Jamie rolled his eyes. "We've been through it enough already. I browse until I'm the only customer left. I ask to borrow her phone, I follow her back into the office, I shoot her in the head—"

"How many times?"

"I empty the gun. Then I pull out the drawers, make a mess and get out the back door. I meet you at the boat race, and we ditch the gun tonight."

She nodded. "Good. And don't touch anything metal or glass or they'll have your fingerprints. Got it?"

"Yeah, yeah, yeah. When do I get my five grand?"

"Don't worry about it. You'll get your money."

"And a crack at your orifices."

"And my orifices."

"And a shot in the Crown Cola."

"And a shot in the damn race. Now get going. She'll close for lunch if you don't hurry."

Jamie opened his door, shut it again. "Hang on a minute . . . That word, orifices." He dug underneath his seat, pulled out a crumpled paper napkin and a pen. "I want to write it down before I forget. I like to use a new word at least three times every day. See? And I've already used it once."

She stared at him as he scratched the pen on his thigh until the ink began to flow. "You gotta be fuckin' kidding."

His eyes opened wide. "Oh no. It really helps. I want to build up my vocabulary. You know that people get their first impression of you based on the kind of words you use? You might want to think about building your own vocabulary, too."

"I don't fuckin' believe this."

"Orifices. How do you spell that?"

She shook her head and spelled it for him.

"Great. And that means: holes." He wrote carefully, folded the napkin and stuffed it into his T-shirt pocket. "Oh yeah, I know what I wanted to ask you. How come you're called Cherry? Is that your favorite fruit or something? I mean, you ain't a virgin, are you?"

She looked at him a moment. "Do I look like a virgin?"

"I didn't think so. So how come Cherry?"

She sighed. "It's French. French for dear."

"Oh." Jamie nodded. "Okay. Cherry means dear." He dug out his napkin. "Let me write that down, too."

Amee groaned, reached for the door handle. "I'm outta here. Meet me at the boat races."

. . .

Pedro. She thought his name was Pedro.

He mulled it over and over. How was he going to correct her without embarrassing her? And if he did embarrass her, would it shame her into avoiding him? Perhaps correcting her could wait a few days. Or weeks. Or months. After all, what was a name? A collection of vowels and consonants chosen by his parents. Douglas. Pedro. What did it matter?

Nolin was lost in the abstraction and therefore didn't notice the Monte Carlo pull up in the circular driveway, didn't see his visitor until he was standing behind him clearing his throat. He turned and smiled. J. R. Van Horne. Just the man he needed to see. "Good morning, Mr. Van Horne."

Nick held up his hand, walked in with legs spread, knees bent, and stood in front of the desk. "I have some legal-type questions for you."

"What happened to your legs?" Nolin asked.

Nick scowled, winced. "Don't ask."

Nolin shrugged, motioned him toward the chair. "Sit down, please."

Nick winced again. "I'd rather stand."

Nolin shrugged again. "Well, Mr. Van Horne, I didn't expect to see you today, but I'm glad you stopped by. There's something I need to discuss—"

"First off," Nick began. "Say hypothetically I hire somebody to do some work, and pay him up front, and then he doesn't do the work. What can I do about it?"

Nolin watched him shift his weight from one leg to the other. "I'd start by complaining to the trade association that represents him. Like if he's an electrician, file a complaint with the electricians guild. There's no legal remedy there, but sometimes they can help resolve things."

Nick thought for a second. "What if there's no trade association?"

"Then you have to sue him. How much did he stiff you for?"

Nick thought again. "Ten grand," he said carefully.

"Then that's circuit court. That's a hundred-and-five-dollar filing fee, and you have to pay to serve the guy with the papers. Then there are attorneys' fees. You can get attorneys' fees and court costs back if you win."

"But in court, would I have to explain what the guy was supposed to do? Or could it be enough that he stiffed me?"

Nolin blinked. "You mean you want to go in there, tell the judge that there's this guy who owes you money, but you don't want to explain why?" He chuckled. "He'd toss the both of us out on our ear."

"I was afraid of that." Nick meditated a moment. "So I guess it's the same if, hypothetically, I hire somebody for a job, and he does something that's got *nothing* to do with our deal. Say, hypothetically"—Nick mumbled now—"he fucks me instead. I guess the judge would want details on that, too, huh?"

Nolin recalled the stiff-legged walk. "Hypothetically fucks you . . . financially? Or physically?"

"Would it make a difference? To the judge?"

"No."

"Then forget it. I'll deal with it some other way," Nick muttered. "I got some other questions, about my wife. If something happened to her, what happens with her legal affairs?"

Nolin raised an eyebrow. "What do you mean *happened* to her?"

"You know. Hit by a bus. Drowned. Anything. I mean, I'm still technically married to her. Do I get stuck with her bills?"

"Ah," Nolin said. "No, I don't believe so. Not bills that she incurred after you were separated. Any debts she had before that, though, are legally yours."

Nick nodded. "Okay. And what about legal problems."

"Problems?"

"Yeah. Like if somebody was suing her . . . Or she was suing somebody. Hypothetically. What happens to those?"

Nolin watched him carefully. The questions had strayed well beyond those of the typical husband seeking a divorce. "Well, if she's a defendant in a suit involving a dispute that predates your separation, then yes, you're a party. As to suits in which she's the plaintiff . . ." Nolin hesitated, saw Nick's eyes narrow. "There, the judge would immediately dismiss the lawsuit."

"A lawyer couldn't keep pressing it," Nick asked casually. "Like in her memory or something?"

"It doesn't work that way." Nolin saw suspicion melt into relief. "Why do you ask? Is your wife prone to falling in front of buses?"

Nick winced, adjusted his trousers. "Don't be a smartass. Just covering all my bases, that's all. So what was it you wanted to talk about?"

"Hmmm?"

"When I came in. You said you wanted to talk about something."

Nolin affected an innocent look, inwardly scrambled. "Oh yeah. No big deal. Just doing some bookkeeping and found that you still have sixteen thousand dollars of your retainer unspent. You want me to transfer it back to your mother's account?"

Nick thought for a moment. "Any way you can just return it to me?"

"Sorry. She was pretty clear when she opened the account. Any refund goes to her."

Nick nodded. "Right. Sure. Well, you hang onto it. I might be needing your services soon." He attempted a grin and turned for the door, walked out in the same bowlegged manner he had walked in.

Through the window, Nolin watched him open the door to his Monte Carlo, heard him curse as he lowered himself into the driver's seat. He waited till the car was gone before he turned to the cabinet to pull out the Van Horne file.

Jamie stood in front of the blouse rack, flipped through them while the lady in the yellow dress helped a pair of high school girls in cutoffs and halters pick out crystal necklaces and earrings. He waded through a bin of scarves as she sold a book on massage oils and three sample bottles to a clean-cut, effeminate young man in a perfectly pressed gray suit.

Jamie eyed him suspiciously, guarding against the likelihood that he'd make a pass at him. He left, though, without any overt moves, and Jamie moved to the large jewelry display while she took care of the only other customer in the store, an older lady with long, brown legs protruding from a black minidress. She, too, finally left with a shopping bag tucked under an arm.

He engrossed himself in the jewelry, picking through gold chains, as he heard his target approach.

"Sorry it's been so busy. Can I help you find anything?"

Jamie turned with a smile, which suddenly froze on his lips. It was his first good look at her face, and he realized at once she was the girl on Cherry's ceiling. His eyes moved to her chest, but the strangely enticing breast in the poster was invisible beneath the flowing fabric.

"Yeah," he began, feeling himself press uncomfortably against the gun jammed in his waistband. "I was looking for one of these, but I need to call my girlfriend to make sure it'll fit."

Barbie glanced at the thin gold ankle bracelet between his fingers. "They're one size fits all." She pointed to a tiny catch on a series of removable links. "They're adjustable."

"I just want to be sure," he said lamely.

She studied his nervous eyes. There was something peculiar about this one. "Why don't you describe your girlfriend for me."

Jamie tried to picture one of his new roommates, but all he could see was that damned poster. The gun's metal felt cold as he pressed against it even harder. He closed one eye and thought of Cherry. "She's got dark hair, about five-foot-two, and she's got really nice tits . . . uh, excuse me, boobs. Although her butt's kinda big."

Barbie suppressed a smile. "I meant, describe her bone structure. Does she have thin limbs, like me? Or thicker?"

"Oh." He blushed. "Thin ones. Like you."

"In that case, any of these should fit without a problem. They all fit me."

Jamie looked down, saw she was wearing a string of pink coral beads around her left ankle. The pink matched her toenails and her cloth sandals. He thought of the thin gold anklet that Cherry wore.

"What's the difference between beads and the gold chains?" he asked.

"Well, it's a matter of personal preference. I tend to feel that coral suggests fun, carefree, casual. Gold is dressier. You see a lot of professional women wearing gold ones nowadays, both with bare legs and over panty hose." And they all happen to be sluts, she thought. "Is your girlfriend a professional woman?"

Jamie grinned. "No. Not exactly." He felt the gun shift slightly when he laughed and remembered his mission. "Well, I guess I need to call her to see what kind she prefers."

Barbie shrugged, motioned to the phone on the counter next to the register. "Help yourself. As long as she doesn't live in Paris or someplace."

He looked at the phone in dismay. It was right out in the main display area, within clear sight of the plate glass windows. "I, uh, need to borrow your phone book." He noticed her brow furrow in suspicion. "To get her work number. I don't know it off the top of my head."

Barbie strode past him toward the rear office. Jamie fell in behind her, studied the back of her head, where the long, straight hair fell over her bare neck. Such a beautiful neck, and those wonderful nipples he was never going to see. A damned waste. Suddenly it struck him: He was going to kill her. He was going to put his gun up against her head and pull the trigger, and her blood and brains would spill out.

"Where does she work?" Barbie asked as she opened the door to her office. "Your girlfriend."

"Oh, uh, Top Shots. Top Shots pool hall." He watched as she rounded her desk and pulled out a phone book. He thought of the various animals he had killed: squirrels, rabbits, deer. How they shivered, less and less alive, until the spirit drained from them and their eyes went dull.

"Let me see . . ." She bent over the desk across from him, head down.

Instinctively he tilted his head to look down her sundress when he remembered the gun. He looked back through the door at the empty store and focused on the top of her head. Her hair swirled clockwise, away from a tiny bare spot. A perfect target. She flipped pages. He drew the gun. It was just like the woods. The small and weak died so the big and strong could survive. He pointed at the center of the swirl. He closed his eyes. He pulled the trigger.

Nothing happened.

He opened his eyes, pulled harder, saw her move her finger down the page. He stuffed the gun back into his shorts, tried to loop the barrel through the drawstring like he had before, fumbled, missed . . .

She was staring at him, mouth wide open, finger pressed against the middle of the phone book, eyes fixated on his hands, which were plunged into his shorts, over a huge bulge that pushed through the fabric.

He smiled, looked down, didn't dare let go of the gun. "You, uh, find the number?"

"I have it right here." She lifted her eyes to meet his. "Shall I write it down for you?"

Jamie swallowed, realized he wasn't going to get his hands out of his pants until he left the store. "You know what? I just realized I forgot my wallet." He turned for the door. "Let me go get it, and I'll be right back."

Barbie watched as he walked briskly past the racks of dresses, pushed the front door open with his shoulder and ran up the street.

God, he realized, was behind him one hundred percent, and hated speedboats every bit as much as he did. The wind had grown even warmer, swung around to the south-southwest and, a consequence of Volusia County's northeast-facing shoreline, completely flattened the waves. Barely a six-inch ripple remained, breaking in long running streaks against the sand.

Conditions couldn't have been more perfect for the flat-bottomed, overpowered, fume-belching behemoths to charge at wide-open throttle down the racecourse, crushing any and all hapless sea life in their path. Conditions also couldn't have been better for the tiny, bobbing aerial to pick up the weak radio signal that would bring the afternoon to a premature but powerful conclusion.

Behind him a covered stage had been erected on the sand, on which the various luminaries had already gathered. One table supported big bowls of ice cubes and various bottles of refreshments to quench the luminaries' thirst. Another table was covered with a large green piece of felt that concealed something that, presumably, the luminaries planned to unveil at some point in the festivities.

He turned his attention back to the water, where the boats were already rumbling. Soon. Very soon. Though the earplugs leading to the

Walkman remained silent, he began shaking his head to the tune that ran through his mind.

At the edge of the crowd, Amee Mosher gyrated to the beat from her Walkman, waving her arms, shaking her buns. She didn't know the song, she didn't even like the radio station. She didn't care. She was going to be rich, and it wouldn't be long now.

She spun, stepped to the side, dropped to the sand, stood straight. She opened her eyes and noticed a scrawny surfer standing before her, mouth agape, staring at her chest. She smiled at him, licked her lips and pulled the errant red triangle back into place, then laughed aloud as he scurried away.

Tonight she would reward that moron, and tomorrow night, she would tell Nicky, and he would reward her. And then they would live happily ever after. Or however long it took for her to devise a way to separate him from his money.

She felt a hand on her waist and turned her head to the beat. It was the moron. She ground her rear against his crotch, pulled out her earphones, settled back into his arms.

"Well? Have you earned a night with Cherry?" she whispered.

"She thinks I'm a friggin' pervert. She thinks I play with myself."

Amee stiffened, turned to face him. "Who thinks you're a pervert? Nick's wife? Why is she still alive?"

"It didn't work. The gun you gave me." He reached into a paper bag. "Here."

"Not here!" she hissed. "Are you nuts?"

Around them, beach bimbos in their bikinis and bubbas in their stained T-shirts stood waiting for the start of the races.

"No one's paying any attention to us," he said defensively.

She grabbed the paper bag from him, stuffed it into her knapsack, then reached into the knapsack with one hand.

"It jammed," he complained. "I squeezed and squeezed, but it wouldn't fire."

She took her hand out of the knapsack, fastened the snaps and thrust it at Jamie's chest. "You moron. You didn't release the safety."

"Safety?"

"Safety. You know. The little thingie on the side? You push it forward before you can fire it?"

"I know what a safety is," he said indignantly. "But *you* didn't tell me *this* gun had one. Not all guns do, you know. How was I supposed to know?"

"Oh, Mr. Great Big Hunter Man can't figure out how to use a fucking little .22. Perfect. Well, a deal's a deal. You go back there and finish it," she ordered. "This time flick the safety off."

"I can't go back there!" he whined. "She'll call the cops if I set foot anywhere near there!"

Amee crossed her arms. "I send you to kill her, and instead you wank off in front of her?"

"I didn't wank off," he whispered, looking around to make sure no one was listening. "It's these shorts. They don't have no pockets. And the gun was gonna fall out. I had to grab it."

She rolled her eyes. "Okay. Here's what you're gonna do. Park across the street from her store. Then, when she leaves to go home tonight, follow her. When she gets to that part of A1A where it narrows to two lanes, you run her off the road and shoot her."

"You want me to shoot her on the street? Out in public?"

"Make sure no one's around." She heard the roar behind her, saw that the boats had started their engines, raised her voice. "You must have seen how empty the road is down here. Just make sure there's no cars coming. Got it?"

"Got it. Run her off the road and shoot her in the head," he shouted, then realized the boats had stopped racing their engines and everyone could hear him. A blond-haired guy with a Confederate-flag T-shirt and ponytail was staring at him. He glared back until Bubba looked away. "Then what?" he whispered.

Amee shook her head sadly. "Come by the pool hall."

. . .

Nick turned the knobs until the glasses focused on the row of bimbos lining the water's edge near the finish line. With the warmer weather, they had broken out their skimpiest bikinis, and all he could see was buns. Big, small, flabby, firm. Buns everywhere.

He groaned and set the binoculars on the table, grabbed the edge until the wave of nausea passed. There was a time, not too long ago, when he could have spent all day staring at young girls' asses. No more. Rear ends were no longer a mystery.

"Where the hell have you been?" Joanna hissed. "I had to lunch with the Budweiser people myself."

She was, as usual, dressed way too young: transparent white blouse, red miniskirt, bright red pumps and the ubiquitous gold anklet. He would introduce her to Crawdad, he decided. Tell him that *she* thought he was gay, too.

"I'm running a little slow today, so back off," he said through gritted teeth. "Mom."

She glared at him for a few moments. "Well, come on over here. The races are about to start." She moved to the front of the platform. "And after the awards ceremony, we'll announce RaceWorld. Why are you walking like that?"

Nick grimaced as he pulled up beside her. "It's nothing, all right? Just pulled something getting out of the car."

The emcee announced their presence over the PA system, and Joanna smiled and waved at the applauding crowd. "Did you take care of everything?" she asked through her smile.

"It's done, okay? Do get off my case."

The first two boats in the series rumbled south to the start line. One bright red, representing Budweiser, the other yellow, sponsored by Chiquita bananas, each carried 1,500 horsepower engines built into its stern, enough to drive them at more than 120 miles per hour across flat water. Three helmeted men in matching coveralls stood behind each boat's console, although only one held the steering wheel.

"You know those things cost ten million each? They could buy five race cars with that," Joanna said.

"Budweiser already *has* five race cars." Nick winced. He had to stop raising his voice. Somehow the muscles in his diaphragm linked up with the muscles . . . farther down.

"I wonder what those other guys do while the driver is driving," Joanna mused.

"Something worthwhile, I'm sure," Nick said. On the sand below him, a beer-bellied bubba had his hand down his girlfriend's shorts. "Something worth the respect of all these classy spectators."

Joanna shot him a glare, then turned back to the start of the race. The course was one mile long and the boats began from an idle. The yellow lights blinked on and off down the pole erected on a flatbed truck, until finally the green one lighted to the accompaniment of a piercing shriek. Suddenly the boats were spewing exhaust, their bows thrust high into the air, rooster tails growing behind them. A few seconds later the roar of their engines arrived, blasting across the beach.

Nick watched the Budweiser boat take a half boat-length lead, then stretch it to a full length. Closer they came, a quarter mile away now. Then only three hundred yards. Then two hundred. And then the bow of the red boat lifted out of the water even farther, dragging her clear out of the water, until she stood upright on her stern, propellers screaming, and then the bow continued its arc, coming over to complete the back flip, coming down, down . . . right on top of the Chiquita boat.

The crowd groaned collectively as space-age carbon composites crunched and smashed, taking loads in directions never imagined by the engineers, until the still-racing propellers on Budweiser finally sheared off, sending fragments of red-hot titanium slicing through her outer hull and into the integral fuel tank.

The explosion drowned out the crowd, which by then was screaming, and the fireball quickly consumed the plastic and metal carcass, sending waves of heat across the water toward the beach. In the ensuing pandemonium, it took some time before anyone noticed the dark fin that sliced this way and that, snatching bits of matching coveralled racers into the depths.

.   .   .

Jamie struggled down the page, one boring paragraph at a time, finally flipped to the next one. He couldn't believe he was reading. He hated reading. It was so slow, so dull. He'd never understood why, after TV was invented, people bothered with it.

But, he had to fit in, and the only place to hang out across from the Harmonic Age was a bookstore that had little tables on the sidewalk where you could sit, drink coffee and read a book. Jamie couldn't see how come they couldn't set out some radios and TVs for people who didn't like reading, but realized that was probably an argument he wasn't going to win.

The owner was probably a snob, some English major in college, probably didn't even own a TV. Besides, everyone else was reading, so he forced himself to grab a book from the best-seller rack and take a table next to the building, facing across the street. He closed the book again, stared at the cover. It showed a dark haunted house, and a bald, evil-looking vampire. He was pretty sure he'd seen the movie, and he even remembered liking it, but how they'd made a decent flick out of such an awful book he'd never understand.

He turned back to his page, picked up where he'd left off. If only he had his Walkman. If he was listening to music, it wouldn't seem like he'd been reading so long. He eyed the waitress at the next table, where a couple wearing matching tie-dyed shirts sat with open magazines.

He smiled at her as she walked by, trying to get another look at her chest. She was wearing a tight, ribbed T-shirt with nothing underneath except a nipple ring. God, he wanted to see her naked. Maybe tomorrow he'd come back with his camera and press passes. Maybe he could get her to come to his new roommates' house. Four girls at once. Now *there* was an idea.

He was busy thinking of pickup lines when, out of the corner of his eye, he noticed Barbie Van Horne shake her front door to make sure it was locked and turn toward her white Volkswagen. It was time. Nonchalantly he set his book on the table, dropped five sticky quarters on the table for the coffee and stood to walk over to his car. He felt his waistband, panicked for a moment, then remembered he'd left the gun under the passenger seat. He allowed himself a smile. This time things would go perfectly, and he'd be $5,000 richer, with a good chance at the $250,000 prize money for winning the Crown Cola 400 come July. He couldn't begin to imagine what he would do with such staggering wealth. But one thing for sure, he'd get himself a new car. Maybe one of those new Trans Ams they just came out with. Now *that* would be cool. With a car like that, he'd be able to get any chick he wanted.

He watched his quarry lower her convertible top, settle into her seat and start her engine. He reached for his door handle, pulled and nearly broke his fingernails off. It was stuck. He turned, saw her look over her shoulder and pull into traffic, and gave another sharp yank on the door, this time accompanied with a kick. Still it wouldn't budge. Panicked, he shook the handle violently, then looked inside the window and realized it wasn't stuck. It was locked, with his keys dangling quietly from the ignition. Why? He *never* locked his doors! There was nothing inside worth stealing.

Then he remembered. This time there *was* something worth stealing. The gun. He had rolled his windows and locked his doors to keep the gun from getting ripped off. Brilliant. He turned to look down Seabreeze but could no longer distinguish Barbie Van Horne's taillights from the rest in the stream. He gave his Datsun a final kick for good measure and turned to go find himself a wire hanger.

FIVE

■ ■ ■

 The floodlights provided an eerie cast to the raceway's infield, giving the grass almost the same blue-green hue the ocean had had that afternoon. Nick stood at the plate-glass window atop the Winston Tower, staring down at the two-and-a-half-mile "tri-oval" of concrete below. Tomorrow was the first day of qualifying. The pits and workshops would be filled with tobacco-chewing rednecks who, somehow, had become the heroes of America's fastest growing spectator sport. The clean, well-kept infield would become home for their beer-swilling kin, who would sit atop their rented U-Haul trucks with binoculars, watching their local-boys-done-good make left turn after left turn, hour after hour, breaking only to get more beer out of the cooler or get into fights with rival clans. By the end of Speed Week, the infield would be trashed, the concrete marred with a few hundred more rubber streaks, and the Van Horne family would be about $20 million richer.

Behind him, Joanna hit the rewind button once again, bringing the tape back to the few hundred feet before the accident. She leaned forward intently and pressed play. Nick sighed, finished his gin and tonic. She had been watching the tape for nearly an hour. On the table beside her sat the still-not-unveiled model for RaceWorld, with its little exhibit hall, its little Van Horne Needle thrusting skyward, its little plastic figurines of parents and children walking the beach and enjoying the many, all-included-in-the-same-low-price attractions.

"There, you see that?" Joanna hit the rewind button, brought it back a few seconds, let it roll forward again. In one frame, the Budweiser boat was charging along in full control. The next, her bow had begun its fatal rise out of the water. "You see that? Sharks."

Nick shuffled painfully forward to just behind the couch. "Where? All I saw was the boat flipping out of control."

"No!" Joanna slapped the remote control onto the coffee table. "One accident, okay. But two? I tell you, it's those same sharks from before. Once they taste human flesh, they never go back to fish."

Nick poured himself another drink, stiffer even than the last, which in turn had been more so than the one previous. "Maybe we just weren't meant for this water thing. Maybe we should stick to racing on land."

She stared at him icily. "How many times do I have to tell you? More than ninety percent of our revenues come from the five big races each year. So the three raceways bring in fifty million, give or take. We have to exploit the other forty-seven weeks out of the year, otherwise we're never going to make any real money. You think Michael Eisner would keep Disney World open just five weeks each year? Or Bill Gates would sell computers for just one month out of the year? Of course not."

Nick took a big gulp, swallowed it down. His headache wasn't getting any better. Neither was his butt-ache. And he wouldn't have either one if not for Joanna's damned beach theme park. "You know, even making money just five weeks out of the year, you're still the queen of Daytona Beach. Isn't that what you always wanted?"

Joanna pressed the eject button, walked over to the VCR to grab the tape. "Now you listen to me. If you think I'm about to abandon RaceWorld because of some stupid fish, you've got another think coming. Now here." She thrust the tape at him. "Take care of it."

"Take care of it?" He looked at the cassette cartridge. "What the hell am *I* supposed to do?"

"Eliminate them. You're having that bitch wife of yours eliminated, right? Find someone to do the fish."

Nick laughed, immediately regretted it as his hemorrhoids throbbed. "Joanna, they're not just *fish*. They're sharks. They're huge! One of 'em swallowed a Jet Skier whole!"

"Kill them."

"Chrissake, Joanna, didn't you ever watch *Jaws*? You can't just kill them. They keep coming back. Year after year after year." Nick caught her glare, held it, finally looked away with a dry swallow. "Who the hell in this town knows anything about sharks, anyway?"

Joanna moved to the couch to step into her heels. "That, Nick, is no longer my problem. Now it is your problem. You have until the end of Speed Week. If we don't announce RaceWorld by then, we'll end up paying a fortune in advertising. No, I take that back. *You'll* end up paying a fortune in advertising."

She strode out of the suite, and he heard her clicking down the hall to the elevator. Nick moved back to the picture window, studied the tape in his hand with disdain, and downed the rest of his drink.

See, Barbie, there's a couple of things I need to explain. First off, my name's not Pedro. Second, I represent your husband in your divorce. And third, I think he might be trying to kill you.

No. Too direct. Nolin shook his head, turned around her mailbox, up her driveway. Perhaps a more casual approach would be better. He'd wait for the conversation to take the appropriate turn, then nonchalantly bring up the salient information. Yeah, right. And how, exactly, would the conversation wind up on the topic of dim-witted, murdering husbands?

He pulled up to the front door, put his finger on the doorbell, then pulled away. He peered in through the glass panel beside the door, saw a long, tiled foyer leading straight back to a sliding glass door overlooking the darkening beach. He turned to face the scraggly lawn fronting the road, looked at the orange sky turning purple.

Another day, that's what he needed. He'd sleep on it, and tomorrow at work he'd think of a smooth way to explain everything. Besides, what was there to explain? The name thing: well, that was just an honest mistake. And the stuff about her husband: again a simple mistake. He didn't realize when he met her that her husband was a client. No big deal. He certainly wasn't trying to trick her. And as for the murder thing. Well, granted he had no definitive proof. And this *was* Daytona Beach, so nothing was too farfetched, and she certainly deserved to know that her husband had been asking about the financial implications of her death.

He turned again toward the door, saw now that it was open and Barbie was leaning in it, arms stretched across the opening.

"I was wondering whether you were going to stand there all night."

She wore a white knee-length pullover and white coral jewelry around her neck and wrists. "I didn't know whether you were going to come over tonight or not." She nodded at the bottle of wine he held in his hand. "No beer tonight?"

He swallowed, handed her the bottle of Chardonnay. "I thought you might like this instead." He followed her into the house, noticed the sparse furnishings. The living room had but an old, beat-up blue couch, a green ottoman and a driftwood-and-glass coffee table. Opposite the kitchen's long counter, the dining room was bare save for a picnic table and some folding chairs. In rooms with redwood-beamed cathedral ceilings and enormous picture windows, the effect was comical, as if squatters had taken over an abandoned mansion and brought in the belongings they'd used on the streets.

"You have a beautiful place," Nolin said.

"Thank you." She fished a corkscrew from a drawer. "Excuse the furniture. Or lack thereof. As you can probably guess, I'm one of those millions of foolish Americans who's cash poor and house rich. I was at an RTC auction and couldn't resist the price, even though it cleaned me out."

Barbie popped out the cork and poured two glasses. She handed him one and clinked her glass against his. "Cheers."

He took a sip, swallowed. Not bad, considering he'd never really cared for the stuff. He watched her pull a tray of cheese out of the fridge, grab a box of crackers from the cupboard and bend over to check the oven. Okay: It had to be now. There would be no better time.

Nolin cleared his throat. "I'm, uh, sorry I'm running a little late, but something came up at the office. Something quite interesting, actually—"

"I've got a chicken in the oven. It'll be another half hour or so. You want to wait in here, or go out on the deck?"

Nolin shrugged, flustered. He almost had it out. "The deck sounds good."

She pulled open the sliding glass door and climbed down three steps onto the weathered gray planking. He followed, slid the screen door shut behind him and watched her set the cheese and crackers beside the sunken Jacuzzi. She lifted off the vinyl cover, folded it and laid it aside.

"I turned the heater on this up about an hour ago." She dipped her toes in, swished them around for a few seconds. "I hope it's hot enough for you."

It took a moment for this to register before Nolin's mouth went dry. She wanted to go hot-tubbing with him! "I didn't bring my suit," he said lamely as he watched her pull the terry cover-up over her head. She was, of course, naked underneath.

She tossed the dress onto the deck chair. "Well, I'm afraid I'm clean out of men's swim trunks. I could lend you a pair of my running shorts. They might fit."

Nolin shook his head. The only thing worse than being naked and staring at her body would be wearing clothes and staring at her body. Like he was doing now. He dropped his eyes and started undoing his belt. "No, that's okay. I guess I don't really need to wear one after all."

Amee put her eye to the peephole, confirmed it was, indeed, Nick waddling up the walkway. She turned nervously to the mirror in the hall. He had that "No Boardwalk tramp can talk to J. R. Van Horne like that" scowl on his face. She'd have to talk fast tonight, reassure him that, yes, Cherry Mosher understood that his station in life was well above hers, and that, yes, she understood completely that he could easily find a dozen others to take her place.

She fluffed up her $29 haircut, mashed her lips together to smooth the bright red gloss and tugged at the uneven seams of her neck-to-toe, red lace body stocking. As an afterthought, she pinched each nipple until it poked through the fabric. As soon as the knock sounded, she pulled open the door, lounged sinuously against the doorjamb, put on her best smile. "I've been waiting for you."

She arched her back to thrust out her chest and, as hoped, saw the scowl disappear, the mouth fall open and his eyes wander hungrily up and down her body. "What's all this about?" he asked finally.

She took his hand and drew him in, immediately started undoing the buttons on his shirt. "I just wanted to make up for the other night. I was mean to you, and I had no right to be."

His eyes narrowed and the scowl returned. She saw he was still determined to teach her a lesson. Quickly she fell to her knees.

"Damn right, you didn't," he said with as surly a voice as he could manage while watching her take his trousers' zipper tab in her teeth and pull it downward. "And don't you forget it," he mumbled.

"Oh, I won't." She pushed the door shut behind him, pulled him onto a couch to finish undressing him. "So tonight, I'm your sex slave." She struck a pose, one hand in the air, the other on her hip, and twirled around. "What do you think?"

He ran his eyes up and down again; she could see that the body stocking had his head spinning. "You look all right," he said guardedly, then seemed to remember something. "Is Lori coming?"

Amee smiled. The greedy bastard. He wasn't going to forget her offer. "Oh, she'll be here soon enough. I've got her at Top Shots by her-self. She'll close up at eleven. In time for round two? But first lie down, I've got a treat for you."

Nick smiled broadly, lay as directed, belly down on the couch. It was clear he'd shown her who was boss. And she was bending over backward to make up for it. He watched as she poured from a small flask into her cupped hand.

"Massage oil. To loosen you up." She placed her greased hands on his shoulders and started kneading. He closed his eyes and moaned softly. "I also got another surprise for you. Wanna hear it?"

"A third girl?" he asked hopefully.

"No." She moved down his back. "It's about that thing we were talking about the other night. About your wife, remember?"

"Oh. Yeah. What about it?"

"Well, I think all your worries are over. I found someone to take care of it."

He opened his eyes, turned his head to face her. "Who?" he asked suspiciously.

"This guy. You won't know him. He's sort of a beach bum. Mooches off chicks. Not bad good-looking. Anyway, I told him you'd pay him five thousand bucks."

She watched as he considered this, his fat lips twisting and poking. What the hell was his problem? Five grand for a killer was a *great* price, even for Daytona Beach. "You know, Nicky, that five grand is a steal. Getting somebody killed usually costs a lot more, especially if you get someone with experience."

He snorted. "Tell me about it. How'd you get him for just five?"

She reloaded her hands with oil. "Well, I sort of also told him you'd let him drive in the Crown Cola 400."

"Drive *what* in the Crown Cola?" he demanded.

She kneaded deeper, moved down into the small of his back. "You know. A race car."

"Hah!" he laughed. "Whadya think, I just pick whoever I want to drive in these stupid things? No sir, they got sanctioning bodies to protect the *integrity* of the *sport*, to prevent just this kind of thing. No way. Tell him forget it."

She bit her lip. By now the deed was done, provided the moron hadn't screwed up again. What was she supposed to do when he came for his money? "But Nicky, you can get just one of your own drivers in the race, can't you? Just this once?"

"Look," he growled. "There's no way I could get something like that past Joanna. Besides, I already found somebody for the job. And yes, thank you very much, I'm paying a whole hell of a lot more than five grand."

She moved her hands down onto his great, pale buttocks. "Maybe you could call your guy off, tell him you changed your mind?"

Nick thought for a moment, grunted. "Forget it. Giving this guy a deposit was painful enough. I don't even want to think about what he'd do if I tried to get it back."

She massaged silently for a while. Okay, she would have to take care of the moron. That should be easy enough: She'd take him out into the woods and pop him, something she would have to do eventually, anyway. So long as *she* was able to take credit for the murder. She was going to be really pissed if *her* guy did the job and *his* guy took the credit.

Oh well. Same as always. She had to work twice as hard to get half as much respect. But never mind. She had bigger fish to fry. Tonight she had to secure her spot as the next Mrs. Van Horne. She leaned forward to kiss him on the neck, poured more oil into her palms, greased her fingers.

"Nicky, you're doing a wonderful job with your wife." She bit his ear. "But have you thought about what to do with Joanna? Maybe I can help, baby."

He grunted. "Do more of what you were doing there."

She smiled. "Oh, you like that, eh?" She slid her oiled hand over loose flab. "I bet your wife never did this for you. Don't you want me to do this to you every night? Don't you want me to live in your house, do this to you anytime you want?"

Amee poked a greased finger down between his buttocks.

Nick screamed.

Nolin took a sip of his wine, munched another cracker. He had a while ago stopped worrying about how to tell her those terribly important things he needed to tell her. Now he was too busy falling for her.

"So how'd you and, what's-his-name, meet?" he asked, sinking deep into the water until the bubble jet was positioned on the small of his back.

"Oh, it's a trite enough story. I guess you have to understand the Daytona social scene for it to make any sense. Everything revolves around the Van Hornes. They're the town's royalty, and everyone aspires to go to the same parties, serve on the same boards, donate to the same charities, and so forth." She smiled over a sip of wine. "It's stupid, I know. But that's the stuff you're made of when you grow up here. And so when Nick actually *talked* to me at a Christmas party, and then *called* me up the next day to ask me on a date, well, that was it. I was Cinderella, about to be rescued. My mom thought it was great. It was in the gossip column of the paper, all her friends were talking about it. We were married within six months."

Nolin stared into her eyes, big and oval, separated by that perfect nose. A model's nose, small and straight. That was it. She must have been a model. That was where he recognized her from. "You know, there's something I don't understand about the Van Hornes. It seems an awful Old World name for such a white trash family."

Barbie giggled. "See what you miss out on not growing up here? That name is a fraud. Joanna invented it after she married into the family. The name was originally Horn. Like what a bull has. Or a car. But Joanna always had this inferiority complex. She bought into that old money thing, where it wasn't enough to be rich, you had to have inherited it from, I don't know, ten generations back. So twenty years ago, she legally changed the family's name to *Van Horne*. She changed all the signs at the track, had the city rename Horn Boulevard *Van* Horne Boulevard. She even went to the paper and sat down with the publisher to explain that they could mention the change in one article, and after that they couldn't refer to the plain old *Horns* ever again."

Nolin chuckled. "And the paper went for it?"

"The publisher decided he wanted to keep his job, so yeah, he went for it. Even Nick had to have his name changed, to John Robert. Joanna thought J. Robert sounded more old-money than Nick. Thought that if they all had hoity-toity names, then the Palm Beach and Martha's

Vineyard set would start accepting her invitations to watch the Daytona 500 from her skybox."

Nolin laughed again. "Interesting family. I can see how you might have felt out of place."

"Like a loggerhead turtle out of water."

She stood suddenly, twisted around to grab the bottle of wine. Again he glimpsed those fantastic nipples. They weren't erect like when she'd pulled off her dress, but still proved fascinating, still almost an inch long. Where had he seen them before? A magazine, maybe? Or a movie? He quickly averted his eyes as she spun back around to refill her glass, then his.

"So," she began as she replaced the bottle behind her. "How come a nice guy like you doesn't already have a wife and kids at home?"

He shrugged, then sank into the water to his neck. "I guess I never really tried hard enough to find someone. Plus, *you* know how hard it is to meet anybody nice in this town, especially if you don't like car racing, or Bike Week or Spring Break or driving your car on the beach. Shoot, you're practically a heretic."

She laughed. "Tell me about it. At least you're not suing to take away one of their God-given rights, like I am."

She sank into the water, lifted her feet out. Instinctively he grabbed her ankles, studied the soles. Long and thin, they were, with toes to match. Just like his.

"I know, I have freak feet." She had lifted herself off the built-in bench so she lay parallel to the surface and a few inches beneath it. "They look okay from a distance, but I could never model sandals, that's for sure."

"No. There's nothing wrong with your feet. I like long toes." He looked up her legs, across her submerged belly and chest to her face. Aha! Modeling. So that *was* where he'd seen her. "I knew I recognized your face from somewhere! You're a model!"

"Not exactly. I did some modeling years ago. You know, to pay bills for college. Ads for local boutiques, stuff like that." She pulled her feet from him. "But that's not where you recognize me from."

"It's not?"

She stood up to reveal her breasts. "I'm the Nipple Girl. From the poster."

He stared slack-jawed. That's right! The girl from the poster! They'd been all over town five years earlier. An artsy, black-and-white profile of a thin, angular model sitting knees bent and head laying on her arms. And one long, dark nipple protruding from her chest.

"That was you?" he asked incredulously.

"You seen tits like these anywhere else?" She sat back down. "That poster gave me the first clue that marrying into the Van Hornes was a serious mistake."

"They were mad you did it?"

She sighed. "See, I never gave permission for that poster. That shot was done in college, when I was modeling for a friend of mine, an *ex*-friend of mine, for his portfolio. I agreed to pose nude so long as he promised not to take pictures that showed anything. Well, he never told me about *that* shot. And it wasn't until years later that he printed the poster."

"Let me guess. Until after you'd married Nick."

"You got it. Two days after I married Nick, to be exact. We went to Bermuda on our honeymoon. When we got back, that poster was in every cheesy T-shirt shop in town. Joanna threw a fit. She screamed, called me a slut, accused me of hiding my past, scandalizing the family." She shook her head. "She considered having the marriage annulled, but decided against it because that would have attracted even more attention to it: 'The Nipple that Broke Up the Royal Marriage.'"

Nolin chuckled. "And what did Nick have to say?"

"Nick had to say exactly what his stepmother wanted to hear, He felt as betrayed as she did, that he had no idea, et cetera, et cetera. And foolish me, I actually felt like I'd done something wrong. Like I *had* betrayed their trust by not remembering those pictures and telling them about 'em. See what growing up being taught that rich people are better than you are just because they're rich does?" She sipped her wine. "I wasted three years of my life in that marriage."

"How come you haven't divorced him?"

She shrugged. "Joanna begged me not to. She thinks divorces in the family hurt them, socially. She attributes her not getting into the Palm Beach set to the fact that she's a second wife, and that Bobby divorced his first wife to marry a girl thirty years his junior. So she didn't want a divorce, especially one so soon after the nipple poster. And I honestly didn't care one way or the other. I had no intention of finding someone else. So I just let it go. Now, with the turtle lawsuit, I can barely afford *that*, let alone the bills for a divorce."

Nolin gazed at her, wondering where she'd been all these years. He thought again of the terribly important things he'd come to tell her. How would she react now if he told her he was her husband's attorney? Even more important, he had to tell her about Nick's peculiar questions about her death.

"So." She smiled. "Do you think I'm a long-toed, long-nippled slut freak, and wish you'd never met me? Or do you think I'm a long-toed, long-nippled slut freak, and wish you'd met me sooner?"

He shook his head earnestly. "I don't think you're a long-toed, long-nippled slut freak. Well, I mean, your toes *are* kinda long. And I suppose your nipples are, too. But that doesn't mean anything. I mean"—he lifted one foot out of the water—"I've got long, thin extremities, too."

She smiled coyly. "So I noticed."

He blushed violently.

"Oh come on. Don't get all shy on me now." She stood, walked across the tub and took his hand. "I mean, it's okay for you to ogle me through your binoculars? But it's not okay for me to notice your . . . extremities?"

He put his other hand on her waist. This was happening too fast. He had to tell her. "Barbie, there's something I need to tell you."

She sat on his lap, put her arms around his head. "What?"

He swallowed. "I heard the oven buzzer go off about twenty minutes ago."

Jamie hit his head against the window, awakened and sat upright with a start. He must have nodded off, that's all. No harm done. The sky behind the house was the same dark gray it had been the last time he looked. More important, the white VW was still parked in the driveway.

He twisted the radio knob to turn up the volume. It seemed to have grown softer as the night had worn on. Or maybe it was just that the miserable choice of music the night DJ had picked had dulled his hearing. The Doors, Van Morrison, Janis Joplin, the Beatles. His favorite station, and more significant, the only station his radio would pick up since the tuning control had broken, had become some sort of oldies-but-goodies station at two A.M. Who listened to that crap? How about some Ace of Base, or Smashing Pumpkins? He ought to call the station manager and tell him that the overnight DJ sucked. Hell, *he* could do a better job.

And there, even before the sun had broken the horizon in the east, came his first brainstorm of the day. He would become a radio DJ. How hard could that be? You played some music, you read some news and took some phone calls when you had a contest going.

He nodded to himself. That's what he'd do. He'd call the station manager, tell him the night DJ sucked and that he had a much better format for those hours and would be happy to help him out. He wondered how much a job like that paid. A lot, he guessed. After all, if you were on the radio, you'd be pretty famous. They'd have to give you pretty good money. Plus there were the fringe benefits, like concert tickets and T-shirts and stuff. It occurred to him that he'd also be able to tip off his friends about contest questions, so they could call in and win.

Jamie stretched his legs to pull his little notebook from his rear pocket, then rummaged around beneath the seat for a pen. He flipped through to an empty page, then wrote in careful, capital letters: NEW JOB—NIGHT RADIO DJ. Beneath the header he wrote out all benefits to such a job: GOOD MONEY, FREE STUFF, FAMOUS—BETTER CHICKS. He drew a solid line, put his pen between his lips to ponder what negatives might go with it. Finally he wrote: LOUSY HOURS.

He flipped back through the pages, glancing at the various headers—video-store manager, bartender, race car driver, airline pilot, used car salesman. He shook his head sadly: so many things to do, so little time. At least he'd definitely have a shot at race car driver, once he finished with this Van Horne chick. He returned his little book of ideas to his pocket, looked up in time to see the front door open and a tall skinny guy step through, turn to kiss Mrs. Van Horne and then walk down the path toward the street.

Jamie slid further in his seat as the guy turned down the street, walked two houses, climbed into the pickup truck in the driveway and then drove back past where Jamie's orange Datsun sat parked, nose pointing out, among some shrubs in a vacant lot.

Jamie peered over the steering wheel to see the taillights disappear in the distance, then wiped the sweat from his brow. That had been close—too close. A perfect witness, the chick's boyfriend, picking him out of a lineup as the suspicious guy in the car across from her house the morning she was killed. Fortunately, the guy hadn't even turned his head toward him as he passed. He did have a big smile on his face, though. Like he'd just gotten laid.

Jamie smiled, turned up the radio again, and sat daydreaming about Mrs. Van Horne. She was the chick in the poster on Cherry's ceiling, all right. He was sure of it. Kind of bony, yeah, but still pretty hot. That was probably why Mr. Van Horne wanted her killed. Caught her sleeping with this other bozo.

The opening riffs of Van Halen's "Pretty Woman" came through the tinny car-door speakers, and Jamie cranked the volume knob as high as it would go. He started strumming his air guitar, realizing that the first thing he would buy with his $5,000 would be a really nice radio for his car, when he noticed Mrs. Van Horne in gym shorts, tennis shoes and a sports bra, a canvas bag slung over her shoulder, unlocking the driver's side door of her VW.

Jamie reached his hand beneath the passenger seat, pulled out the towel-wrapped pistol, carefully unwrapped it, checked to make sure the safety was off and set it on the seat. He waited for her taillights to come on, then her white reverse lights, and then turned his ignition key.

The radio went dead as a soft click came from under the hood.

Sweat beaded his lip as he frantically released the key and tried again. Again the click, and then nothing. Across the highway, the VW backed into the street, stopped, then lurched forward.

Jamie pounded the wheel with his left hand, ran through the familiar procedure step-by-step: left foot pushing in clutch, right foot ready on the gas, gear shift in neutral, ignition key to "on."

Still nothing.

He pounded the wheel with both hands, swore that his stupid, piece-of-crap car had screwed him for the last time, when he noticed that now no sound whatsoever was coming from the radio. Slowly at first, then with increasing speed, he slammed his forehead on the steering wheel.

S I X

■ ■ ■

Nolin drove slowly, studying the small houses on either side of the road. A casual visitor might not notice anything out of the ordinary, he decided. The streets were tree-lined and tidy, the homes well tended and neat. But here and there were hints that Cassadaga wasn't just a run-of-the-mill town in the Florida Bible Belt.

In the backyard of a concrete-block house, he caught a glimpse of half a dozen men, all bald, all wearing bright orange robes, sitting in a circle on the grass. Two houses down, a three-story Colonial had a giant wooden cutout of the Hindi symbol for "Om" mounted above the portico. And up the street a bit, a front yard was decorated with a small white-flowering shrub arranged in an enormous pentagram.

Nolin grabbed the "Guide to Spiritualists" he'd picked up at the visitors' center, unfolded it and scanned it as he drove, making sure of the address.

He slowed his truck, came around a gentle curve and saw the white mailbox with the red lettering: MADAME ROSA CASTILLA MURDO, SEER AND MEDIUM. He turned into the driveway, set the parking brake and stepped out.

He chuckled to himself as he saw the number on one of the posts supporting the porch—777—and wondered how much of a fight there'd been for *that* address when street numbers had been assigned.

"I have been waiting for you, Meester Nolin," a Hispanic voice sang out from inside. "Please, won't you come in?"

He hesitated a moment, then pulled the screen door open and stepped through. Inside was dark, intentionally dark, with cloth hangings over the windows. As his eyes adjusted to the gloom, he saw a Spanish motif: a bullfighter's cape and sword, a pair of castanets, a small photo of the Alhambra. She smiled when she saw him, and waved him to the seat across the table from her. He moved to it, pulled out his chair and sat.

"How are you today?" she asked pleasantly.

"I'm very well, thanks." He studied the bright blue eyes, the makeup, the long, manicured fingernails on short, stubby fingers. "You know who I am?"

She laughed. "Madame Rosa knows many things, Meester Nolin. How may I help you today?"

He smiled. "Don't you know already?"

"Ah, a skeptic. It's so nice to have one every once in a while!" She laid her hands on the table, on either side of the grapefruit-sized crystal ball. "How was your drive here? From your home in Holly Hill, in your 1989 Ford pickup truck?"

And suddenly he knew. Suddenly he understood why the receptionist at the visitors' center had a computer and modem on her otherwise quaintly decorated nineteenth-century desk, why a pair of binoculars lay on the little table by the window.

"It was fine." He grinned. "Except, of course, I traded in the truck two nights ago for a BMW, although I suppose the new registration hasn't made it into the state Motor Vehicles database yet."

Madame Rosa's smile remained frozen on her lips as her eyes narrowed slightly, then widened again. "Ah, yes. Now I see the new car, although you still have the truck's aura about you. You like the new car, yes? It is very beautiful."

"I was only kidding about the new car. Don't you think your spy in the visitors' center would be able to tell the difference between a Ford pickup and a BMW?"

She lifted her arms from the table and crossed them across her ample bosom. "Is there something I can help you with? Or did you just come here to insult me?"

A bit of the Spanish accent had fallen away; Nolin noticed a touch of Texas or Oklahoma underneath. He reached into his jacket pocket and pulled out a money clip, laid it on the table. Madame Rosa's eyes fixated for a moment on the folded stack of fifty-dollar bills.

"I'm sorry if you feel insulted. I didn't come here to do that." He pulled off the silver clip, counted out two bills. "How much is your normal fee?"

"Fifty dollars for a half hour, eighty for an hour."

"More than a mechanic, less than a chiropractor." He nodded his head, counted out five $50 bills on the table. "Well. I'm prepared to give you three hours worth of money right now for your help. Help which, by the way, will not take any more of your time than normal."

She nodded for him to continue.

"You see, a very good friend of mine is one of your clients. She believes what you tell her. Don't ask me why, but she does. Anyway, I have some information that I want to tell her but, because of my own personal circumstances, I can't."

"What kind of information, Mr. Nolin?"

"It's about her husband. He's up to no good with her, and I've got this uneasy feeling he may try to hurt her. Now, I can try to protect her, but I think she'd be a lot safer if she was on her guard, too."

She eyed the money, then looked up at him. "You're asking me to base my evaluation on your information? How do I know it's true?"

He snorted. "You don't have a problem using Department of Highway Safety and Motor Vehicle information in your *evaluations*, and you know how inaccurate a lot of *that* stuff is. Plus the reason I'm here is I really care about this woman. But I think she'd be very angry with me if she knew how I came to learn this stuff about her husband."

She sighed. "It's unethical to influence a psychic forecast for the sake of two hundred and fifty dollars."

"Really?" He counted out another bill. "How about for the sake of three hundred?"

She shook her head. "If people learned that Madame Rosa changed her predictions because of bribes, they would never again trust—"

"Three-fifty?" He counted out another bill.

"— what I or any of my colleagues here—"

"Four hundred."

"— tell them, for fear that—"

He peeled off two more bills. "Five hundred dollars."

Madame Rosa looked at him, looked at the pile of fifty-dollar bills, leaned across the table to gather them up and stick them in her blouse. "Who is she, and what do you want me to tell her?"

Crawdad sat crammed in one of the tiny painted iron chairs the Book Nook had on its stretch of sidewalk, his massive legs stretched out under a glass-topped patio table. With fingerless leather gloves he poured back his third beer, motioned at the passing waitress that he wanted another.

"Just a little while longer, Jasmine." He stroked his old lady's bare arm.

It was a gray day, and although not quite cold, was on the chilly side. That morning had promised sunshine and he'd had her wear her usual warm-weather costume of high-heeled ankle boots and ruffled socks.

"It's okay," Jasmine said demurely, crossing her arms to keep herself warm.

"That chair's not too cold for you now?" he asked, recalling the yelp as she'd put her newly tattooed but otherwise-bare bottom in it.

"No. I'm fine."

Crawdad resumed his study of the Harmonic Age storefront. It looked like a terrible place for either a hit or a snatch, with big windows facing one of downtown's busier streets. Inside, his target was showing a skimpy dress to a great, big, fat woman.

The more he watched her, the more he knew he should snatch her, despite what that dipshit Van Horne said. She looked five-foot-nine, five-foot-ten, easy, with most of that in her legs. He wished the hair was blond. Light hair typically fetched a better price than dark, although that depended on the total package and the tastes of the individual customer. A lot would depend on eye color. Blue had fallen out of style, but gray or green would up the price considerably.

The fat woman left the store, and Barbie bent to pick up something off the floor. Crawdad nodded in admiration as her dress hiked higher up her thigh. Yes sir, she'd bring a nice price indeed. And he'd just tell Mr. Bigshot Executive, Mr. J. Robert Van Homo, that he'd shot her and buried her in the forest, and where the hell was his remaining fifteen grand? Shoot, he might even ask for a little tip on top, and royalties every few months probably wouldn't be out of line, either. He smiled, thinking of the pudgy, nervous little weasel. It would be just like collecting lunch money back in junior high.

"Baby, why don't you go check out that store? I need to know what color eyes this chick's got."

Jasmine nodded, took another sip of coffee from her mug and got up to walk across the street.

Nick shut off the motor and stared through the windshield at the dilapidated old house. Stucco flaked off the walls, which themselves leaned pitifully, as if weary of a long, dreary existence and just waiting for the big storm that would sweep them into the sea. The building had no number on it, yet there could be no mistaking it: the only house on the east side of A1A just inside the Flagler County line. Just like the *Daytona News-Herald* article had said.

As proof, parked right in front of him, was the car: a faded orange Karmann Ghia with the personalized tag BLCKTIP, Romer's long-ago surfer nickname, according to the article. Nick opened the door and stepped out, slowly standing upright. The soreness was gradually diminishing. With the help of Preparation H, so was the burning.

He walked to the door, rang once, twice, a third time, then, despite the NO TRESPASSING sign, started through the dune grasses and sea oats around the house to the sound of a power tool. A side window looked into a room piled high with surfboards and lumber, but Nick saw no sign of Romer and continued around to the rear of the house. There, a sliding glass door opened onto a vast workshop filled with surfboards in various stages of assembly.

The power tool noise had gone away; Nick looked around nervously, stepped inside. Tiny bits of fiberglass, foam and wood littered the bare concrete floor. He took a step forward, saw a hallway leading back into a darkened room with a blue glow, took another step and saw the source of the light. It was one of those glass wave tanks with the blue fluid that rolled back and forth, except it was bigger than any Nick had ever seen.

He moved to it, transfixed by the waves as they slowly rolled one way, broke against the side, then back the other way.

He never saw the forearm that dropped him to the thin carpet until it was already across his throat, holding him down against the cold floor. He looked up in terror at blazing eyes set amid a face constructed entirely of acute angles.

"What are you doing in my house?"

Nick managed a choked gasp in response, tried futilely to push the arm off his throat.

"You're trespassing. I'm within my rights to shoot you. You were a burglar. I was asleep. I feared an imminent threat to my person and my property. So I shot. I can guarantee you the police would buy that lock, stock and barrel. So explain why I shouldn't kill you right now."

Tears came to Nick's eyes as he kicked his legs, tried again to free his throat. "Can't breathe," he finally squeezed through.

The arm relaxed a millimeter, and Nick sucked in air. "I rang the doorbell. Three times," he explained.

"And I didn't answer it. What did that tell you?"

The tone and the eyes demanded a response, Nick realized. "That you didn't want to be bothered?"

A wicked smile curled the lip, exposing two rows of sharp teeth. "Very good. So why, then, did you choose instead to invade my privacy and break into my house?"

"I need to talk to you. It's very important."

"So talk."

The man still lay across Nick's chest, his arm still securely pressed against Nick's throat. Nick thought about asking if he could sit up, decided against it. "You're Randall Romer, right? The guy who used to be the state attorney? I mean, I only assumed because this is the house—"

"I'm Romer," the man said flatly.

"I came here because—" Nick blinked. "Don't you know who I am? Don't you recognize me?" Nick tried to turn his head to the angle in the flattering publicity shots the paper always used.

"No," Romer said.

Nick tried to hide his disappointment. "Oh. It's just that I'm on the TV every once in a while. And I'm in the paper all the—"

"I don't watch television, and I *never* read the newspaper." Romer squinted. "You're not that stockbroker I sent away for ten years, are you? The one who ripped off all those old people?" He smiled his wolfish smile. "Oh, I bet your dance card was filled every night, huh? Bet you were the belle of the ball. Tell me: Was it better with soap? Or without?"

It took a moment for Nick to realize what he was talking about, and when he did, sweat broke out on his brow as he recalled Crawdad's savage grin afterward. *No, not again!* "No!" he shouted. "I mean, I'm not him at all. I've never sold any stocks. I'm, that is, my family . . . You know who the Van Hornes are, right?"

Romer cleared his throat like he was about to spit. "You're not one of those scum, are you? That's my biggest disappointment: Eight years in office, and I was never able to put a single one of those bastards away."

Nick's mind spun gears. "Uh, no. I'm not *one* of them. I just work for 'em."

"That would have been my crowning coup: the Van Hornes, Daytona's white-trash-turned-royalty. A bunch of thieving scum, the whole lot. Another couple of months and I could have had the old man, his tramp wife and the kid. All three on bribery and mail fraud. I think I could've gotten state time for the kid."

Nick gulped. "Well, I don't really know them that well. The old man died a few years ago, though. The tramp wife is running things now. That's who I work for."

Romer scowled. "So what does she want?"

"Sharks. I guess you're some kind of expert?"

Romer's eyes narrowed. "What do you mean? Who says I am?"

"Lots of people, I guess. I asked a friend of mine for a shark expert, he sent me down to a surf shop in Ponce Inlet. The guy there said Randall Romer was the closest thing to an expert Daytona had ever seen." Actually the guy had said: that crazy son-of-a-bitch state attorney. "He even dug up an old article from the newspaper. They quoted you about surfing at the Inlet, and how come so many sharks bite surfers—"

"Screw the newspaper. Endorsed my opponent, the bastards. Over the porno tapes. Editors didn't want anybody interfering with their God-given right to rent *Debbie Does Dallas* and whack off. To hell with Florida law. Just enforce the laws we *want* you to enforce."

Nick lay very still, watching Romer stare vacantly at him, through him. The details of the controversy came back to him now, how God-fearing Randall Romer had taken a literal view of the obscenity statutes and gone beyond shutting down the peep shows and sex clubs on U.S. 1 like he'd promised in his campaigns. Instead he'd gone after video-store owners for carrying porno cassettes, even subpoenaing them for their lists of customers. Romer had put his flawless record on the line for his crusade: In twenty years as a prosecutor, first as an assistant U.S. attorney, then as the elected state attorney for Volusia County, trying everything from racketeering and counterfeiting to extortion and murder, he'd never lost a case. Ever. Not until the blue-haired grandmother and jury forewoman had stood up after a full ten-minute deliberation and told the judge that while *she* personally wouldn't watch such filth, she didn't think it violated obscenity laws for others to do so.

Romer's fall afterward had been swift and complete. He failed to return to his office, or even call in, for two weeks after the verdict and when he did return, it was as a surly, withdrawn tyrant. His wife left him, took the house, took everything. And when it came time for re-election, the voters disavowed him as well. Though he'd taken nearly seventy-five percent of the vote in his first two elections, he won only thirty percent in the election that threw him out of office.

"I personally think it's a lousy newspaper, myself," Nick offered.

Romer's eyes regained their focus. "So what about sharks?" he asked suspiciously.

"Well, sir, you seem to be as much an expert as there is about them, at least here in Daytona Beach, and I was hoping—"

"Most misunderstood fish on the planet, the shark." Romer's eyes lifted up to the wave tank. "Absolute apex predator of the sea. Perfect in every way, and everybody hates it."

Romer lifted his stringy body off Nick, brushed bits of Styrofoam and wood from his shirt and moved to the wave tank. On the wall above was a varnished teak plaque displaying five triangular teeth. One by one he pulled them from custom-carved indentations and turned back toward Nick.

"This is from *Carcharhinus limbatus*, the blacktip." He handed Nick a hard triangle, an inch on each side. "This accounts for ninety percent of shark attacks in Florida. Almost all of them are on surfers."

Nick felt the serrated edges of the tooth, nodded admiringly.

"They don't mean to bite us. We're not their normal prey. But the water's so murky near river mouths, the visibility is terrible, all they can feel is the vibration as the surfer paddles out. These they can sense from miles away, along the lateral line that runs right back to the tail. They can also sense the surfer's actual electrical field through tiny little holes, the ampullae of Lorenzini. Biologists still haven't figured out exactly how they work. Just like they haven't figured out why sharks never get cancer."

Nick felt more than saw Romer's evangelical gaze as he turned the tooth over in his hands. "Really?" he answered pleasantly. "That's interesting."

"Oh, it's more than just *interesting*," Romer mocked. "Here we are, helpless before this dread disease that, sooner or later, will get every one of us if something else doesn't get us first, and this primordial fish, something that's barely evolved in millions of years, is completely immune. Of course, when you're that perfect, why would you *need* to evolve?"

Nick nodded, passed him back the blacktip tooth. "It seems that you might be just—"

"This one is from a tiger shark." Romer handed him a slightly larger triangle. "Another species classified as dangerous. Because, I guess, it has the audacity to defend its territory. This is from a bull shark. This is from the favorite of the big and small screen: *Carcharodon carcharias*, the great white, the best known and the most feared. Which is not completely deserved. Because this one"—he held up a narrower tooth, slightly smaller than the great white's—"comes from the most unpredictable, most ferocious thing out there: *Isurus oxyrinchus*, the mako."

Nick took the tooth, studied it with genuine curiosity. "Really? Worse than the great white?"

"*Worse* is pejorative, but in that context: yes, worse than a great white. A great white will hit when he's hungry. When he's not hungry, he'll just bump or even go away. Not a mako. He hits for the sake of hitting. Voracious feeder. Easily excited, faster than hell. Bite first, ask questions later. Nothing's safe in the water when a mako's around."

"Huh." Nick looked up from the teeth. "Sounds like the one that showed up at the boat races."

Romer fell silent, studied Nick closely for a minute. "Actually, no." He grabbed the teeth out of Nick's hands and replaced them in their plaque. "A mako is a pelagic fish. He doesn't hang around shallows. Whatever it was, it wasn't a mako."

He smiled broadly at Nick, then stepped back into the workshop, put his face down close to an eight-foot-long board with a gentle hollow ground out of its centerline. Nick looked around the room, counted four other boards in various stages of completion. He peered through an open door and noticed stacks of finished ones, brightly colored and shiny, nearly filling the side room. Other boards were mounted on the walls. Every one was more than seven feet long.

"Nice boards," he offered.

Romer turned from his examination, looked Nick up and down "Are you a surfer, Mr. . . . ?"

Nick glanced around the room quickly, noticed a large stainless steel box under the kitchen counter. "Mr. Box," he said. "Nick Box. That's Box: B-A-C-H-S. Am I a surfer? I guess anybody growing up in Daytona has done his share of surfing. Not much anymore, though."

Romer shot him a look of disdain, picked up a sanding block and turned back to the board. "It's actually a highly complicated means of locomotion. Much more complicated than these nose-pierced cretins nowadays understand. The management of kinetic energy along a wave front, constantly remaining at the point in the curve where the forward vector just balances the down vector. It's a beauty these kids will never appreciate. All they want to do is chop, chop, chop. Up the face, down the face, tear it up. Like those moron snowboarders they have out West. Everything's me, me, me. Look what I can do. Look how I can deface God's creation."

Lightly, he sanded a high spot on his board. "Barely a step above Jet Skiers, they are. This board, for instance, I'm experimenting with a displacement-saving hollow that runs from the midpoint aft to the fins. Since we lose laminar flow at about a third of the way back, it doesn't do much good to continue a foil shape past that point. Try and explain that to any of the geniuses down at the pier and they look at you like you're from Mars."

Nick listened politely, wondering what the hell laminar flow was, and why Romer thought he was in the least bit interested in it. Still, he was the shark expert. Finally Romer seemed to have shut up.

"About those sharks, then," Nick said pleasantly.

Romer didn't look up from his sanding. "What about sharks?"

"I was hoping you could help me with a problem." Nick waited for a response, got none. "Like I said, I work for the Van Hornes, and as you might know, they sponsored those races where sharks showed up and ate the racers."

Romer reached for a torpedo level, laid it against the board and sighted down it with one eye closed. "They were in the sharks' domain, and the sharks ate them. Besides, they were Jet Skiers and speedboat racers." He put the level back down. "I'm a busy man. I don't have time to serve on any panel of inquiry or committee or whatever else the city might be doing to cover its ass. I frankly—"

"Oh, no," Nick interrupted. "We don't want you to study the sharks. We want you to kill them."

Romer stared at him silently. "You want *me* to kill *sharks*?"

Nick nodded. "Oh, yes. Joanna was quite clear. Kill the sharks. All of them. She'll pay you quite well. In fact, I'm authorized—"

"Get out."

"But you're the only guy in Daytona—"

"Get out before I kill *you*." Romer picked a cordless scroll saw off the floor, revved it. "Yeah. They'll think *you* were attacked by a shark by the time I get through with you. Now, get out!"

He stood, advanced on Nick with eyes blazing and power tool screaming.

Nick stumbled back over a foam slab, caught himself and waddled quickly out the back door.

Jamie stared straight ahead through the windshield, unable to blink for fear he would miss her. His Datsun sat parked on the street, four spaces behind her VW. The meter had a good two hours worth of quarters in it, even though her store was scheduled to close in another few minutes.

The pistol lay on the passenger seat beneath the sports section of the newspaper. The safety—he had checked it four times—was off, as was the car radio. The engine, however, was on, and idling roughly. He wasn't about to risk another screwup over a balky engine. And, for the first time since he'd traded a nice video camera for the car a month ago, gas wasn't an issue. He could idle all night, if he needed to. The needle stood at full, courtesy of the $15 that Monica, the most generous of his new roommates, had lent him after borrowing a set of jumper cables and rescuing him.

Yup, that Monica sure was a classy chick. Not only was she the best looking of the three, with the tightest ass and the firmest tits, but she was the nicest, too. He would have to reward her somehow, he nodded to himself. Maybe as soon as his photography gig started taking off, he'd do a special spread with just her. Help her get into *Playboy* or *Penthouse* or one of the other top-shelf magazines. Maybe put in a good word for her, too, if someone wanted to use her in a movie or on TV.

Unlike others he'd heard about, ol' Jamie Hotchkiss wasn't about to forget those who helped him on his way up. No sir. Once he made it, he would reach down with a helping hand. That's how he'd been taught. One good turn deserves another. He'd help out Kristin and Tiffany, too. Probably not get them into the movies, like Monica, but maybe something else in show biz. Shoot, he could be their agent, set up gigs, arrange publicity, for a cut of their contract.

He wondered how much an agent got. Thirty percent? Forty? He would need more clients, then. More chicks. He gazed out across the street at the Book Nook, where the waitress with the nipple ring worked. She was probably working there tonight. She was pretty hot, too. He would be sure to sign her up. Maybe after he finished tonight he would come back and have a cup of coffee out on the street, maybe get to know her a little—

A giant Harley-Davidson roared by his door, startling him. He watched it rumble down Seabreeze, the enormous rider straddling it, a tiny German war helmet sitting comically atop the mop of red hair that flowed to his shoulders. Maybe that's what he'd get with the $5,000 instead of a car: a Hog. Man, that would be cool, tearing up the road on a big machine like that. And chicks dug Hogs, especially in Daytona. He'd have to look into it.

He turned back to the Harmonic Age and his heart nearly stopped. The lights had been turned off. Quickly he craned to see the parking spot four spaces ahead of his. Sure enough, the VW was gone. He swore to himself as he pulled into traffic, cutting off a Cadillac that honked in anger. He ignored the other driver's hand waving and gunned ahead, tailgating the car in front of him as he searched desperately for the convertible. How the hell had she driven off without his noticing?

God damn it, James, you have to pay attention! What the hell had he been thinking of? Helping out Monica, that's what it was. Well, that's what he got for being too smart for his own good. Always thinking, never an idle moment: that was his hyperactive brain. He couldn't imagine what it would be like *not* to have ideas all the time, to be brain-dead like some of the kids he'd grown up with, but Christ Almighty, he wished he could keep it in check sometimes, stay focused on the task at hand . . .

There! Three blocks ahead, just now turning onto A1A. He pressed the accelerator to race through a yellow light, then another and he, too, was turning south onto A1A.

Methodically he weaved through traffic until only the Harley separated him from the VW. Okay, easy does it, he told himself. He had plenty of time before the road narrowed to two lanes and grew deserted. He just had to make sure he was directly behind her by then. No problem. The Harley was sure to turn off on Dunlawton, just like most of the other cars.

He rehearsed in his head the steps he would take: first, wait until no other cars were around on that empty stretch of Wilbur-by-the-Sea. Then, pull around her like he was trying to pass, cut her off and drive her off the road. He'd stop like he was checking to make sure she was okay and then, after checking for cars again, he'd pop her in the head four or five times and get the hell out.

Simple and sweet. He'd meet up with Cherry, get his money and find out about when he could start practicing for the Crown Cola. He'd never raced on a big track before, never even raced on a paved track, for that matter, and he'd need a little bit of work. He fully intended to finish in the money, whatever it took, so he wanted to start early.

Ahead of him the Harley was still between him and the VW, and Jamie started to get a little nervous. The traffic lights of Dunlawton Avenue were in sight now, and still the Harley hadn't moved into the right lane. With his luck, this would be the one biker who lived in the ritzy South Peninsula. Most of the other traffic slid to the right to turn and cross the high-rise bridge to the mainland, but the Harley kept going straight, through the light, barely a car length behind the VW.

Great. He *had* found the one biker who lived on the South Peninsula. He ran a hand through his hair to calm himself and consider his options. He could pass the biker and get between him and the VW. But that wouldn't help, not if he kept following them. No, he would just have to stick it out, hope that the biker got impatient enough with Barbie's just-over-the-speed-limit driving to race past her. And if he didn't, well, he'd have to think of something, and fast.

The VW sped up a touch, and Crawdad twisted the throttle a hair to keep up. She lived down here, he knew, but wasn't sure exactly where. Not that it mattered.

He'd watch her go into her house, wait a few minutes, park nearby, break in from the beach side, grab her, tie her up, throw her in the back of her car and be in Miami by midnight. She'd be out of the country within forty-eight hours, and in the harem of some sultan or prince or tribal chief by the end of the week, the lucky bastard. With $30,000 from Van Horne and, say, $50,000 for delivering a nice, tall, green-eyed white woman to his old Union Correctional acquaintance Gatortail, he'd be flush for a while, a couple of months at least.

It would be enough to have the bike detailed, maybe get that airbrush painting of Pamela Anderson he'd always wanted on his gas tank. Hell, he could probably spare a couple of grand to send home to Ma. He could get something nice for Jasmine, too. Maybe a leather vest or a new pair of boots. Although the waitress at that bookstore had looked pretty fine, as well. He'd noticed her checking out Jasmine's tattooed bikini. Maybe he'd get her to move in with them for a while.

He smiled at the thought, then glanced at the rearview on his handlebar. The dickhead in the little Jap car was still there, and still riding his ass. He had half a mind to pull the big Colt revolver from his jacket and fire through his windshield a couple of times. That would make him back off.

He thought again of Barbie Van Horne's long, long legs, and what a waste it was just to sell her off like that without getting a piece for himself. But, no, she was certain to put up a fight, and every scratch, every bruise was hundreds or even thousands off the price. It was bad business to damage the goods like that. Maybe he'd take it out on her husband again. He smiled at *that* thought, nostalgically remembered his prison days.

Ahead, the VW sped up again, and Crawdad turned the throttle again to keep pace.

Barbie looked into her rearview mirror in annoyance, saw that awful Harley still there. It was the loudest motorcycle she'd ever heard, even after suffering through two dozen Bike Weeks in her lifetime. The thing was behind her, yet loud enough to drown out her radio.

She turned up the volume button and, finally, the strains of Van

Morrison's "Moondance" overcame the bike's exhaust pipes. She nodded to the music, flipped the lever on the rearview so the single headlamp wouldn't blind her and let her foot rest a bit more heavily on the accelerator.

Her new friend Pedro was supposed to come over again tonight, and she was going to attempt to cook him dinner, having charred the previous night's chicken to a crusty, inedible black lump. But, boy, had it ever been worth it. They'd eaten cold-cut sandwiches in bed, instead, and talked and made love through the night. She should be exhausted, she knew, but felt instead a boundless exhilaration. She'd been anticipating this evening all day.

It had been years since she'd felt anything like this, not since . . . Well, come to think of it, she'd *never* felt like this. Not with the guys she dated before she married Nick, *certainly* not with Nick, and not even remotely with the one or two losers with whom she'd had dinner-and-nothing-else-thank-you-for-a-lovely-evening since her separation. Finally, she'd met someone whose idea of conversation wasn't bragging about how he'd picked up two coeds at once last Spring Break by telling them he was Don Wheat, the founder of Tahitian Tropic sunscreen. Or explaining to her in excruciating detail how that no-account bum Dale Earnhardt had cheated Ernie Ervin out of the Winston Cup points lead with that dirty piece of driving last Sunday. Had she seen that? No? Well, they were replaying it on ESPN 2, and they could go over to his place and watch.

Quickly she went through in her head what she needed to pull together for dinner, what she would wear, what to drink. There would be no burned chicken tonight, no sir. It wasn't until she'd pulled into her driveway that she noticed idly that the annoying biker had disappeared.

SEVEN

∎ ∎ ∎

Nick paged through the file again, this time actually reading the clippings and reports in the half-inch-thick folder. He'd had the publisher of the paper drop the packet by his office the day before, but he'd only skimmed it to find an address. Now he read more closely to learn more about the man who had dared to threaten him. The man who'd knocked him to the ground, humiliated him. Who the hell did he think he was? Well, he'd find out all about him and then decide how to make him pay.

He struggled to keep his place in the long article about his record as state attorney after his first term: higher conviction rates for murderers, rapists, child molesters. Even tax cheats and embezzlers. *Blah, blah, blah, blah,* the article went on and on. Best front-line prosecutor in the state, maybe the nation, according to some bar association survey.

Yeah? If he was so fucking smart, how come he was living in a dirty little shack? He paged backward through the clips, came to a profile from before he was elected. There was a photo of him holding a crossbow and the head of a boar he'd shot on the two hundred acres he had lived on at the time in backwoods Flagler County. He looked even more intense and angular than he did now, Nick thought with a shudder. He began skimming the article, and a chill went up his spine: youth surfing champion three years running in high school, valedictorian of his senior class, appointment to Annapolis Naval Academy, two tours in Vietnam with the Navy SEALs, a stint at the postgraduate school in Monterey, then Stanford Law School, then back home to northeast Florida and a job with the U.S. Attorney.

A SEAL. A fucking SEAL. Nick didn't know a lot about the Navy's elite corps, but knew enough to be afraid. A trained killer, he was. He trembled again, reconsidered his vow to punish Romer. Perhaps, since there'd been no witness to his insults, there would be no need to make him pay. Perhaps it would be better just to let it go.

He paged back some more, blinked at a *Washington Post* story about a secret Navy project in Key West, an offshoot of the one where they'd trained dolphins to plant explosives on the hulls of ships. This one, though, had instead tried to work with sharks, trying to train them to respond to certain sounds, to perform certain tasks. The article was slanted toward the idea that the whole thing was a complete boondoggle, even though a couple of experts said they thought it might work, if the sharks were trained early enough after they were born.

The Navy's official comment was no comment, as was the comment of a northeast Florida prosecutor who, according to documents obtained by *The Washington Post*, had spent two years in Key West on the project, part of it ostensibly during a second tour in Vietnam. Romer had flatly denied knowing anything about it, and the local paper didn't seem to have followed up.

Nick nodded his head. No *wonder* the guy had reacted so violently to Nick's proposal to kill the sharks. They were like his pets. He trembled again, flipped through more pages, came to an article about Romer's wife of twenty-one years divorcing him over the porn-tape crusade. Nick blinked as he read the next part: He had not fought for anything: not the house, the cars, the boat, anything. He clucked to himself, shaking his head, wondering what kind of mental illness must have possessed a man to do something like that. He'd never heard of such a thing. A man capable of that was capable of anything, he realized apprehensively. Well, he'd figure it out later.

Right now, he needed a drink. He stretched his arms, eased his buttocks forward to the edge of the couch and only then noticed the face that filled the muted big-screen television across the room.

It was Crawdad, taken off his driver's license. Nick scrambled for the remote control, patted all the cushions, finally found where it had slid down between them, pointed it at the set and hit the mute button.

. . . Stanko is among the first of this year's motorcycle enthusiasts to visit Daytona Beach. He remains comatose at Halifax Medical Center, where doctors treated him for two broken arms and a shattered kneecap. Police are looking for the hit-and-run driver who left the scene before a resident noticed Stanko lying in the street underneath his motorcycle. . . .

The news anchor and his willowy blonde co-anchor shook their heads sadly, reminded viewers of the importance of Motorcycle Week to the local economy and admonished everyone to pay extra careful attention in the coming days to watch out for our two-wheeled friends on the road. In other news, there was another huge turnout for the Daytona 500 practice session, Marty would have details . . .

Nick hit the mute button again, shook his head slowly. Amazing. Just fucking amazing. Of all the bikers in this ridiculous town, of all the fat, grungy thugs terrorizing the streets on their noisy toys, some road hog had to choose *his* to run over. He pieced through the implications and, slowly, his amazement and anger turned to loathing and fear: He would have to return to that biker bar and find somebody else.

His sphincter puckered at the thought. Then he remembered the $15,000 he'd already given to Crawdad and it puckered some more. He would have to get that back! Or else tell Joanna what had happened.

He heard footsteps on the stairs, turned to see Joanna in her nightgown, coming to watch the Raceway clips. She sat in the chair beside him and reached over to grab the remote control from his hand. As always, a wave of Oedipal guilt washed over him. She always wore a sheer nightie in the evening hours. And she never wore a robe. And he always found himself sneaking a peek.

"How's your little project coming?" she demanded in an icy tone.

The guilt receded immediately, replaced again with fear. He gulped, nodded at the television, where a police spokesman was offering a reward for information in the hit-and-run on the innocent motorcyclist in Wilbur-by-the-Sea earlier that evening.

"Not too good," he admitted.

The steam from the hot tub rose into the cold air, condensing into a thin mist that stuck to Nolin's face and hair. He leaned back against the jets and sighed contentedly.

"Thanks for a wonderful dinner. It's the best meal I've had in . . . ever. It's the best meal I've had ever."

Barbie laughed, slipped back into the tub across from him. "Now I *know* you want something."

"I'm serious. You should open a restaurant."

"No way. I took my business courses. Most restaurants fail. Especially in this town. The favorite food of the natives is fried shrimp, and the favorite food of tourists is Pizza Hut."

"So what's holding you here? Your umpteenth annual Speed Week–Bike Week–Spring Break?"

She groaned, lifted her feet onto his lap. "You know, I had the loudest biker—"

"Motorcycle enthusiast." Nolin wagged a finger. " 'Biker' is pejorative. The Chamber doesn't like it."

"Sorry, the loudest *motorcycle enthusiast* on the planet behind me most of the way home. I couldn't hear myself think."

Nolin nodded. "Yeah. They could muffle their exhausts, but they don't. And then they ride around at full throttle outside your house at two in the morning all Bike Week. I've always wanted to figure out where they live, drive up there on my vacation, take the muffler off my truck and then drive in circles around *their* houses all night. See how *they* like it."

"They'd like it fine. They'd just come out and shoot you."

He shook his head sadly. "Another pejorative myth about motorcycle enthusiasts. As the Chamber and the City Commission tells us, our two-wheeled friends are *not* mother-rapers and father-stabbers. They are doctors and lawyers, dressed in costume to enjoy a week of camaraderie each year among ten thousand fellow motorcycle enthusiasts. And each spends an average of three hundred dollars a day during a week-long visit, so, after factoring in the multiplier effect, they have a positive impact on our local economy of about seven hundred trillion dollars."

She laughed. "You've got it down, haven't you? What do you do, work for the Chamber?"

"I had a client who tried to sue them one year to keep the biker, er, excuse me, the enthusiast parade from passing by his store. He was tired of the vandalism and the litter and the doctors and lawyers pissing on his door."

"And? What happened?"

Nolin ground his thumb into the palm of his other hand. "Squished like a bug."

"It's amazing. This whole town is so completely brainwashed by this stuff. And then they wonder how come we attract every deviant and escaped psycho on the East Coast. You know this afternoon I had a woman, good-looking, about twenty-seven, twenty-eight years old, walk into my shop. She was wearing a pair of biker boots."

"So? Lots of women in Daytona wear biker boots."

"That's *all* she was wearing. Except for a black thong bikini that was either painted on or tattooed on. I couldn't tell."

"Really," Nolin muttered, trying to picture it.

"And the day before, this surfer guy came in, asking about an ankle bracelet for his girlfriend. Next thing I know, he's got his hands down the front of his shorts, grabbing himself, and then he runs out. He dropped a little piece of paper. It said: Orifices, holes, cherry, dear. I think maybe it was supposed to be a poem."

"So when you say 'good-looking,' how do mean? Like blonde? Big bazoongas?"

Underwater, she grabbed a bit of thigh between her toes and pinched. He let out a howl.

"Let that be a lesson to you. Not only are they freakishly long, they're astonishingly powerful, as well."

He grabbed her foot and lifted it out of the water. "It's funny, mine are freakishly long, too. But they're not even a little bit powerful."

She lifted his foot out to study it. "It's all in the breeding. My great grandmother was a trapeze artist in the circus, and my grandfather was the first man to free-climb the face of El Capitan in Yosemite."

"Wow," he said, impressed. "You're kidding."

She smiled. "Yeah. I am."

He dropped her foot disgustedly, shook his head. "Serves me right."

Barbie traced a finger down his big toe, around his ankle and up his calf. "I wonder what would happen if a man with freakishly long toes were to mate with a woman with freakishly long toes."

"You'd either get a baby with chimpanzee toes, or no toes at all."

Her mouth fell open. "You're kidding."

Nolin smiled. "Yeah. I am." He pulled her toward him. "You want to practice some more?"

She turned up her chin in a pout. "I thought you wanted a blonde. A blonde with big bazoongas. I thought—" But his mouth was already on hers.

"We've got a slight problem," Joanna said quietly. This time the album remained in the safe behind the aerial photo. This time, he had called her.

"I can tell from here in Tallahassee that you got a problem," Weathers said, his Panhandle drawl firing on all cylinders. "I keep looking in the Daytona paper for a certain obituary, maybe an article about a prominent local lady in a tragic accident. But I ain't seen nothing. And then I hear from a buddy of mine who happens to be a golfing pal of the good Judge Anthony Antoon that he can't wait for Monday to stick it to that quote pompous lardass county attorney unquote. I put two and two together, and the outlook don't look promisin', does it?"

Joanna breathed silently into the phone. He had no right to talk to her like this.

"Now maybe you can explain what you plan to do about it."

She held her temper. She could destroy him. End his career overnight. It would take one phone call and a messenger to run the photo over to the paper's city desk. "I told you, we just had some bad luck."

"Well, let me tell you: There ain't no such thing. I didn't get to my position by relying on luck. You're responsible for making your own luck, and you obviously haven't been taking that responsibility seriously. So don't go tellin' me about bikers and car wrecks. Serves you right for relyin' on that idiot son—"

"Stepson. And only technically. He's older than me."

"So you say."

She waited through an awkward silence. "Look, I told you I'd handle the lawsuit problem down here, and all you have to do is—"

"Don't tell me what I have to do. I already done it. There's eighty million hidden in the appropriations bill for RaceWorld, and we ain't gonna see a dime of it 'cause of some fuckin' turtles and *your* daughter-in-law."

"Estranged daughter-in-law."

"Look, just shut up, okay? Let me think a moment. You obviously have no idea of the political risks I'm taking monkeying with the budget like that. Just shut up for once in your life."

Joanna shut up, her hands shaking with anger. One phone call. That's all it would take. But no, not yet. She still needed him. Until the $80 million was safely in her account, she needed him.

"All right. I'll take care of it," Weathers said finally.

"But I thought—"

"Shut up, already. I'll take care of it. If there's one thing my daddy taught me, it's that you want somethin' done right, you'd best do it yourself."

"Do you want me to meet you somewhere, give you—"

"No. I don't want your help. It's likely to get me killed. You just keep that idiot son out of my way, that's all."

Joanna listened to the silence after the click for a few seconds, then hung up.

· · ·

Nick pressed the fake mustache firmly against his upper lip, held his breath to stifle another sneeze. He glanced down at the $26.95-plus-tax Pick-Me-Up Bouquet in his hands with disdain; he'd be glad to get rid of those. Still, to get into a hospital without a lot of questions, there was nothing like them. The elevator pinged three times, the doors opened and he strode out, following the signs for patient rooms to the right. Quickly he came to 316, turned the knob and stepped in.

Immediately his sinuses were under assault. Through watery eyes, he scanned the room, counted fifteen, twenty, twenty-five, thirty, *thirty-seven* floral arrangements. They covered every inch of bureau, desk, chair space and much of the floor as well in the private room. Nick made his way through the foliage toward the sounds of a tinny television, stepped between two giant rubber tree plants to where Lon Stanko was propped up in the adjustable bed watching a *Baywatch* rerun.

"That you, Jasmine?" Crawdad growled, then turned to see Nick emerge through the greenery. "The fuck do you want?"

His bulk was covered in a cotton gown from pasty white feet to a sunburned neck. Each arm was in a cast from bicep to wrist, as was his left leg from mid-thigh down. They had apparently bathed him, for the grime from around his malignant eyes and squashed-in nose was gone. Even the red curls of his beard glistened softly. In belated response, Nick sneezed violently. With the third explosion, his mustache flew across the bed in a cloud of mist.

"Chrissake," Crawdad roared. "You come to a hospital with a raging cold? What are you, some kind of psycho?"

Nick sneezed again. "Allergies. From all this." He waved a hand around the room.

"Oh. Tokens of sympathy from the community. Those tulips over there are from the mayor, the mums from the Chamber, the roses from the Hotel/Motel Association. Plus they're giving me a complimentary week at the Marriott. That big mixed assortment is from the police and one of those rubber plants is from the sheriff. The rest of the stuff came in while I was asleep this morning."

Nick stared in disbelief. Only in Daytona would a hired thug on his way to a murder be given the red carpet. "What happened?"

Crawdad shrugged. "I was followin' her home. This punk tried to get past me and cut me off. I wouldn't let him in. He tried again, only this time he was wavin' a gun. I reached in my jacket to grab mine when the cocksucker ran into me. I went over the top, landed on my arms. So here I am."

Nick studied him silently, up and down. Casts meant broken limbs. Meant he was out of commission for at least several weeks.

"I can tell you this much," Crawdad continued. "I hope he's settlin' his affairs, saying goodbye to his momma and his sweetheart. Because he's a dead man. No doubt about that, no sir."

Nick cursed his luck under his breath, wiped his nose on his sleeve. "So when do you get out?"

He stared at the television, where big-bosomed lifeguards dragged a wiry surfer out of the waves and gave him mouth-to-mouth resuscitation. "The doctors want me for about a week. They tell me I was in a coma through the night. Fuck if I know. Don't remember no coma."

Nick chose his words carefully. "So in other words, you can't do the job."

Crawdad turned to him slowly. "What are you, deaf? I told you: I was on my way to do it last night when this happened. It's because of *you* that I'm here, all busted up."

Nick studied the cast on the leg, decided there was no way he would be able to stand, let alone walk. He swallowed, growing braver. "Look, I appreciate the effort. But I'm not paying for effort. I'm paying for results. You obviously are in no position to do what I need done, by the date I need it. Because if it's not done by Monday morning, it's of no value to me. Therefore I need to find someone else immediately." He held Crawdad's stare, swallowed again. "Therefore, I have to ask you for my deposit back."

Crawdad's eyes narrowed slightly, his mouth turned up on one side. "What did you say?"

"I said," Nick began, more confident now, "that I want my fifteen grand back, and I want it back now."

In a flash, Crawdad's hand shot out toward Nick, and tears of allergy became tears of pain. "What did you say?" Crawdad asked again, his voice barely a whisper.

Nick's mouth opened, closed. His hands squirmed, moved toward Crawdad's cast-encased arm, moved away again. No, he reasoned through the agony, if he tried to pull the arm away, Crawdad would make it hurt even worse. "Nothing," Nick managed finally.

Crawdad eased his grip slightly. "That's nice. Because the first time, I thought you said you was backin' out of a deal. And I don't like people who go back on their word. Do you?"

Nick shook his head, his breaths coming fast and shallow, his hands squirming. Crawdad shook his massive head, too. "Good, 'cause I don't like 'em, either. Fact is, I hate 'em. Now. I'll do what I told you I'd do. And I expect to see the rest of my money, plus, say, ten grand to compensate for my injuries and my lost time. Sound fair?"

Crawdad tightened his hold. Nick winced, nodded furiously.

"Well, I knew we could come to a reasonable agreement." Finally he opened his hand, drew his pulleyed and counterweighted arm back inboard of his bed, and returned his attention to *Baywatch*. "You know, just once before I die I'd like to have Pamela Anderson."

Nick, still hunched over, hands covering crotch, turned and shuffled through the foliage toward the door.

"Thanks for stopping by," Crawdad called. "Just leave the flowers on the nightstand."

Lori bent at the waist, lined up the cue ball with the solid yellow that lay inches from the corner pocket and missed it completely. Not just missed it completely, but managed to scratch, yet again. With a pout, she stamped her foot on the floor as a middle-aged tourist retrieved the cue ball and set it on the felt.

Amee sighed and turned back to her rumrunner. It was hopeless: Lori was never going to get any better. She had been playing pool now twelve hours a day, every day, for over two weeks, but she still hadn't picked up the slightest bit of game. Not, judging by the size of her Joe's eyes as he stared at her over the table, that it seemed to matter.

And there, Amee decided, was the secret to getting rich. It didn't matter how well Lori played or didn't play. Just so long as customers came in primarily to see her falling out of her bikini top, and so long as she brought in more than Cherry was paying her, she could remain the world's worst pool player and still make Amee a lot of money. And if one dumb blonde in a thong could nearly double Amee's income, then how much would a second dumb blonde, or a third, or a tenth bring in?

That's what she would do, Amee decided. After she'd gotten her hands on some of Nicky's dough, she would add three or four more tables and hire another couple of chicks. And all she'd have to do would be to count the money. Or maybe she'd hire somebody to do that, too. Isn't that what rich people did? Hire other people for things they couldn't be bothered with anymore? Even fun things like keeping track of all their money?

Speaking of which, she wondered, where the hell was the moron? He hadn't shown up the previous night, like he was supposed to, but that wasn't really surprising. No doubt he'd freaked out afterward. Probably hadn't expected so much blood and stuff. Probably hiding out somewhere, gathering his courage to come collect his money.

She'd give him his money, all right. No problem, Jamie boy, let's go out for a ride in your car. Out to the woods by the river, where I buried it to keep it safe. Too bad he wasn't more reliable. She would have liked to have kept him around awhile, at least until she'd gotten rid of Joanna, maybe even Nicky, too.

She glanced at the clock over the bar, saw it was already past noon. She sighed, realized he wasn't going to come to her, that she would have to go find him. A billiard ball clattered onto the floor, rolled toward her with Lori in hot pursuit. Amee bent to pick it up, handed it back to Lori. "It's supposed to stay *on* the table," she said dryly.

She followed Lori back toward the table, patted her bare bottom encouragingly, smiled at the customer and watched his eyes light up. That's right, we're lesbians. And if you hang around long enough, we might let you watch. She winked at him, knowing he'd be good for another hour now, at least, and walked back into her office.

Jamie Hotchkiss. She picked up the phone book, replaced it immediately at the notion of Jamie paying a monthly bill. Where did he say he lived? She thought back through their meetings, recalling the first, when he'd stood at the side of the pool hall holding a beer. He hadn't told her, she realized, had only bragged about the three girls he'd shacked up with. She snapped her fingers and reached for her desk drawer, grabbing the envelope with the nudie pictures. Sure enough, there was the address on the front. She tore off the receipt and stuffed it into her bikini bottom, closed the door to her office as she left and gave Lori another fondle as she passed.

"Be back in a bit, Peaches," she sang as she opened the front door. "Hold down the fort."

The airplane rose and rose, pointed its nose toward the ceiling and immediately tumbled out of the air, well short of the wastepaper basket, joining two dozen other failures on the hardwood floor.

Nolin squinted at the wedge of paper. Obviously a design flaw. The craft was not balanced. The center of effort was too far forward, giving the nose the tendency to pitch upward at the slightest disturbance. He grabbed another sheet from the respondent's brief and began folding it. First in half, then each half over on itself. Not everyone could make paper airplanes like this. It would be something he would teach his son. Or his daughter. Or both.

He smiled to himself again. She had mentioned children, and he hadn't freaked, hadn't made excuses that he needed to go, that he had an early day tomorrow, that he had a load of laundry that needed to go in the dryer. Before he was hopeful, but now he was certain: He had found her.

He creased his final fold, bent the nose downward for improved performance at supersonic velocities and let it fly. The long, narrow craft flew fast but low and nose-dived into the edge of the Oriental rug. Back to the drawing board.

He thought again of his visit to Cassadaga and Madame Rosa, and the $500 he'd thrown down the toilet because of his paranoia. *Of course* Van Horne was hoping Barbie would have a terrible accident. He knew that he would have to pay through the nose for alimony, and couldn't bear the thought of giving her a cent, let alone tens of thousands of dollars every month. How could that dumb, fat slob know that his ex was already getting serious with somebody else, that he probably would have barely a month or two of payments before she remarried?

He smiled to himself again. Finally, in his life, everything was working out. He would finish the beach house, and, depending on which one they liked better, they would live together in one and sell the other. That money would be more than enough to pay off her legal bills. She could keep the store, maybe even hire a part-time clerk to help run it, in case she got pregnant or something, and they would live happily ever after. Now all he had to do was dump Van Horne. And, at some point, explain to Barbie that his name wasn't Pedro. But that could wait. And, if it came to it, he could rename the dog, and keep Pedro for himself. It was, after all, just a name.

He glanced again at the letter he'd typed that morning:

Dear Mr. Van Horne: Due to a recently discovered preexisting relationship that could constitute a conflict of interest, I must at this time end my representation of you re: your matrimonial. Blah, blah, blah, blah, blah. Douglas Nolin.

Short, sweet, to the point. Leave me alone. Find some other shyster. That would be that. He could forget that he'd ever had any dealings with Van Horne, and he'd never have to explain anything to Barbie. He'd already pulled another sheet of paper from the long, tedious brief he should have been reading and started yet another airplane design when he saw the big green Monte Carlo pull into his driveway and jerk to a stop. The door opened, and J. Robert Van Horne lurched out of the car and, bent at the waist, staggered up the stoop. Nolin turned to his desk, grabbed the one-page letter and stuffed it into an envelope as Van Horne wobbled through his door.

"Ah, Mr. Van Horne, what a surprise. In fact, quite a coincidence—"

"Here." Nick threw a brown paper bag onto Nolin's desk. "I need you to hang onto that."

Nolin carefully tugged at the bag's opening, peeked inside at two videocassettes and a plain white envelope. His stomach sank. He didn't even want to know. "What're those?" he asked warily.

"Never mind. You just stick 'em in your safe. I'll be back for 'em in a week."

Nolin studied Van Horne. He didn't look at all good, with dark circles hollowed out beneath bleary and bloodshot eyes. "*Why* do you want them in my safe?" Nolin asked finally.

"You're my damned lawyer, aren't you? I want you to hang onto 'em. That's all. If for some reason I *don't* come back for them next week, then you open the letter."

Nolin nodded sagely. "And then what am I supposed to do?"

"It's all in the letter, okay?" Nick straightened, grimaced, bent back over.

Nolin twisted to look into the bag again. He didn't like any of it. Still, he had to know what was on the tapes. . . . "Why don't you just keep them in your own safe?" he asked.

Nick scowled like he'd never heard anything so stupid. "Then who's supposed to open the letter if I don't come back?"

What the hell could be on the tapes? Barbie had posed naked for a poster. Could she have done a video, too? No . . . She *wouldn't* have . . . No. That was ridiculous. Van Horne wouldn't be asking him to hold onto dirty videos of his ex-wife. That didn't make any sense. No, it was part of some paranoid fantasy, that's all. A part he had no interest in, and wanted only to wash his hands of once and for all. The longer he saw Barbie while continuing to represent her husband, the worse the Florida Bar would come down on his head.

"I don't know, Mr. Van Horne. I'm awful busy. In fact"—he reached for the envelope containing the letter he'd written—"that's what I was getting ready to tell you when you walked in. I've got some big trials coming up and I really need to lighten my caseload—"

"What?" Nick demanded. "What don't you know? All I'm asking is that you put this bag in your safe for one week. How much could that possibly add to your *caseload*?" Nick began to laugh, then stopped short, grabbing himself in the crotch. "I mean, I'm paying you *money* to leave something in your safe and not do anything. What could be easier?"

He really didn't look good, Nolin decided. In fact, he seemed to acquire a new ailment each time he saw him. *What the hell was on those tapes?* He knew now that he just had to find out. If it was something about Barbie, he wasn't going to be able to sleep until he knew.

Slowly he nodded. "Okay. I'll do it."

Nick nodded back. "Good. Now was that so hard?" He turned and started hobbling through the office door. "I'll see you in a week."

Nolin watched him ease himself slowly into the enormous sedan and drive off before he went back inside and sat at his desk. He pulled the cassettes out of the bag, laid them atop the clutter, stared at them. They were black, with not even any labels on the side. He pulled the white envelope from the bag, studied it, front and back. It was high-quality, 25 percent cotton rag, letterhead stock. Rich man's stationery. Except for the Van Horne logo, it was completely blank, and sealed.

He set it down and turned back to the tapes. He drummed his fingers on them, imagining their contents. *They were blackmail tapes of Barbie screwing another man, two or three other men, to make her agree to a fast, free divorce.* His eyes widened. What if they were of Barbie screwing one *particular* other man in her hot tub?

He stood up quickly and walked the tapes into his living room, plugged the first into his VCR, flipped on the television and stepped back a few feet.

On the screen, a dozen Jet Skis roared through a turn, their riders' left legs stuck out into the water as they rounded the floating mark. The camera followed the racers for a while, then panned the crowd at the beach, focused on a trio of bikini-clad girls who stood facing the water, moved to a mother holding her little boy's hand, then to a profile of a middle-aged man sitting cross-legged in the sand, listening to a Walkman.

Nolin hit the pause button, rewound it slightly and let it play. He knew the man on the screen from somewhere. Even in profile, he recognized the face. He just couldn't recall where . . . The middle-aged man adjusted his Walkman, and the camera moved back to the racers. Suddenly, the lead racer went down around the far mark.

He hit the fast-forward button. The rest of this he'd seen, repeated a million times, on the news. He grinned. Despite the savage shark attack, the city had done absolutely nothing. No extra lifeguards, no beach closures. This close to the prime tourist season, they had hoped the whole thing would just go away. The recording ended, turned to snow. Nolin pressed the eject button and pushed in the other tape, fast-forwarded through the leader.

This one was the speedboat race. Again the camera panned the crowd, lingering longest on women who were both young and unclothed. The race began, and the camera followed the two boats as they tore through the water along the beach until they neared the finish line. Then the red boat leapt into the air. Again Nolin hit the fast-forward button, watched as the camera pulled back for a wide-angle shot of the spectators all lining the beach, pointing out toward the flaming wrecks of the boats.

Except for one. Nolin slowed the tape down to normal speed and saw the Walkman guy again, walking back to the line of parked cars on the beach, getting into a Karmann Ghia and driving off.

Nolin ejected the tape, rapped the remote control onto his palm as he racked his brain about the tall, angular man with the Walkman. Finally he walked to the kitchen to set a kettle on the stove to steam open Van Horne's envelope.

E I G H T

■ ■ ■

The numbers on the wooden post holding up the sagging car-port were faded, but legible. Amee rode her bike up the side-walk and let it fall on the grass, cursing loudly as the pedal caught her calf and drew a thin red scratch across brown skin. She was already in a foul mood and could feel it getting worse.

She had ridden up Seabreeze to get to the house, fully expecting to see police tape and a CLOSED sign on the door of Harmonic Age. Instead, she'd seen Nicky's wife, wearing a cute little top and miniskirt, showing scarves to some blue-haired tourists from up north.

Amee rang the doorbell and waited impatiently until a tall brunette wearing a long T-shirt answered the door. Inside, two other girls still in nighties peeked across the dim living room.

"I'm here to see Jamie," Amee announced. "You must be Monica."

Monica eyed her up and down, lifting her nose slightly at Amee's bikini. "He's not feeling good today. Can I give him a message?"

Amee snorted. "He's gonna feel a fuck of a lot worse by the time I get through with him."

She squeezed past Monica and marched over the faded orange shag rug in the living room, began poking her head through doorways. She'd checked two bra-and-panties-strewn bedrooms and one bathroom on one side of the house and crossed the main hall leading to the other when the short brunette and the chesty blonde took up station in front of a closed door. Each wore panties and a T-shirt and stood with crossed arms and a defiant look. Monica joined them and crossed her arms, too.

"Excuse me. But I need to talk to your boyfriend," Amee said.

"He's sick," Monica said. She seemed to be their spokeswoman. "What about?"

Amee smiled broadly, put her hands on her bare hips. "Private business."

This was too much for the blonde. "Screw you! Who the hell do you think you are, busting in our house like this?"

She smiled again. "I'm Jamie's photography agent. You know, the one who sells all his pictures?"

The girls traded worried looks, unfolded their arms. The blonde pushed a strand of hair behind her ear, thrust out her chest a bit. "Oh. Have you, uh, seen any of the stuff he took of us?"

Amee nodded sadly, sighed. "Tiffany, right?" She ran a hand down her side from breasts to buttocks. "You got great tits, but you need to work on your ass. Cottage cheese don't sell pictures." She turned to the short brunette. "And you, you got a nice firm butt. But really. Don't you think you ought to invest in a boob job?"

Both girls stared at Amee in horror. Tears came to their eyes and they ran down the hall into their rooms, slamming doors behind them. Monica stood quietly. "You got any complaints about me?"

Amee reached past her for the doorknob. "With you I got no problems. Well, nothing a pair of scissors won't fix. Guys don't want to see the Black Forest down there, know what I mean? They get scared they might get lost."

Monica blushed and stepped back. Amee stepped forward, turned back. "You don't, by any chance, play pool, do you?"

· · ·

Nick drove north along A1A at below the speed limit for the first time in his life. Inside, his stomach was a tight ball, spewing out acids that burned his throat.

He couldn't believe what he was about to do. But what choice did he have? Besides, it would be better to get killed by this lunatic than sodomized by another foul-smelling biker. He'd heard those SEALs could crush a man's windpipe with their fingers, or jab a pencil into the brain through the nose. He nodded to himself soberly. He'd have to keep Romer away from his windpipe. Or any pencils.

More quickly than he wanted, the high-rise hotels of Daytona gave way to the expensive mansions of Ormond and the subdivisions and condos of Ormond-by-the-Sea. Before he knew it, he had crossed the empty dunes of the state park and had pulled onto the gravel fronting Romer's ramshackle beach house.

Cautiously, every nerve ending on high alert, he stepped from his car, crossed to the front door, peered through a narrow jalousie window. Nothing but gloom. The whole house was nothing but mildew and gloom, except for the workshop in back.

Remembering Romer's lecture about his privacy, he rang the bell once, twice, three times. No answer. Back in the driveway sat the Karmann Ghia with the ubiquitous long board sticking out the back, as if Romer had to be ready to hit the road at a moment's notice to track down the big wave.

He rang the doorbell twice more, got no reply and slowly started around back. Step by step, stopping twice to pick sandspurs off his socks, he moved through the brush until he was on the back porch. He knocked on the sliding glass door, called out Romer's name, turned in frustration and gasped. Quickly he crouched behind a rusty barbecue grill.

Out in the water, maybe a hundred feet from shore, stood a man in a wetsuit. And beside him was a dark gray dorsal fin, at least two feet tall. Nick's jaw fell as the man stroked the fin, eliciting a fast thrashing of the giant tail that broke the surface. Nick breathed heavily, felt himself losing his balance and grabbed the grill for support.

Rusted legs gave way and the grill toppled off the concrete patio with a loud crash. In the same instant, Nick half stood and Romer snapped his head around. For a moment their eyes locked, Nick's bulging and wide, Romer's dark and narrow, before Nick stood, turned and ambled into the fastest run of his middle age. Through the sea oats and dune scrub, ignoring the sandspurs that dug into his flesh, across the gravel drive, into the driver's seat.

He felt for the ignition key, remembered it was still in his pocket, shifted his bulk uncomfortably to jam his hand into his hip pocket, down, down, down further. There! He pulled his hand, but it wouldn't budge. It was stuck! He leaned back and forth, tugging at his hand, looking out his window at the corner of the house where Romer would emerge at any moment, an official, hardened-steel Navy SEAL knife in his hand. He began to whimper, struggling with the damned keys—*why in God's name did they make the pockets so small?*—when he felt the cold metal under his chin.

He stopped struggling, wondered how Romer had snuck up without him hearing, turned his eyes to the left, saw him standing outside the car holding a spear gun through the open window. He still felt the point under his chin.

"Hello again, Mr. Bachs," Romer said coolly. "Mr. Bachs who works for the Van Hornes but isn't part of the sleazebag family. Particularly not that fat, lazy lardass J. Robert Van Horne."

"Please don't shoot me with that thing."

Romer nodded to the spear gun. "This? You won't feel a thing. You see, I've always thought it crude to kill fish with those pivoting tips that don't come back out the way they come in. So I make my own tips: razor sharp. So that I need to hit a vital organ and kill the animal instantly. Of course, if I miss even a little, the spear goes clean through and the fish gets away. Of course, I never miss."

Nick gulped. "I came to talk to you."

"You came to spy on me."

"Nuh-uh, I came to talk. I just, uh, got a little panicked. But I came to talk."

Romer nodded once. "So talk."

Nick swallowed again, his mouth dry from the prick of the point under his chin. "Can you please move that thing away from my throat?"

Romer smiled. "The spear? I already have." He showed Nick the whole spear gun, now completely outside the car. "What you feel is the cut the tip left behind."

Nick looked down in horror, saw the blood staining the front of his shirt, moved his hand to his warm, wet neck and fainted.

"Please, please, pleeeeeeeease, let go!" Jamie wailed.

Even in the darkness under the bed, Amee saw the tears in his eyes. She kept a constant pressure between thumb and forefinger. "I'll let go when you get your ass out from under there."

"Okay," he relented. "I'm coming. Don't pull!"

He wiggled slowly toward the edge. As he moved, Amee moved back, keeping her grip, slowly getting up on her knees. When he emerged, she squatted to stand, yanking him upward.

"Don't pull!" he shouted, scrambling to keep pace. "Now what?"

"Lie down," she demanded.

When he complied, she finally let go. Immediately he covered himself with his hands, shielding himself from her awful fingers. "You don't have any idea how much that hurts," he protested. "How'd you like it if I did that to your tit?"

She got in bed with him, shrugged. "I might like it."

"Not if I did it that hard," he pouted.

"You deserved it." She began stroking his chest and belly. "So what happened after you ran the biker off the road?"

"I didn't *mean* to run him off the road. He was being a dick. I was trying to get in behind her and he wouldn't let me. So I showed him my gun. You know, to scare him."

"Great. So now he knows you have a gun. My gun. Perfect. I bet he told the cops."

"I doubt it. 'Cause otherwise he'd have to tell 'em about the gun he was pulling out of his jacket. That's how we wrecked. I saw his gun and turned to get away. I musta skidded. Anyway, next thing I knew, I was turned around in the ditch and the car was stalled. The biker was lying on the road near his Harley."

"You didn't check on him?"

"Jesus Christ, Cherry, the cops were gonna be there any minute. Plus the guy was gonna shoot me, and you think I shoulda stuck around to make sure he was okay?"

Amee stroked lower on his belly, started sliding under his hands that still formed a protective shield over his privates. "Not check on him to make sure he was okay," she said calmly. "Check on him to make sure he was dead."

Jamie blinked. "What, kill *him*, too?"

Amee shrugged. "Why not? You just said he was ready to shoot you."

He shook his head. "I don't know, Cherry. Killing Mrs. Van Horne, now I got a good reason for doin' that. But that biker, I got nothing against him. He wasn't doin' nothing."

She sat up. "I think there's something you don't understand about life. If there's something you want, you have to go out and get it. You don't let anyone stand in your way, especially not biker trash. If you want to make some money, if you want to drive at Daytona, you're gonna have to get the job done. Mr. Van Horne's getting impatient. Now. What did you do with the car?"

Jamie timidly opened his hands to give her better access, ever mindful of the terrible pain she could inflict. "I ditched it in the woods up near High Bridge. Covered it with some branches."

"And the gun?"

"Buried it. About a mile south of the car."

"You'll need to go dig it up this afternoon. And tonight you'll go take care of Mrs. Van Horne. It didn't work at her store, it didn't work on the drive home. Fine. Do her at her house."

"At her *house*? How?"

"You're a smart boy. You think of a way." She reached around back and undid the knot, pulled her bikini top over her head. "And to help you think, I'll give you a kiss to make it better."

Jamie's eyes widened in terror at the thought of the permanent disfigurement she could do, then relaxed a bit, then closed as a wide smile spread across his face. A light knock sounded on the door.

Amee lifted her head slightly. "Come in."

Monica stepped in, closed the door behind her. She had lost her panties and was holding the bottom of her T-shirt up above her navel. It was clear she had spent the past twenty minutes with scissors and razor. "You think the magazines would be interested in me now?"

The boat was bobbing, going nowhere. Just bobbing. Fishing, probably. Nick hated fishing. He hated water, period. Just the though of it nauseated him. In fact, he felt like throwing up right now. Why would he dream about boating? He hated boating. He wished he would wake up.

A splash of cold water hit him in the face. "Wake up," a voice commanded.

Nick woke up, saw Romer's dark face surrounded by blue sky. He realized he was freezing, turned his head to look around and wished he'd remained asleep. He was buck naked, tied to a surfboard, bobbing up and down in the slight swell. Romer stood next to him. The deserted beach was about 150 feet away.

"So, you ready to tell the truth?"

Nick tried to move his hands, realized he couldn't budge them. Of course he couldn't. A Navy SEAL would certainly know his knots. He felt nauseated again. "You're not going to let me drift out to sea, are you?"

Romer laughed. "It amazes me how a guy can live by the water all his pathetic life and still not know a damn thing about the tides." He grabbed the surfboard and spun it around so Nick's head pointed offshore. "See, the prevailing wind this time of year is southeast. The easterly seabreeze is even stronger. So unless there's an unusual westerly to take you well offshore, all the tide does is take you away from shore, then bring you back to shore, away from shore, back to shore, until at some point a spring tide washes you up on the beach. That's why drowning victims almost always come back."

Nick felt the vomit rising, struggled to keep it down, knowing Romer would probably let him choke on it.

"That's the good news, as far as drifting out to sea goes. Now the bad news: This is the time of year we *do* get lots of westerlies with all the cold fronts coming through. Right now for instance. Feel how warm the air is?"

Nick shivered, his pale, doughy flesh covered with goose bumps.

"Well, you probably don't, being naked and all. But believe me. It's warm. Unseasonably warm. That's because the wind is out of the south, pulling up all that warm, moist air out of the Gulf of Mexico and the Caribbean. And you know what that means, right? Exactly. It'll go west as the cold front approaches. And this time of year, it might sit in the west for, oh, a day or two. Perfect surfing wind, a westerly. Especially with a big northeast swell, that west wind makes those big boys stand right up. Nice, clean, long break. California conditions."

Romer shook his head wistfully. "Anyway. That westerly will also push things out beyond the reach of the daily tides. In fact, if it can get you fifty or sixty miles offshore, it'll put you in the Gulf Stream, and then God only knows where you'll wind up. Maybe Cape Hatteras. More likely, Ireland, or even Norway. Of course, there's a chance you'll catch the Canary current off Cape Finisterre and be pushed southwest right into the trade winds and the northern equatorial current." Romer laughed. "And that could put you right back on this beach: in about two or three years. What's left of you, anyway."

Nick retched violently, sending a spume straight upward. Romer dodged it easily, then turned the board on its side to let Nick puke into the water.

"But to answer your question: No. I'm not going to let you drift out to sea."

Nick finished vomiting, took a series of deep breaths. "You're not?"

"Nope." Romer shook his head, let the board down into the water again. "I'm going to flip you upside down and let my trained shark devour you."

Nick felt his mouth go dry, saw a wicked smile on Romer's lips.

"See, that's why I took your clothes. The cops, they aren't too good with bone fragments. But clothing, that's where they'll make an ID every time." He laughed softly. "I know what you're thinking. You're thinking: He wouldn't feed me to the shark like this; it would ruin his board. But that's the best part. Remember I said *trained* shark. Lots of people, even ichthyologists who should know better, think sharks are mindless brutes, nothing but strength and hunger. They have no idea how intelligent these animals are because they've never bothered to study them. Well, I have. And I've found that not only are they trainable, some also *want* human contact. Take Bruce, for example. I've trained Bruce since he was born. He comes when I call him, and he'll be as playful as a kitten or as hungry as, well, I guess as hungry as a shark, depending on the signal I use. But he won't even damage my board. No, he'll just pass by right next to you, and his rough skin will slice right through those ropes. Then he'll tear you to pieces. Or he'll swallow you whole. I never know."

Nick's jaws moved, but nothing was coming out. Quickly, he had to tell him about the tapes he'd left with his lawyer, the letter. Why wasn't his voice working?

"Well, I'm sure after listening to me blather, being eaten by sharks will seem a welcome relief. I'm sorry I go on so; I guess I'm used to rambling. You know once in a conspiracy case I did a five-hour closing argument? Convicted all seven, too." He reached for his waist and unclipped the bright yellow Walkman, started adjusting the knobs. "Anyway, I'm sorry it has to end like this, but I suppose there are worse ways to go."

"Like the electric chair," Nick finally blurted.

Romer blinked. "Excuse me?"

"That's what they do to murderers, you know," Nick spouted self-righteously. "They fry 'em in the electric chair. And that's what'll happen to you, too. I've got a lawyer."

"I *am* a lawyer, and a fat lot of good it did me. Anyway. They'll never prove anything. Especially if Bruce eats you whole. They'll think you ran away to Tahiti with your bimbo—"

"I gave him some videos. And a letter. To be opened if I don't return by the close of business."

"Videos." Romer watched Nick carefully. "Videos of what?"

"You know of what. Dead Jet Skiers. Dead boat racers. You. Your shark." Nick swallowed, gambled on a hunch. "Your Walkman."

Romer's eyes flashed, and Nick pressed his advantage.

"Yeah, I read all about you. You hate TV. You hate music. You don't even have a radio in your car. But you go out and buy a two-hundred-dollar underwater Walkman? And you, who hate Jet Skis and power-boats, you go out of your way to watch them race? And take your Walkman with you? So you can listen to music, which you also hate, while you're there?"

Romer stood still, stared at Nick with cold, unblinking eyes. "You're lying. You're making this up as you go."

"I'm not!" Nick croaked. "Believe me, I'm not that smart."

Romer stared another minute. "No. You're not, are you? But you *are* smart enough to watch tapes of the races and figure out what happened. You probably watched them a million times to see why your races kept blowing up. Of course, there's nothing provable. Hell, there isn't even probable cause to come search my house, let alone bring me in," Romer mused aloud. "But with the police chief in your pocket, you wouldn't need probable cause. And they'd bring all the evidence they need with them. So you could have already gone to the cops with what you got. But you didn't. You came here instead. Why?"

Nick swallowed again. "Because—"

"To blackmail me," Romer continued. "Of course. The tapes are at the lawyer in case something went wrong. Well, with all your resources, you must know I don't *have* anything. All the money's gone. I gave it away. And my surfboard business hasn't exactly taken off. So the question recurs: Why are you here?"

"I'm not here to blackmail you," Nick said, now more confident that he wasn't going to die in the jaws of Romer's pet. "I'm perfectly willing to pay a reasonable fee for one night of your . . . cooperation."

Romer stood silently for a moment. "How much?"

Nick calculated quickly. "Five thousand?"

Romer scoffed, started fingering his Walkman.

"Okay, twenty!" Nick blurted.

The angular head tilted for a moment, considered the offer. "What do you want?"

Nick licked his lips. "I need to borrow your shark."

. . .

Weathers stroked the long barrel one final time and tucked it into the specially cut slot in the foam. He patted the night scope, its power pack and the ten shiny cartridges all in a row. He shut the case, flicked the snaps, hit the light on his way out and climbed into the forest-green Ford Expedition. The $30,000 sport utility vehicle still had that new-car smell Weathers loved so much, despite his frequent jaunts to the hunting lodge. He got to the end of the dirt road, looked left and turned right, flicking the truck out of four-wheel drive for a smoother ride down to Daytona.

God, he hated leaving the lodge like that. It belonged to the cable television lobbyist, who'd given it to Weathers for the week in anticipated appreciation of his personal interest in a bill that would, in the now highly unlikely event that it passed, levy the telecommunications surcharge on the cable industry.

Perhaps he'd mention to the lobbyist that he'd had a harder time than expected lining up the necessary votes in the Finance and Taxation Committee, and another week or so in the lodge should ensure the bill's defeat. That and maybe an evening with one of his firm's younger associates, he was thinking in particular of the blonde with the long legs.

He had seriously considered preserving his long weekend by hiring out the task at hand. In fact, he was reasonably sure one of his colleagues from Miami a few years earlier had had a similar thing done with a loud-mouthed community activist who was threatening to run against him. But he knew if he asked for a referral it would come back to haunt him. Soon enough, either the colleague or the contractor would no doubt need a favor, or two, or ten. Joanna with her damn pictures was bad enough. One blackmailer was plenty in the life of any politician.

Garth Brooks skipped a note on the CD player and Weathers grimaced. Why bother if it wasn't going to work right? Now he'd have to take it back to Capital Ford and complain to the owner, the one who wanted an exemption to the state's Growth Management Law so he could build a Hyundai dealership on land that had been set aside for a state park, back when the bunny-huggers had held sway in the House. Maybe he'd try the next Expedition in a different color, maroon perhaps. If he didn't like it, he could always go back and get green again.

He flicked on the cruise control and stretched out his legs. Another five hours to Daytona to clean up Joanna's mess. Damn her and those wretched Polaroids. He should have taken care of them, and her, a long time ago.

On the other hand, had he done that, she never could have given him 10 percent of RaceWorld. An easy million and a half a year. *That* he could live with: a safe, reliable income he could depend on as he struck out for higher office. After all, it would take a while before an investment in a congressional seat started paying dividends. He'd need a few years to acquire the power and seniority necessary to attract the favor of Washington lobbyists, particularly those with the really well-heeled clients. And a man had to eat in the meantime.

Those Polaroids, though. He really would have to do something about them. It wouldn't do at all if, one day as chairman of the House Armed Services Committee, he were to get a breathless call reminding him of the gory details and asking for yet another favor for Van Horne Enterprises.

Yes, he would make those pictures a top priority. A nice, clean burglary would do it. Grab all the jewelry, all the silver, everything in the safe, including, most likely, a well-worn photo album. How much might such a thing cost? Perhaps he would check into it tomorrow or the next day, whenever he finished.

He sighed, wiggled his hips and stretched his legs some more. Another four hours and fifty minutes to Daytona.

Madame Rosa held up both palms, eyes shut tightly. She began swaying to and fro.

Nick checked his watch impatiently. "Cut the crap, all right?"

Rosa opened her eyes, studied him suspiciously. He was in full disguise mode: beard, mustache and plain-glass, horn-rim spectacles.

"I know all about you. Your real name is Rosalind Jones. You're from Tulsa. You're about as psychic as I am." He waved a hand around the room at the faux-Spanish decorations. "This is all bullshit."

Rosa pulled the shawl off her head, picked up a folding fan and began fanning herself. "Who are you?" she asked, the Spanish accent gone.

Nick pulled open his jacket and removed a money belt. Quickly he counted out ten $100 bills and laid them on the table. "You don't need to know that. You just need to know that I'm good friends with Mr. Franklin here." He held up one of the bills. "You have a regular Friday customer. Barbie Baxter."

She looked down at the stack of bills, back up to Nick's face. "I don't discuss my clients with others. Everything's strictly confidential. Sort of like a priest, or a lawyer."

Nick snickered, picked the money off the table. "Really? Then I guess we have nothing to talk about." He turned for the door.

"Wait a minute!" Rosa called out, an Okie twang infecting the words.

Nick turned slowly.

"I might as well hear you out. Now that you're here, I mean."

Nick laid the thousand dollars back on the table. "You're the one who got Barbie on this sea turtle kick, right? Don't try to deny it. I know it's true. Anyway, I just want you to give her one more piece of advice about the ocean, okay? How does that sound? A thousand bucks for one sentence. And another thousand if she follows through."

Rosa stifled a gasp, but couldn't keep her eyes from widening: Two thousand dollars for one sitting! Plus Barbie's regular $50 fee, plus the $500 her boyfriend already put up; more than five weeks worth of income! She could take a vacation. Go to Atlantic City, or even Las Vegas!

"Tell me what you wish me to say and let me meditate. If it is in her aura, I will pass it along," Rosa said, the Spanish pronunciations and inflections creeping back into her voice. "Otherwise I cannot."

Nick groaned. "Whatever. She loves to go swimming at night. In the ocean. Tell her she has to go tonight. Tell her all the turtles and dolphins and fishes and whales and all the other animals will be having a harmonic conference. That this is the one night when all the kindred spirits of the sea meet in the ocean of life."

"Señor, I will not speak of harmonic convergence." Rosa turned up her nose. "I am a traditional seer."

"Tell her whatever the fuck you want. Just make sure she goes swimming tonight."

Rosa set her hands on either side of her ball and closed her eyes. "I must see."

Nick shifted his weight from one foot to the other, checked his watch, bent to peek out the window. "Come on, Madame Jones. I ain't got all day. She's gonna be here any minute."

Rosa opened one eye suspiciously. "Why do you wish for her to go swimming tonight?"

"It's her birthday." Nick turned away from the window. "And, uh, we're having a party for her on the beach. A surprise party."

Rosa shut her eyes again. It didn't make any sense, a surprise party on the beach. Where would everyone hide? Well, that was *their* problem. Two grand was two grand. "I see it is in her being, in her spirit to do this."

"Well, hallelujah. You'll tell her, then?"

"When will you bring by the second thousand?"

Nick grinned. The almighty dollar had won again. "Tomorrow." He turned for the door. "If Barbie shows up at her party tonight, I'll come by first thing in the morning."

He hurried down the dim hall, pushed aside the screen door and waddled to the car. Things were still sore, but the salt water had actually made him feel better. Or maybe it was the prospect of finally getting rid of Barbie, and actually having a hand in it. Maybe that's what all the fuss of do-it-yourselfers was about.

He slammed the door, pulled a U-turn in the narrow street and headed back out toward the interstate. He hadn't gone two blocks when he saw approaching the familiar outline of the VW Cabriolet. Quickly he slouched as low as he could, put a hand over the left side of his face and held his breath.

Barbie drove down the street, parked in her usual spot and got out, just slightly off balance. Something had happened. She'd seen something, but couldn't figure out what. She looked back down the street, shrugged and turned down the path to Rosa's parlor.

NINE

■ ■ ■

Weathers set the parking brake, stepped out of the truck and stretched out his once-lanky, now filled-in frame. He grabbed his hunting case and an overnight bag and walked up the rest of the drive to the stately river mansion, the property of Jimmy Poole, the lobbyist for Daytona Raceway. He entered the empty house, walked past the art-gallery trinkets, through the back door and down a wooden walkway toward the *Checkered Flag,* the Van Hornes' fifty-four-foot luxury trawler, tied to the end of the dock. A fifteen-foot, rigid-bottomed, inflatable runabout hung on hoists off her aft deck.

Weathers ignored both vessels and instead grabbed a four-foot-long, three-foot-thick bundle of plastic and unrolled it onto the gray planks. Aluminum slats clicked into place as he put a bellows pump to one of the valves and began pumping. In twenty minutes, he had prepared himself a ten-foot dinghy, complete with a 9.9-horsepower Evinrude outboard, and had it tied to the dock at the bottom of a wooden ladder. Weathers looked at the quickly darkening sky and checked his watch. Sure, he had time. At least for one beer.

He headed back up toward the house, hoping that good ol' Jimmy kept a supply of cold ones in his fridge.

Outside, the sky over the ocean was dark, dark blue, with the few clouds reflecting back the orange from the sunset across the river. Amee ignored it, instead scanned the Boardwalk up and down for Jamie's familiar blond head. The moron was late again, and she had important instructions.

She turned and watched Monica, her new thong-clad billiards hostess, line up a shot and knock it in. What she lacked in breast size, she made up for with long, long legs and a decent pool game. She was already out-earning big, blond Lori at the next table.

Monica sunk her final ball and walked over to her Joe, an acne-faced kid in Bermuda shorts, T-shirt and baseball cap, a Canadian Spring Breaker. She gave him a big hug, kicking her foot up in the air like in the old movies, and a demure kiss on the cheek. She didn't object when the kid's hands slid down and grazed her bare buns. Nor when he pulled out a twenty to pay for his game and told her to keep it.

Amee smiled. Now *that* was customer service. She wondered again what it would cost to pay off a couple of city commissioners and the Boardwalk cops to let her girls play topless. She could easily double, maybe triple her income. Make it that much sooner that she could pick up a third and fourth table. And then a third and fourth girl. Between that and the money she'd make off Nicky, she was finally going to be rich.

The bell at the top of the door jingled as three Joes, their pockets and fanny packs emptied, went out and Jamie and his goofy smile came in. Amee marched to the door, grabbed his arm, dragged him past the tables, past Monica's waving, through the back door and into her office.

"The fuck have you been?" she snapped when the door was shut behind them. "You were supposed to be here two hours ago."

He put his hands on her shoulders, let them slide down her arms. "Whoa, take it easy. I'm here now, ain't I?"

She pulled his hands off her and sat on the desk. "Did you get the gun?"

Jamie lifted his shirt to show her the handle sticking from his waistband. "That's what kept me. I couldn't remember if it was fifty paces east and sixty paces north or sixty east and fifty north."

Amee lowered her head into one hand and squeezed. "Why didn't you just do it fifty and fifty? Then you woulda had to remember just one number."

He blinked, nodded slowly. "Oh yeah. Good idea." He patted his pockets for a pen. "I oughta write that down. Anyway, I ended up borrowing a metal detector from this guy on the beach. Told him I'd lost my keys hiking in the woods. What a nice old guy."

She rolled her eyes and sighed. "Okay, now that you got your gun back, there's been a change in plans. You're not going to Mrs. Van Horne's house tonight. You're going to the hospital."

"The *hospital*? Why, what happened? Is she okay?"

Amee sneered. "Your concern is touching. No, it's not her. It's some business partner of Nicky's. He screwed him somehow. I didn't get all the details. Anyway, he's in room three-sixteen at Halifax. You go in, put a pillow over the gun and shoot him in the head until it's empty."

"Wait a minute," he said, raising his hands. "I ain't killing *two* people for five grand. I ain't *that* cheap."

"No one's telling you to. You get five grand for this one, plus another five for the wife, all right?"

"And a chance to drive in the Crown Cola?"

"And driving in the Crown Cola. Now go get some clean clothes. Buy some flowers like you're visiting somebody."

Jamie stroked his chin. "Are you sure this is a good idea? Shooting somebody in the hospital? Won't somebody hear?"

"It's just a .22. If you use a pillow, nobody will hear a thing. Here, gimme the gun." She grabbed a cushion off the mildewy old couch in the corner and pushed the muzzle into it. A "pop" sounded in the office and a cloud of cotton filling blew into the air. "See? You can hardly hear it."

Jamie stared at the ceiling. A small round hole had appeared in the paper poster, barely an inch above Barbie's head. "Did you know that's her?"

"That's who?" Amee asked.

"The chick in the poster. That's Mrs. Van Horne. Amazing, huh?"

Amee stared at the photo. *"That's* his wife? Nicky's married to the Nipple Girl?"

"Ummm. And I gotta say, she's just as pretty in person."

Amee scoffed. "Gimme a break. Except for them freaky nipples, she's as flat as a board. You couldn't get her pictures into *Screw* or *Jugs* or *Hustler* if you paid *them.*"

Jamie shrugged. "I'm just tellin' you like I see it. Speaking of which, that was pretty good, this afternoon, huh?"

"Yeah. I suppose it wasn't bad." She remembered Jamie lying there like a log, waiting for her and Monica to work on him. Now, Monica was a different story altogether. She wouldn't mind getting together with *her* again. "Where's Monica from, anyway?"

Jamie nodded with pride. "I guess I'm pretty good in the sack. I suppose I must be, huh? To satisfy two good-lookin' chicks at once? You know, a couple of years back I had four at once. Did all four of 'em, too, one after the other: boom, boom, boom, boom."

Amee pushed herself off the desk. "Right, Jamie. You're the best. Now, why don't you get going. Nick said the nurses have a shift change at ten. That'll be the best time."

"You really think I'm pretty good? 'Cause I been thinkin' a good way to make a little extra money might be to be like a male hooker, you know? I figure, I get laid a lot anyway, I might as well get paid for it, you know?"

She pushed him toward the door. "Sure, Jamie, anything you say. You can be a NASCAR driver, and an airline pilot, and a tree surgeon, and a submarine captain, and a gigolo, and whatever the fuck else you want, all right? But tonight, right now, you got to be a killer, okay?"

He turned toward the door, then turned back for a final point. "I mean, it's not like I'm making this up. Just the other day, a guy on the Boardwalk asked if I did tricks. So you figure there's gotta be a pretty good market."

She stared for a moment in renewed amazement. "He was *gay,* you moron! He wanted to know if you'd let guys stick their dicks up your ass. Now *go!*"

Jamie considered this new piece of information, shrugged. "How much you suppose they'd pay for that?"

Amee shook her head, pulled open the door and shoved him out.

Nick scanned the beach in one direction, then the other. Nothing. Completely deserted. He set down the binoculars, grabbed the black metal box with the attached coil of wire and ran down the dune, fell in the soft sand at its base, got up and continued waddling toward the water.

He stood for a moment at the border of wet sand and dry. He'd always hated this moment. The water was always cold. And usually it had slimy things floating in it that brushed up against him and scared the daylights out of him. Why would anyone want to swim in the ocean, anyway? That's what pools were for, for God's sake.

He looked nervously up and down the beach, then cautiously waded in, sneakers, jeans and all. A small wave approached and suddenly wet his legs to his knees. He suppressed a shout. Somehow it was colder, a *lot* colder, than that afternoon. With gritted teeth he waded out until he was thigh deep. There. That would be perfect, he decided. With a clumsy thumb he pressed the single button on the metal box. A tiny green LED bulb began blinking. Just like when Romer had demonstrated it.

He undid a garbage-bag tie from around the coil of wire and flung the black Styrofoam ball at the end away from him. Quickly now, with chattering teeth, he reared back and threw the softball-size metal box as far as he could. It flew about ten feet and plopped into the water. He shook his head; he'd always hated softball.

As Romer had instructed, he made sure the Styrofoam ball was floating and still attached to the box by the wire. He watched it sway in and out with passing waves and decided he'd checked it out just about enough. He turned, waddled, then splashed through the surf, out onto the beach, and started running back up toward the gutted house he'd picked as his base. The wind stung through his soaked blue jeans and his teeth chattered all the more as he climbed the dune and retreated into the shelter of a plywood wall.

He huddled for warmth and swore aloud, first at Joanna for making him go through all he'd endured, and then at Barbie for tricking him into marrying her in the first place. He'd get even, though. Tonight was it. Tonight he'd take charge, once and for all.

"You know, I haven't got a lick of work done on my house since I started seeing you."

Barbie flipped herself around in the tub, nestled against him. "Yeah, but you've been getting laid a lot more."

His hands began caressing her neck, moved down to her shoulders, her chest. Her back arched in anticipation. He wondered whether to broach the subject of Nick Van Horne's strange videotapes and even stranger letter, the one that spoke cryptically about a business arrangement and advised police to search Randall Romer's house. What the hell was all that about? Drugs? Counterfeiting? And what exactly were the videos supposed to show? Sure, they proved Romer was in town the days of the Jet Ski and speedboat races, but surely there were easier ways of proving *that*. As long as none of it had to do with Barbie, he really didn't care what the tapes and the letter were about. Still, his uneasiness about Van Horne had returned.

He stroked down her smooth, soft sides, down past her hips. "Maybe, but getting laid doesn't pay the bills."

"No, but it's a hell of a lot more fun, isn't it?" Barbie collapsed in a soggy heap against his body, sighed. "Tell you what. Starting tomorrow, I'll help you with the house every day. I can handle a hammer and a nail as good as the next six-dollar-an-hour, pot-smoking bum."

Nick's eyes widened. "Seriously? You'd help me?"

"We could get up early every morning and do it before work. That way we'd have some daylight, too."

He had never hired casual help because he'd been trying to save the money. But a second pair of hands would get him through the grunt work in half the time. "God, that would really speed things up. We could finish the exterior in the next week, and then all the drywalling the week after that." He stroked her damp hair. "We could be finished this spring."

"Good. Then you can stop obsessing about it while we're making love."

"I *never* think about the house while we're making love. Trust me." His hands wandered down her thighs. "And you know what else? In return for helping me with the house, I'll take over your lawsuit for you."

She turned around to face him. "You don't have to do that."

He shrugged. "Why not? I want to."

She bit her lip. "The lawyer I got now said he's losing half his clients because he's representing me. The same thing would happen to you. There's a lot of pressure to make sure I lose."

"I doubt it. My clients aren't as politically well connected as his. Anyway, I thought Antoon was so pissed about the chicken-eggs thing that he was going to rule against the county."

"My lawyer says even if that happens, the county would appeal, and appeal again, and keep appealing right up to the U.S. Supreme Court. He said it would cost a fortune."

Nolin tilted his head, lifted his chin. "I could get into that. Arguing before the United States Supreme Court. I guess I'd have to call myself J. Douglas Nolin."

She blinked. "Douglas?"

He froze for a moment. "My middle name," he answered weakly. "Anyhow, appellate procedure was my favorite thing in law school. I'd really enjoy going before appeals judges. They're a sharp bunch, you know."

She leaned forward to kiss him. "You're so sweet to me."

"Sweet nothing. I just can't see you pissing away all that money on some shyster. What's he charge, like a hundred an hour?"

"One-seventy in court, a hundred out of court."

Nolin shook his head. "What did Shakespeare say? Kill all the lawyers?"

Barbie laughed out loud. "*You're* a lawyer!"

"True, but I never tell anybody. Have you ever noticed, that's why lawyers call themselves attorneys? It's because *lawyer* sounds so sleazy.

You know, there's a technical difference. You're not an attorney until you're representing somebody. Like if I take on your case, I'm your attorney. But I'm still a lawyer."

She kissed him again. "Well, I think you're a very sweet lawyer. I hope Shakespeare doesn't kill you." She smiled broadly. "You remember you were making fun of me for going to a fortune-teller? Well, she predicted I'd meet you. She said I'd get another lawyer, and the turtles would win their beach back, and all my problems would be over."

He raised an eyebrow. "Really? She said that? What else did she say?"

"Well, I saw her again today, and she saw more about my past lives. Turns out I had several in the sea. Most of my psychic history, in fact, has been in the ocean."

Nolin nodded. "Interesting. Anything else?"

"I was a dolphin. Before I was a turtle, I mean."

"Hmmm. Nothing else? Nothing about any dangers on the horizon? About sharks lurking in the waters?"

Barbie shrugged, shook her head. "Why? Should I be looking out for one in particular? One with long, thin fingers, and long, thin toes, and a long, thin—"

"*Okay,* no need to get into that." He kissed her neck. "Seriously, though, she didn't say anything about any dangers?"

"No. Why are you so interested? I thought you didn't believe in psychics and seers and all that stuff."

"I don't." Especially when they took your money and didn't keep their end of the bargain, he thought crossly. "Just curious, that's all."

"Well, she didn't say anything about dangers." Barbie sat up straight with a grin. "But she *did* say I had to go swimming tonight. In the ocean. You know, I haven't done *that* since we started seeing each other, either."

He recalled instantly the many nights he'd watched her through his binoculars running naked in and out of the water. "No, I suppose you haven't. What's so special about tonight?"

"It's something about all the spirits of the water creatures coming together in Pisces. It won't happen again for fifty years or something. I'm not too clear on it. All I know is it's tonight and I want to do it. And I want you to come with me."

He thought of how cold the water would be this time of year, and of how the sharks had torn the Jet Skiers into so many bits of flesh and neoprene. "Gee, Barbie, I don't know. I'm not into this cold-water stuff. Why—"

"Come on!" She tickled under his arms until he squeezed them against his sides. "Don't be such a baby. Besides, you said you liked to go skinny-dipping every now and then, remember?"

"Yeah, but in the middle of winter? Can't we wait for the water to warm up a little?"

"Oh, I guess the water's warm enough for *me* to go in while you ogle through your binoculars, but it's too cold for *you* to go in?"

His face, already flush from the hot water, darkened even further. "I *wasn't* ogling, I was looking at the sky; I . . ." He saw her smirk, gave up. "All right, you win. But at least let me get good and hot in here first, okay?"

Through the night glasses, the single house with the tall, pointed roof stood out in bright detail among its squat neighbors. The tall privacy fence hid the deck area, and a long dune crossover extended to the beach.

Weathers put down his binoculars, tossed the small dinghy anchor overboard and pressed the kill switch on the small outboard. A damp mist hung in the air, and he zipped his hunting parka against it. At least it was a calm night. It could be hours, he knew, or perhaps not at all tonight. That was okay. He was used to waiting and not even getting a shot at something. Those were the dues you had to pay whenever you hunted anything: ducks, moose, deer. Troublesome wives.

Quietly and efficiently, he attached barrel to stock, night scope to barrel and battery pack to scope. With practiced ease he slipped five cartridges into the breech and worked the bolt to move one into the firing chamber. He lay down across the inflatable to face the shore and peered through the glasses at the empty beach. Over the privacy fence, steam rose in intermittent clouds: a Jacuzzi. A good sign, he knew. She was home. And what would feel more refreshing, more bracing after a soak in the tub than a nice, cold dip in the ocean?

With his free hand he searched the floor for his open can of Miller Genuine Draft, drained the last few ounces, crushed the can and flipped it into the water before opening another. With any luck she'd come out soon; he only had four cans of beer left.

Jamie tiptoed along the deserted corridor, searching the doors for room numbers. Just as Cherry had promised, the floor was empty of nurses; he'd seen only one since getting off the elevator. If challenged, he would tell them he was visiting his cousin in room 216. Oh, he was on the *third* floor? His mistake, sorry. He held the basket of pink carnations surrounding a stuffed Winnie-the-Pooh he'd lifted from the nurses' station counter like a talisman, proof that he belonged there. Sweat, meanwhile, accumulated under his arms and on his forehead.

This was crazy. Why had he agreed to it? Oh yeah: another $5,000, he remembered. That was it. Enough for a motorcycle, although not a nice one like that Harley. He could probably get a pretty decent Hog for $10,000, if he could wait until after doing Mrs. Van Horne for a new set of wheels.

He had a bad feeling about her. It was like she had some sort of guardian angel, and no matter what he did, he wouldn't be able to hurt her. He shook his head to clear away negative thoughts. *Come on, James:* Be all that you can be, he told himself. Finally he came to a door with 316 on the smoked acrylic sign next to it. He turned the knob and pushed silently inward, stepped into a forest of green growth.

Bewildered, he closed the door behind him and turned to step among the potted plants and trees. Ahead he heard faint noises, like animals. A television, he guessed. Jamie wiped the sweat onto his sleeve, pulled the gun from his pocket and set it inside his basket of flowers for quicker access. Quietly he began stepping among the flowers, over a cactus and through a jumble of rubber trees and ferns.

Ahead and to the left came the soft noises. He edged in that direction and soon came to the wall. Carefully, one soft step after another, he eased through the greenery, his heart hammering in his ears, almost over-coming the soft grunts that seemed just ahead . . .

Gently he pushed aside a heavy fern, and his breath caught in his throat. Not two feet away was a darkly tanned blonde, naked except for a black, seemingly painted-on bikini and sitting astride the chest of a very hairy man, presumably the room's patient. And behind her was the wait-ress from the Book Nook: *his* waitress! She was also naked except for her nipple ring, which she teased between the fingers of one hand while the other hand groped the painted-bikini woman. Both girls smiled at him demurely.

The man on the bed noticed something amiss, lifted his head and grunted, *"You!"*

Even upside down, Jamie recognized the pushed-in nose, the blaz-ing eyes of the biker he'd run off the road.

"You!" he screamed again and began waving his cast-bound arms on either side of his women. "I'll kill you, you son of a bitch!"

Jamie screamed, dropped the Pooh basket and tripped twice on var-ious potted plants on his way to the door.

It would be pneumonia, Nick knew. Crouched on the concrete slab, naked from the waist down, with the wind swirling through the framed-in porch, he would catch his death. He shivered again, rubbed his arms to keep warm and again cursed Romer for not telling him to bring a set of clothes to change into after he'd planted the transmitter.

No, instead that maniac had suggested a wetsuit. Like he would even own one. He was catching a nasty cold, and it was all Romer's fault. Romer's and Barbie's. Romer's and Barbie's and Joanna's. Romer for not warning him he wouldn't dry out after he'd been in the water, regardless how warm a night it was. Barbie for tricking him into marrying her, then leaving him, then filing that pain-in-the-ass lawsuit and finally for not dying two nights earlier and causing him all this extra trouble. And Joanna for, well, being Joanna. For torturing him through the years with that plump, ripe body she would tease him with, then make him feel guilty for wanting, and finally for putting him through this ordeal just for a stupid theme park.

Sure, it was easy for *her* to sit and criticize. She hadn't been swindled, sodomized, threatened at spearpoint and prepared as a shark hors d'oeuvre. She'd get hers, though. And soon. Maybe he would rent the shark gear from Romer again. Problem was, though, that Joanna never went in the ocean, either. He'd have to find a way to get the shark into the swimming pool. But then afterward he'd have to get the shark out. And clean up all the blood before the cops got there.

He shuddered at the thought. No, he'd need some other method for Joanna. Certainly Romer would think of something. He seemed pretty resourceful, although expensive. It had cost him $20,000 just to rent his equipment. That, plus the $10,000 he'd wasted on Lance the Gay Biker, $15,000 on Crawdad the sodomizing biker and another $5,000 to have Crawdad taken care of so he wouldn't come after him for the remaining $15,000. . . .

That was his $50,000 right there, not counting the $1,000 he paid that fortune-teller out of his own pocket. He wouldn't be able to skim any of it for himself, and wouldn't have any left to pay for Joanna's demise. Maybe Romer would work on credit? After all, Nick would be a wealthy man after Barbie and Joanna were gone, with full control over his own money. No more running for Joanna's signature every time he wanted to cash in a CD or savings bond. No more of those insufferable parties Joanna kept dragging him to. And no more races, either. He might agree to award the Winston Cup trophy at the end of every season, but that would be it.

Nick felt a sneeze coming, braced for it and still smashed his head on the two-by-four he was leaning against. He rubbed his forehead gingerly, thankful, he supposed, that there hadn't been a nail protruding from the stud. He picked up the binoculars and stared at her house. Still the same lights on, still the steam rising from the back porch. Still no sign of her.

He shifted slightly to rearrange what portion of his bare buttocks contacted cold cement; he had sat in soaked pants and underwear for a while before finally deciding they weren't going to dry anytime soon. He reached to check his jeans, draped over a sawhorse. He sighed: still no drier. Eventually he was going to have to pull those wet clothes back on to go home.

What if that phony gypsy hadn't told her to go swimming tonight? What if Barbie had missed her regular appointment? What if she already had plans for the night, and couldn't go swimming, regardless of Madame Rosa's suggestion? Nick scowled, realizing his elaborate scheme was pretty much a house of cards, ready to fall apart at any instant, leaving Barbie rich and him dying in intensive care with fluid in his lungs.

He sneezed again, less violently this time. As he twisted to wipe clear, sticky snot onto his sleeve, he noticed a blur on the dune crossover two houses down. Quickly he pushed the binoculars to his eyes, saw his estranged wife, tall, thin and naked, tugging at something behind the gate. Finally she pulled it out, and Nick saw it was a man. Equally tall, equally thin and equally naked. Together they scampered across the walkway and down the stairs and ran across the sand, steam rising from their bodies.

Nick fumbled for the yellow Walkman, found it on the floor behind him, held it out in front of him between two studs, and pressed the play button. A small red LED began to blink slowly. Still pointing the Walkman, Nick lifted the binoculars to his eyes and held his breath.

Weathers laid his binoculars on the dinghy floor and picked up the rifle, flicking the safety with his thumb and activating the battery for the night scope. In a few moments, the image through the scope was bathed in soft green hues.

At the center of the cross hairs was the outline of a woman with long flowing hair, then a man, then the woman again. He swore at the motion of the dinghy, which, magnified through the 20-power scope, seemed to lurch beneath him. He shifted his weight so he lay completely athwart the little boat, the rifle resting on the inflated gunwale, his duck-booted feet dipping into the water.

There, much better. The images of the woman and man came together, then apart, then together again. The cross hairs lined up on the two heads as they turned as one. Well, if the boyfriend had to die, too, that's the way it was going to be.

He took a deep breath, had begun slowly exhaling through his nose and gently squeezing the trigger when the rest of the wind was knocked from his chest and sky became water and water became sky.

"Jesus Christ!" Nolin yelled. "This water's fucking freezing! Did your fortune-teller say anything about the spirits of the sea dying of hypothermia? Or maybe heart failure?"

She ducked under, arose and splashed him. "You know, I shouldn't tell you this, because it will only encourage you, but I don't feel any particular kinship with ocean creatures tonight." She thought a moment. "Which reminds me. Rosa also wished me a happy birthday. And my birthday isn't for another three months. Isn't that weird? The first time I went to her, she knew my birthday, and my middle name, and where I lived and everything."

Nolin rubbed his arms. "I recommend a new psychic, before this one gets me killed."

Barbie sidled next to him, put her hands on his hips and pulled him closer. "Come on. It's not that bad when you get used to it. Actually, it feels kind of warm now, doesn't it?"

Nolin snorted, sputtered, nodded at her chest, which alternately surfaced and sank in each passing wavelet. "If it's so goddamn warm, then how come you got your high beams on?"

She reached out a hand underwater. "Funny, it seems to have had the opposite effect on you."

She stretched upward to kiss him, spun him around. He pulled her close, felt the chill fall away and suddenly froze. He had seen it out of the corner of his eye: a glint of green, then an enormous black shadow bursting through the surface, the silhouette of a man, then a splash, then nothing. He pulled his lips away and stood very still, put a hand over her mouth when she tried to question him. Whatever it was, it was gone.

"We need to get out," he said quietly. "Right now. Without a lot of noise."

"What? What did you see?"

"Later," he hissed, and turned her toward the beach. Slowly they walked toward the shore, then faster as they got into thigh-deep water, then ran as they were in the surf.

Safely on the sand, he turned to her, panting. "You're never going to believe this."

T E N

...

 Nick stood up, stumbled backward, barked his shins on a stack of two-by-fours, finally sat down again. He put his hand over his heart, willed it to slow down. The shark had come, all right. The same one he'd seen that afternoon at Romer's underwater petting zoo. But who the hell had it eaten? His binoculars had been trained on Barbie and her boyfriend when he'd noticed a green wink, searched for it, fearing it was the box he'd thrown out into the surf, somehow risen to the surface.

It wasn't though. He'd seen it clearly enough, for that split second before the view was instead filled with the head of the shark, rising straight upward from beneath. He shook his head. He had to get out, before Barbie and boyfriend called the cops. He crawled to the sawhorse, and that's when he noticed the dog.

It stood silently, staring, a curious expression on its face. Nick froze, stared back. He hated dogs, and dogs generally hated him. He tried a stilted smile. "Nice boy," he said, voice quavering.

The dog tilted its head slightly, stood its ground. Nick reached slowly for his pants and underwear, grabbed them with one hand and started drawing them back. The dog lunged, snapped the pair of jeans and BVDs from his hand and raced out between the studs framing the rear of the porch. With brisk strides, he was down the dune and out on the beach.

Nick scrambled to his feet, stepped through the frame for a sliding glass door. "Come back here right now!" he hissed. He watched the dog run in a quick circle, drop the clothes and start barking loudly. Nick glanced nervously up and down the beach, saw a light come on in the house to the south, and ducked back inside. On the sand, the dog grabbed the clothes, ran in another two circles, dropped them, and barked some more.

"Owwww!" Jamie yelled, shaking his head. "Be careful, will ya?"

Amee straightened, pulled the levers on the vise grips apart, grabbed the cactus spine between thumb and forefinger and laid it on her desk, adding it to the existing row of eight.

"Just shut up, okay? Stop being such a baby." She leaned over his face, positioned the vise grips over a short spine sticking from his forehead and locked the tool down.

"Aaaaaaahhhhh!" he screamed, pulling his head violently away, leaving the blood-tipped spine between the vise grips' jaws. "Don't you have a pair of tweezers or something?"

"Sure. At home. I'll go there in another three hours. You want to walk around like that till then? This is the only thing Rick had that would work. So shut the fuck up." She laid the spine with the others and prepared to pull another. "So how do you know it was the same guy? I thought you didn't get a good look at him the other night."

"No! *He* recognized *me*! I told you, he had these two chicks on him, and then he looked up and said he was gonna kill me!" Jamie became still as she approached with the vise grips again, stared up at the bullet-scarred poster on the ceiling. "This whole thing has been a disaster, right from the get-go."

"No, *you've* been a disaster right from the get-go." She pulled another spine. "Let's see: You've screwed up with Nick's wife, what, four times? Now this one tonight makes oh-for-five."

"Well, I ain't going after that biker guy again. You can just forget about it. No way. That psycho's liable to tear my head off with his bare hands. In fact, I'm thinking maybe I ought to get out of town for a while. You know? Let things settle down for a bit?"

She reached for his face and yanked another spine. "Don't be a pussy. Besides, I thought you said both his arms were broken."

"He's still dangerous." Jamie shook his head warily. "You know, they say a crazy guy has the strength of ten normal guys. Forget it, Cherry. I ain't goin' anywhere near him."

Amee realized he'd dug in his heels. "Okay. Forget about him. Besides, he isn't going anywhere for a while. We need to concentrate on Mrs. Van Horne. That's the important one." She stroked his face, pockmarked and red. "How'd you manage to fall on a *cactus*, of all things?"

"The guy's a celebrity or something. He's got like a million baskets of flowers, potted plants, boxes of candy." Jamie gazed at Amee's chest bursting from her bikini top, remembered the painted one worn by one of the biker's chicks. "I wonder why your boyfriend wanted him killed?"

Amee recalled her argument with Nick about using Jamie. He already had Barbie taken care of, Nick had said. Right. By the biker who Jamie ended up putting in the hospital. Whatever happened, she had to make sure Nick never found out about that. The guy was probably putting the screws to Nick, now that he was laid up.

She shrugged. Who knows? Nick hires guys from time to time. You know, to help out at the Raceway. I guess this guy didn't work out."

Jamie shook his head. "So he's havin' him killed. Great. I hope *I* never piss him off."

She paused over the last spine, stuck in the corner of his lip, and yanked it out. "You won't. So long as we take care of his wife. Tomorrow night. We'll do it together." She reached a hand down his pants. "Tonight we'll do something else, at your place, okay? Me, you and Monica."

Jamie instantly forgot the biker. His eyes lit up greedily. "Can we bring in Tiffany and Kristin? It's been a couple of years since I've had four at once. And I'd kinda like to keep in practice."

Nick tiptoed up the stairs, got to the landing and took a deep breath. So far, so good. He'd made it home without incident, wearing only his windbreaker, his still-soaked shoes and his golf shirt wrapped around his waist. The last thing he needed was to explain any of it to Joanna. He snuck down the hall, to where the light shone from her open bedroom door. He steeled himself and quickly strode forward.

"John Robert!" she called.

Nick stopped, swallowed, turned into the room and opened his eyes. Joanna was sitting at her vanity, brushing her hair. She was wearing one of her see-through peignoirs, unlaced in the front, so that her bosom seemed on the verge of tumbling out. She looked at him in the mirror.

"Why are you wearing your shirt like that? What happened to your pants?"

Nick shrugged carelessly, like he couldn't be bothered to keep track of such minutiae.

She frowned. "Well, you'd better get your black suit ready. We'll have to make an announcement to the press, probably before the race. But the race will go on as if nothing had happened, and we'll carry on through our grief."

Nick gulped. "What, uh, will have happened?"

Joanna turned to face him. "After finally realizing you are incapable of performing even the simplest task, I decided to take care of the Barbie problem myself."

Her left breast had escaped from the peignoir, bobbed slightly up and down as she breathed. Nick felt a twinge in his loins, tried to suppress it. She was his *stepmother,* for Chrissake. "You mean, she's, uh, already taken care of?"

"As we speak. An old friend of mine is handling it personally." Joanna flipped some loose strands of hair back with a shake of her head. "If not tonight, then tomorrow morning. Certainly by the race."

Old friend. Old friend. The phrase referred to someone specific, he knew, but couldn't remember exactly who. Someone important. Nick felt a cold sweat break out on his lip and brow, remembering the long, thin shape in the shadowy figure's hands before he was snatched by the legs and dragged under. "How? How's he doing it?"

"Oh, he mentioned something about the versatility of a deer rifle. But don't you worry about it. Let's just say your beautiful wife will be permanently cured of her habit of running around naked on the beach. And the police will have yet another one of those unsolved mysteries."

Old friend. Suddenly Nick remembered. It was that politician, Withers, Walters, Webber. Whoever. The guy Joanna had the pictures on. The guy making sure RaceWorld got all that state money. A wave of panic overcame him, and he struggled to keep his composure. No matter what happened, he had to make sure Joanna never even suspected his involvement. She would kill him, without a doubt. With her bare hands. Worse, she'd hold it over him the rest of his life, take it out of his trust fund. No more cars. No more girls. He'd be better off dead.

Nausea built in his stomach, spread slowly upward. His stepmother turned on the stool, exposing a smooth, just-waxed leg up to her hip, but he'd lost all interest. Fear had overcome lust.

Joanna stroked lotion up and down her legs, only then seemed to notice the loose breast. She tucked it back in coyly. "You know, Nick, there's no reason to be embarrassed about having . . . desires for me. We're not *actually* related, you know. And as you point out so often, I *am* younger than you." She teased her hair between her fingers. "So, now with Barbie gone, there's really no reason for us . . . not to get to know each other a little better, don't you think?"

The nausea climbed up his throat. He grabbed his mouth and turned for the bathroom, big white buns flapping in his wake as the golf shirt fell off his waist.

Joanna clucked disgustedly. "Remember we have our party tomorrow night, after the race, and then the Thompsons' on Sunday," she called after him, then turned back to her vanity and resumed brushing her hair.

. . . .

"It was a guy with a rifle, and a night scope, and he was aiming right at us." Nolin waved the flashlight as they walked down the sand. "Right out there."

She clung to his arm, still damp beneath her sweats. "Out in the water? Standing or swimming?"

"I'll give you standing or swimming." He pinched her bottom through the thick cotton fabric, drew a howl of protest. "I told you. He was in a raft, or maybe a little boat."

"And you saw all this, how? On such a dark night?"

"There's enough light. The stars. The lights onshore."

"Sure. And then a giant shark came up and grabbed him." She nodded agreeably. "And this guy had a rifle, with a . . . what again?"

"A night scope. You can get 'em in military surplus stores, gun catalogs." He noticed her eyes narrow suspiciously. "I know because I defended a gun nut once. Boy am I glad I lost that one. He was a real kook. Militia commander, survivalist, the whole bit. Anyway. There are two kinds of night-vision sights: one that shows you stuff in infrared, and one that makes everything look green. That one gives off a green glow when you look straight through it. Which is what I saw, and which is why I know it was aimed right at us."

Barbie nodded again. "Right. Of course. And this person wants to kill me . . . why again?"

Nolin sighed. "Look. All I'm saying is that there's a whole town here that wishes you and your lawsuit would go away." He again debated telling her about Nick Van Horne's strange behavior, again decided against it. The more he thought about it, the more outlandish the whole thing seemed. Maybe she was right. Maybe he *had* had a bit too much wine. "I don't know. After all that shark stuff with the Jet Skis and the boat races—"

"The sharks didn't have anything to do with the boat accidents," she said quickly. "They only showed up afterward. I mean, what do you *expect* them to do when you got a bunch of bleeding bodies in the water? You can't blame 'em for that!"

Nolin smiled. "No. Far be it from me to blame a sea creature for anything bad. I mean, hey, sharks are people, too. Oooowwww!" he howled, rubbing his butt where she'd pinched him. "I didn't pinch you that hard!"

"You deserved it. You were making fun of me."

"Still, you didn't have to rip my flesh off. I'm gonna have a bruise for—"

"Give me the light a second." She pointed it down the beach, broke into a jog, stopped over a dark piece of flotsam. "A raft like this, maybe?"

He studied the gray rubber, about two feet square, torn at its edges. He poked it with a stick, as if afraid it would spring back to life. He turned the swatch over, immediately saw the Zodiac logo.

"Where's the rest?" Barbie whispered. "It wouldn't have eaten it, would it?"

Nolin shrugged. "Beats me. All I know about sharks is from movies. I guess they'd eat anything." He looked out to the mist-shrouded water. "But I suppose that if the boat was torn up, the weight of the outboard would sink it transom first. Maybe the rest of it's at the bottom, out there."

A familiar bark sounded down the beach. They both waited, heard it again.

"That's Pedro," Nolin said. "Pedro! Come!"

Barbie scrunched up her nose. "Pedro? You named your dog after yourself?"

Nolin realized his slip. "It's a long story. Pedro! Here, boy!"

Pedro bounded out of the fog, a package of rags in his mouth. He deposited them at Nolin's feet and then turned to Barbie to get his head rubbed. Nolin sifted through the clothes, separated a pair of forty-two-inch white cotton briefs from a tattered pair of blue jeans. He felt the pockets, removed a brown leather wallet. He opened it quickly and, though it wasn't a total shock, his breath still caught in his throat when he saw the driver's license. Wordlessly he passed it to Barbie, who took it in both hands and studied it for a long minute before looking up, mouth agape.

He reached out for her shoulder. "I guess I've got some explaining to do."

. . .

Nick absolutely dreaded returning to Romer's place in Flagler. His first visit, Romer had nearly choked him. On the second, he'd come at him with a spear, then tied him naked to a surfboard and threatened to feed him to his shark. This time he'd probably want to dissolve him in acid or something. Quietly Nick crept through the sea oats, past the window of the room filled with surfboards, turned the corner onto the patio and nearly ran right into Romer.

Romer held up his belt sander threateningly, pulled the mask off his nose and mouth. "Where is it?"

Nick resigned himself to his fear. "Where is what?"

"The radio transmitter. The Walkman. You didn't bring it back."

Nick's eyes widened as he tried to recall what he'd done with it. He remembered pushing the button, waiting, seeing the fish hit the rubber dinghy and eat Joanna's friend. What had he done next? Stumbled backward, reached for his clothes, lost them to the dog . . . He must have dropped it on the floor!

"I forgot it," he mumbled. "It's at home. I'll bring it by. Don't worry."

Romer tinkered with the belt sander, ran his fingers along the curves of the surfboard. "So why are you here? If you forgot the Walkman, then why'd you come?"

Nick swallowed hard. "I need your . . . expertise again."

"Why? What went wrong?"

"It ate the wrong guy."

Romer set the sander down. "The wrong guy."

"Joanna had arranged with one of her friends to take care of it. He was out in a dinghy with a rifle, and I guess he was splashing his legs or something."

Romer shook his head. "Well, Bruce might not be so hungry if he ate last night. Depends if he's in a growth spurt. You might have to wait awhile before you try again."

"I don't think she's ever gonna want to swim in the ocean again. Not after last night. The shark jumped clear out of the water with that guy in his mouth." Nick shivered. "Anyway, I can't wait a few days. She's gotta die this weekend."

Romer held a wooden template against the board, marked a high spot with a piece of chalk. "I'm not a hired killer. I rented you some equipment because I needed the money. What you did with it is your concern. Now I want the equipment back."

"Don't worry about the equipment." Nick gulped again. "You'll get it back. I promise. But look around: I bet you could do with a little more than twenty grand, right?"

Romer put his tools down, crossed his arms.

Nick licked his lips, on a roll. "Like, here you are, making all these surfboards, and what do you do with 'em? Stack 'em in a spare bedroom." He gently stroked the board on Romer's workbench. "I bet babies like these are worth, what, two hundred, three hundred each, right?"

Romer scoffed. "More like seven or eight hundred. You offer me three hundred, and I'll have to kick your ass."

"You're right, eight hundred. Maybe even a thousand each. But you can't sell them out of a broken-down shack up in Flagler. No offense." Gears turned in his head as Nick remembered friends who owed him favors. "In fact, I know a store with a fantastic location that'll come vacant, if something should happen to Barbie. She sells crystals and incense and all that New Age shit, but I bet you could do a hell of a business selling surfboards."

Romer studied his half-finished board, glanced at the stack of finished boards overflowing from the spare bedroom. "What's it cost?"

"That's the best part. The banker who holds the note is a personal friend of mine." Nick smiled, tallying the race tickets he'd given him, all the pert, young Raceway groupies he'd sent his way when his wife was out of town, "He'd be more than happy to let you have it for free for the first year, and something *real* reasonable after that."

Romer tapped his fingers on the surfboard, thinking. Nick saw that he was close, real close, realized he would have to start promising money he didn't have.

"And to help set up the place, decorate, advertise, so on, maybe I could kick in a hundred grand? Cash? And if you do Joanna, too, say, another two hundred grand?"

"And when"—Romer shot Nick a sardonic smile—"would I be *doing* her?"

Nick shrugged. "Soon. But after Barbie. Definitely after Barbie, but I'd leave the specifics up to you. Surprise me."

Romer thought for another few moments, sighed and shook his head. "As tempting as the prospect of earning a living off my work is, I'm afraid I can't accept. I can't justify killing for money. I put too many of those scumbags in prison to become one. Thanks, but no thanks."

Nick's jaw dropped. "Are you serious? You killed, what, five Jet Skiers and another five offshore boat racers, but you can't kill two more? What are two more?"

"Yeah, but Jet Skiers and boat racers are subhuman. Jet Skiers especially. They hog the waves, they have no sense of grace, they stink up the air with their fumes, and that incessant whine from those engines . . ." He shook his head, picked up his belt sander. "It's grounds for legally justifiable homicide. Same with the boat racers, to a lesser degree. They deserved to die. And I'll bet you there are fewer Jet Skiers out on the water right now because of what happened. You could say I've performed a public service."

Nick's brain went into overdrive, began spitting out a whole new pack of lies. "Well, that's all *I'm* doing!" he blurted. "Who do you think sponsored those races? That's right: Joanna and Barbie! The two of them want to bring those assholes to Daytona six times a year. Race after race. They think Jet Skiing and boat racing are the fastest-growing spectator sports in the country! I'm just trying to stop them!"

Romer set his sander back down. "So now you're some kind of environmentalist? You want to kill your ex-wife and stepmother because they're bringing dirty, polluting boats to Daytona? And I'm supposed to believe you?"

Nick licked his lips for a moment until the right answer came to mind. "No, I won't bullshit you. I'm doing it because I'm tired of them pissing away my inheritance. *I'm* the only *real* Van Horne among them, but they spend it like it's theirs! There'll be nothing left by the time they're done."

"So it's nothing more than basic, craven greed, then." Romer nodded. "All right. I can live with that. You're telling me that if they die, then this RaceWorld theme park and all its Jet Ski rentals and races and all that shit dies with them?"

"Mr. Romer, you're talking to one of the laziest men you'll ever meet. All I want to do is let Daytona Raceway take money from dumb rednecks and give it to me. I shake the winner's hand, give him a trophy and that's that. I couldn't give a rat's ass about RaceWorld, or Jet Skis or any of that crap." Nick raised his left hand, palm outward. "Scout's honor."

Romer eyed him suspiciously. "It's the right hand, and it's supposed to be three fingers. You were never even a Cub Scout, were you?"

Nick lowered his head, recalling the long-ago humiliation of being thrown out by his den mother. She had caught him playing with himself while spying on her as she changed into her bathing suit. "So you'll do it?"

"Tonight." Romer lifted the mask back over his mouth, pulled it back down to speak. "I'll expect that hundred grand tonight, too. The deed to the store can wait until Monday, but the money I want to see tonight. Here. Ten o'clock."

"You got it. I'll be here." Nick turned to leave, suddenly had an afterthought. "She seems to have this new boyfriend she's hanging around with a lot. If you happen to, uh, eliminate him, too, I wouldn't have any problems with that."

"Really? I'll keep that in mind. Oh yes, and just so you understand completely: If those ocean races continue after Barbie and Joanna are gone, or if you so much as turn one shovel of dirt for RaceWorld, then, Mr. Van Horne, you and I will have some business to discuss. Fact of it is, I'll hunt you down like a dog. Just so you know."

Romer scowled, fired up the belt sander and turned his attention back to the surfboard, grinding with a practiced touch at the chalk marks. Nick shuddered and walked back to his car.

Nolin knelt on the floor, ran his fingers along the irregular line marking the stain on the concrete slab. "Someone was definitely here last night. Someone wet." He pointed to the fallen sawhorse. "The piece of white cotton on that nail matches the hole in the underwear. I think it was Nick. He must have waited here, then gone down to the inflatable after dark."

Barbie surveyed the half-finished Florida room with arms crossed over her T-shirt, hands rubbing her forearms. "So he's really dead."

Nolin stood and put his arm around her shoulders. "I think so, yes," he said softly, massaging her neck. "Are you all right?"

Barbie shrugged. "I guess, considering that my husband, who was trying to shoot me, was instead swallowed by a shark. And that my boyfriend was technically working for him, and technically has a different name than what I've been calling him all this time. Apart from all that, I guess I'm just peachy."

He pulled her into his arms and squeezed tightly. "I'm sorry. That's all I can say."

Barbie nodded. "I know. I just wish you'd told me from the beginning, instead of waiting until everything went to hell."

"I'm sorry," he repeated. "It's just, I didn't have any idea, none, that you were his wife, until we'd already started seeing each other. And the only reason I didn't dump him as a client was because I got suspicious about what he might be up to. You know I even went out to that psychic of yours and gave her five hundred bucks so she would warn you about him? I guess looking back it sounds pretty stupid, but at the time, I couldn't think of any other way of doing it without your finding out that I represented him."

She stared over his shoulder at the water, flat now with a strong southwesterly knocking down the ground swell. "Well, you ought to go get your money back from her. She never mentioned a word about it." Barbie pulled herself free and walked to the framed doorway, stared up at the thickening cirrus clouds. "So what do we do now?"

"I don't know what we *can* do." Nolin came over to stand behind her. "I mean, I don't think we can prove a word. The rifle's somewhere on the bottom out there. Like the rest of that dinghy. But all we got is his wallet and some clothes. Maybe we should just let Joanna deal with it."

"I suppose." Barbie shrugged. "I guess this takes care of all my financial worries, though. Nick's father wrote his will so I'd be taken care of if Nick were to die before me. He knew Joanna didn't much like me. I guess it's sort of funny how things turn out, huh?"

Nolin nodded, hugged her from behind.

"Can we go now? I'm not feeling too well." She turned to grab his hands. "I think I'd like to lie down for a while."

He nodded again, started to follow her through the framing, stopped, broke away to step back inside. He returned a moment later with a bright yellow Walkman.

"I didn't know you had one of those," she said.

"I don't." He turned it over, shook it. "I guess Nick must have brought it. To help him pass the time while he waited."

"I guess. Although he never had one while we were married." She started leading him down the path to the sand. "Then again, he never had a rifle when we were married, either."

Pedro fell in step behind them, pausing once to stare at something in the breakers. He barked twice and bounded to catch up.

"So when I ring the doorbell, you sneak up behind her with the wrench. Hit her as she's opening the door, then I'll help you carry her to the back. Then we'll figure out how to get her down to the ocean. All right?"

Amee waited for a response, heard only the chatter of a sports announcer and the whine of race cars. Finally she stuck her head out of the bathroom and saw Jamie, still naked from their afternoon romp, sitting at the foot of the bed, eyes transfixed by the television, mouth open. She emerged from the bathroom, a towel around her body and hairbrush in hand and stood between him and the thirteen inch RCA. He craned his neck to look around her. Without warning, she raised the hairbrush and brought it down hard between his legs, earning a tremendous howl.

Jamie curled into a ball, grabbing himself. She turned and looked at the television, where a green car and a red car bumped each other as they chased a yellow car. The announcer chattered, the engines whined. Amee turned back to the bed where Jamie lay grimacing, his eyes watering but still locked on the television set.

"Whatcha do that for?" he protested.

"You haven't been listening to a word I said, have you? Just watching that stupid race."

"*Stupid?* It's only the biggest Winston Cup race of the year! Wallace and Martin, neck and neck, with Earnhardt just two car lengths back until he had to pit early last lap. Now—"

"Shut up. I'm gonna go over the plan one more time, and you better pay attention."

Reluctantly Jamie pulled his eyes from the TV. "Yeah, yeah, yeah. I'm listening."

"You get there just as it's getting dark, break in from the beach side and go hide. She comes home after closing the store. Remember, she closes a little early on Saturdays. I show up and ring the doorbell—"

"And I come up behind her and whack her in the head as she's opening the door. I know. See? I was listening the first ten times. You didn't have to hit me."

"And what do you do if she's late?"

"Hang tight."

"And if I'm late?"

"Hang tight."

"Good." Amee smiled. She should have taken a more active role a long time ago. Jamie was basically good, just needed a lot of guidance. "And now, I have a surprise for you. Remember what Monica did the other day?"

She dropped her towel and ran a hand over the razor-burned pink skin between her legs. "Doesn't this turn you on?"

But Jamie's eyes had migrated back to the television, where a black car was trying to pass a yellow car. His penis lay unprotected, a dark purple welt running across it diagonally from her blow. Amee wound her arm back and let fly with the hairbrush once again.

Madame Rosa leaned back in her chair, lifted her feet onto the table and took another long drag from her Virginia Slims cigarette, grimacing as the orange-and-yellow Tide detergent car tried and failed to squeak past the Miller beer car. The Tide driver was from her hometown, in fact, had been a boyfriend once, if having done it with him in the girls' locker room, up against the door in the towel closet counted as having had him as a boyfriend.

She'd toyed with the idea of walking up to him after a race and seeing if he remembered her, if he wanted to have another go at her in the locker room. But he'd never finished in the Top Ten in points, though, had never even won a major race. She couldn't see throwing herself at a driver who wasn't consistently in the Top Five, or who hadn't won Darlington or Talladega at least once. It wasn't like she was some cheap NASCAR tramp.

She flicked the cigarette over the base for the crystal ball she was using as an ashtray; the ball itself lay on a crumpled Cheetos bag on the floor. The front door had a CLOSED sign on it, and Rosa lounged in spandex leggings that stretched over an ample bottom and a loose tank top that barely contained a sagging bosom. It felt nice, she thought, not to have to be in costume all day. It was a luxury she gave herself only on race days, when much of her clientele was either screaming their heads off in the Raceway's littered infield or hunkered down over a television set with a twelve-pack of cheap beer.

The TV went to a commercial, one of the annoying car dealers with the shouting salesman, and Rosa reached for the mute button on the remote. She set down her cigarette and reached for the travel brochures she'd picked up the previous evening: Las Vegas, New Orleans, Atlantic City, as well as a splashy booklet describing the Carnival Cruises from Fort Lauderdale to the Bahamas. She'd never really considered a cruise before she'd picked up the brochure, but the more she thought about it, the more it appealed to her. There was gambling, the chance to pick up men but also sunbathing and shopping. Best of all, it promised five gourmet meals a day. All you could eat. It wasn't that much more expensive than a nice hotel, either. All she needed was to collect the $1,000 from that guy.

She sighed and popped a can of Busch. It figured the weasel wouldn't pay up. She should make him. She ought to go to his house and collect it. Just show up and make a scene until he paid. In fact, tonight would be the perfect night. He and his shrew stepmother would host their annual post-race bash at their house on the river. Watered-down drinks, black-tie, moldy-oldies wedding band, the works. Yes, that's exactly what she'd do. She'd go down there in full Madame Rosa regalia and demand payment for services rendered, or else threaten to put a hex on the house and everyone in it. That ought to make him cough up the money in a hurry. Even if it didn't, it would certainly get the attention of the gossip columnist for the local rag and win some free publicity. She would need to remember to take some business cards with her.

The television was showing the race again, and Rosa turned the sound back up. Yes, that's exactly what she'd do, as soon as the race was over. In fact, she'd run by Barbie's house first, to make sure she'd met her friends for the surprise party on the beach. That way she'd have proof that she'd held up her end of the bargain.

Rosa took a long swig of beer and settled lower in her chair. It was funny, though. She didn't think Barbie and her ex were on speaking terms, and suddenly here he was planning a surprise birthday party for her. She thought about it another moment, then shrugged. She'd long ago given up trying to understand the Daytona marriage.

She gave a long belch and leaned forward as the Tide car made another run at the leaders.

Crawdad jabbed his finger as far as it would go between the cast and his arm, scratching furiously. Then he switched arms and repeated the procedure, gritting his teeth until pain drowned out the itch.

If only he had a hanger; he cursed again his stupidity for sending both Jasmine and Lola out at the same time. But he supposed it was a worthy sacrifice. Lola was starting on a bikini tattoo, in bright red, and Jasmine was getting a nipple pierced. He supposed he should also consider himself lucky. It wasn't every biker who could find two old ladies who got on so well together. Still, he wasn't happy. And, as usual, it was money problems weighing heavily on his shoulders.

Jasmine told him the bike-shop guy had come out to the hospital to check out his Hog, and it wasn't pretty. He was looking at $15,000 to make everything right, including a new paint job. And that was just to put it all back the way it was, never mind getting Pamela Anderson air-brushed on the gas tank.

He needed money, and he needed it fast. More than anything, he needed to get the hell out of the hospital. He couldn't do deals lying on his ass all day. He was losing his edge, doing nothing but watching talk shows and getting blowjobs. It had been days since he'd kicked the shit out of anybody. He would get out; that was that. That very night, as soon as Jasmine got back to help him on his Harley, he'd go over to that chick's house and finish what he'd started when that dipshit kid had run him off the road. He shook his head, recalling the scared face above him the previous night. What the hell had he been doing? Who had sent him?

Someone was trying to take him out, that was sure. But why send some kid, especially some kid who couldn't tell his ass from a hole in the ground? His first guesses would have been Walnut or Squid. Neither had ever liked him, and both would love to get their grubby little hands on his tittie bar take. On the other hand, both had the balls to do the job themselves, not send some pimple-faced punk.

Well, that would be his next job, after he sold the chick in Miami. He might have to wait for the casts to come off before he took out whoever was after him, but that didn't mean he couldn't start asking questions.

He lifted his eyes back to the television and smiled. The black Mr. Goodwrench car had just knocked two others into the wall and taken the lead. Now *that* was good car racing. One day he'd have to meet that Dale Earnhardt, maybe buy him a beer, or a chick. Hell, he might even lend him one of his.

Slowly at first, then unbearably, the itch started under his right cast again. Crawdad cursed aloud and contorted his arms to cram a finger underneath and scratch like crazy.

His nose pressed against the glass in the owners' box, Nick watched idly as the two cars knocked from the race by the black car limped off the track and into the pits. Two skinny, helmeted guys in coveralls that matched their dented wrecks crawled out the windows and stormed around, kicking the crumpled fenders and waving their fists at the far turn, where the black car was opening an ever-wider lead.

Good, Nick thought. No caution flags. The damaged cars had come off the track under their own power without anyone else running into them and stopping the race. The faster that son of a bitch won, the faster he could get the hell out of there.

He racked his brain, trying to remember the combination to the safe in Joanna's room. He'd come upon it once, snooping around in her lingerie drawer, but hadn't thought to write it down. He could have kicked himself. Oh well, it just meant he had to root around in there first, get the number, and then get Joanna's little pocketbook out of her safe. The one with the emergency "grease" money, in case a city commissioner or county council member became suddenly recalcitrant just before a key vote.

He'd overheard her talking about it to the chair of the Planning and Zoning Commission once, and thought she said she kept $250,000 there in large bills. He couldn't decide whether to take just $100,000 or the whole quarter million.

If he took only what he needed, the rest might get locked up in probate upon her tragic death. On the other hand, if he took it all and she noticed it missing before she died, she'd kill him. First she'd cut his nuts off, and then she'd kill him. Of course, she was likely to do that even if he took just the hundred grand. Of course, he didn't even know how much was really there. Maybe she'd just bribed somebody last week, and hadn't had time to replenish it. In which case *Romer* would cut his nuts off and feed them to his shark.

Nick shuddered at the thought and looked back down on the Raceway. More than 150,000 people *paying* real money to watch cars drive in circles for four hours. Morons, all. But morons who kept him rich, so he supposed he shouldn't be so harsh. He checked his watch again impatiently, and looked for the black car leading the remaining pack. One hundred and seventy laps done, thirty to go. It took close to a minute for each lap, so he had another half hour of this, barring any yellow flags.

He groaned and glared at the black car. Come on: *win*, already.

• • •

Once again the pinging sound came from shallow water, and he dutifully turned around to home in on the signal. It had never sounded without food having been nearby, so he picked up his speed, swishing through the water with his massive tail. Yet just as it seemed he was close, the pinging stopped.

He lunged through the surface, just in case, but there was nothing. Bewildered, he turned back toward deep water. He'd eaten a full meal just the day before, but rational considerations weren't his forte. If there was food, it should be eaten, and four times now, food had been signaled, then not delivered.

He began a slow patrol of his territory when the signal sounded once again. And once again he turned his giant snout toward the shallows and raced in.

Nolin popped the cassette back in, snapped the lid shut and pushed the play button. A small red LED came on, but neither spool on the tape moved. He shook the machine and stared at it. Still no movement. He hit the stop button and the light went off. He pushed play and the light came on, pushed stop and it went off.

"Baby, do you have earphones for one of these?"

Barbie kept flipping through the channels of her old, rabbit-ears, nine-inch black-and-white set. "No. I don't believe in tuning out the outside world like that."

"Yeah. I kind of figured." He opened the battery panel, pulled out four AA cells and pushed them back in place. "Well, I can't figure this out. It seems to come on, but nothing happens. How are you supposed to listen to a tape if the tape drive won't engage?"

"Maybe it's broken." She flipped through the dial, stopped at the channel that had been showing the race. "Can you believe they haven't said a word about it? They just ran the race like nothing happened."

Nolin set the Walkman on the table and walked over behind Barbie. "Well, honey, given what you've told me about Joanna, did you think she would postpone her single biggest cash cow of the year just because her stepson died?" He began massaging her shoulders. "Plus, she might not even notice his absence yet. Maybe she thinks he just stayed out late, didn't get home by the time she left for the track."

Barbie shook her head. "Not Joanna. Not on the day of the Daytona 500. She'd have a stroke if he was a minute late, let alone miss it entirely. No, she must know he's missing. You're right, though. Whatever reason he's missing can't possibly be important enough to stop the race."

The tendons in her shoulders tensed even more, and Nolin pushed down hard with his thumbs. "It's okay, baby. Remember what he was trying to do when he died, all right? There's no reason for you to feel guilty."

"Oh, I know." She let her head loll back, her shoulders droop. "I guess I can't help but blame myself. If I hadn't filed that turtle lawsuit, none of this would have happened."

Nolin moved his thumbs to her back, rubbed until she groaned. "Come on, baby. That's crazy talk. Just because you sued—and I might point out, sued the *county*, not him—just because you sued doesn't somehow justify his trying to kill you. Nick died because he got unlucky while he was trying to shoot you in the head. In my opinion, he got what he deserved. And now it's done."

Suddenly she was tense again, leaning toward the television. "No, it's not," she whispered. "Look."

The television scene had shifted to the winner's circle, where perennial anti-hero Dale Earnhardt was spraying a bottle of champagne over a crowd of cheering groupies. Behind him stood Joanna and J. R. Van Horne, applauding sedately, waiting to present a giant trophy to Earnhardt and his team.

"So he's alive after all," Barbie said softly. "I guess it wasn't him last night."

Nolin knelt to study the black-and-white picture more closely. "Apparently not. But that *was* his wallet we found. Whatever it was I saw last night, Nick had something to do with it."

He stood up again, went to the table to retrieve the dysfunctional Walkman. Quickly he pressed play, then stop to watch the LED light come on and go off.

"Baby, remember I told you about those videotapes? Well, I think it's time we see what Randall Romer had to do with this."

ELEVEN

■ ■ ■

Jamie crouched low among the dunes, carefully scanned the houses fronting the beach. There were no lights on, no movement visible through the windows.

Suddenly he was sprinting up the dune, reaching for the top of the wooden privacy fence, swinging his legs over. And then he was falling, falling, falling. His right ankle crumpled under him as he hit a bed of white pebbles. He looked back up with a grimace and realized that the ground inside the fence was a couple of feet lower than outside.

Jamie struggled to his feet and limped past the hot tub, past a chaise lounge to the sliding glass door and knew he was in luck. The door was centered between two tall, thin, multipaneled windows. Quickly he pulled off his T-shirt and balled it around his left hand. He steeled himself, punched a pane of glass. The pane shattered, but left a curious stinging in his hand. He pulled his fist back and felt himself growing woozy: Sticking into the T-shirt was a triangular slab of glass the size of his palm. The white cloth turned dark red in an expanding circle.

He bit his tongue and gingerly pulled out the glass, tossing it aside. He unwrapped the T-shirt, saw the shard had sliced cleanly between middle and index fingers; as he moved his fingers, he could see the tendons shifting inside. Lightheaded again, he reached out for support, resting against the glass door, which slowly began sliding open.

When he realized what was happening he wanted to kick himself. It was unlocked. Unsteadily he limped inside, closed the door behind him and picked broken glass from the floor. A potted plant stood nearby; he dropped the pieces into the pot and slid the plant to hide the empty pane.

He noticed a clock on the kitchen wall, saw it was already past six and began to panic. She'd be home any minute. Quickly he knotted the bloody T-shirt around his hand and scurried through the darkening rooms looking for a place to hide. He settled on the kitchen and wedged himself beneath the sink, his head tucked between the side of the cabinet and the disposal, his wounded hand between his knees. He shifted around so the small pipe wrench in his pocket didn't dig so much into his hip.

His hand began to throb, and he felt his ankle swelling inside his tennis shoe. That, he decided, was the last straw: He'd had enough of the killer's life. He'd been in a car wreck, his face still hadn't healed from falling on the cactus, and now he'd sprained an ankle and cut himself open. The money sounded good, but it was going to get him killed.

His hand throbbed harder, and he remembered the white tendons moving around inside his hand, the blood squirting out through the gaping hole. The lightheadedness came back, accompanied by a claustrophobic attack.

Jamie hyperventilated, then passed out.

It was a strange feeling, Crawdad decided, to have cars honking at him, flashing their lights, weaving, before finally swerving out and passing him, usually with an angry gesture. Crawdad didn't care. It was his goddamned road, too, and he had as much right to it as they did, a sentiment he dutifully expressed to each passing motorist with a scowl and a flipped middle finger. Otherwise he just leaned against the backrest of his Hog, crutches lashed to the rear fender and a cast-encased arm on each handlebar as he rode along at fifteen miles per hour: the fastest he could go in first gear.

That was the only thing he couldn't manage because of his injuries. He could work the clutch and the front brakes despite his broken arms, and the rear brakes with his good leg. But working the gear shift with the broken leg was out of the question, something he'd learned in the hospital parking lot while acquiring some bruised, maybe broken, ribs.

He swore aloud as a pothole sent ripples of pain through his limbs, and swore to himself that the next time he saw the punk who did this, he would first break every bone in his scrawny little body, then run over him several times with the Harley.

As he neared the stretch of A1A where the chick lived, though, he again wondered how he was going to drive her down to Miami by himself, and hoped to hell that her car had automatic transmission and cruise control. If it didn't, he'd have to have one of his old ladies drive him down. Either that or steal a car with automatic and cruise. Come to think of it, he would steal a *nice* car *and* have one of his old ladies drive him down. Sure, he'd take Lola. Sort of introduce her to the business a little.

He passed a deserted stretch and slowed the bike until he was barely moving, eased it into the overgrown vacant lot across from the house. There he leaned on his good leg, pushed the heavy machine onto its kickstand, untied his crutches and hobbled unsteadily across the road.

The convertible VW was in the driveway, and he paused by the driver-side window. Stick shift. Fucking figured. He continued up the pathway, up the two stairs to the door and tried the knob. With a quick glance up and down the deserted road, he pulled the gun the punk had dropped in the hospital room from his waistband and shoved it into a jacket pocket, then pulled out a canvas satchel.

Balancing on his good leg, he pulled out two stiff pieces of wire on wooden handles, felt around the keyhole and quickly heard the soft "click" from the knob. With a sneer, he turned the knob and hobbled in.

. . .

Romer pushed his little inflatable through the tiny swell, waded until he was thigh deep and hopped aboard. The wind was already blowing nearly twenty-five knots from the west, and he let it push him offshore.

His life in the morning would be very different from his life these past years, he thought ruefully. He'd be rich again, and reintegrated into society, such as it was in Daytona Beach. He'd have a business to run, bills to pay and appearances to maintain. Chamber of Commerce dues, Kiwanis breakfasts, those insufferable Halifax Club luncheons. The mere thought sickened him.

Still, it was a way to win the recognition he deserved for his work, his lifelong pride: the best hand-carved surfboards on the East Coast. Those money-grubbing weasels at Big Kahuna and Ron Jon who'd turned down his lines, they'd be knocking down his door. And he could tell them to screw themselves. With his own store, he wouldn't need them. And maybe after he'd built up a name for himself, he could ignore all the crap that went with running a business and just stick to shaping boards.

He glanced down in the black water and wondered where Bruce was. He'd miss him. With the shop all day and making boards at night, he wouldn't have much time to play in the water. Perhaps it was just as well. Ultimately Bruce was a wild creature, and deserved the opportunity to roam the oceans like his cohorts, not remain tied to some freak human. Tomorrow, maybe, he would say bye to him, and then avoid the water for a while. In a few days, or weeks, a month at most, Bruce would understand that he was on his own.

There was already a slight northerly component to the wind, and the dinghy was drifting south as well as east, away from the empty beach. Along the shore, the western sky had acquired an unhealthy, pale orange cast. The front would be a doozy, he could see already. He would need to wrap things up quickly before it hit; there'd be no fighting a strong norther in a ten-foot inflatable.

Romer leaned to pump the bulb on the gas tank and flip the choke switch on the big Evinrude. At twenty-five horsepower, he was seriously overpowered, and could skim over the waves at nearly twenty knots. He lowered a crude wood-and-foam muffler over the engine cowling and yanked on a cord.

The motor instantly roared to life. He adjusted the choke, fitted a blue-painted length of PVC pipe over the handle, slid to the front of the dinghy and twisted the pipe to open the throttle.

Nick stood in his underwear and socks, his ear at his bedroom wall. It had to be soon; all of Daytona's leeches and suck-ups would be in his home soon, and he wouldn't get an opportunity later.

Come on, bitch, he thought impatiently. Finally he heard the noise he was waiting for: the gurgling of water pipes. He kept his ear to the wall a half second longer to make sure he wasn't mistaken, then ran out his door, down the hall and into Joanna's room, shutting the door softly behind him. She was in the adjoining shower and, as usual, she'd left the door to the bathroom open. He saw the occasional white flash as her butt bumped the shower stall's glass door.

Quickly he crept to her dresser and opened the third drawer down, began sifting through the various nightgowns, teddies and other lingerie Joanna liked to parade around in. He came upon a black fishnet body stocking and held it for a second; it still had the store tags on, and he wondered for a moment what she would look like in it.

He heard splashing from the bathroom, and tossed the fishnet aside. There, in the corner, was the slip of paper he'd remembered. He grabbed it and ran to the safe across from the desk, hurriedly dialed the numbers. He pulled it open and rooted through envelopes and a photo album before seeing the purse in the back.

In a moment he had it back in his room, next to a leather overnight bag he'd pulled from his closet. His heart pounding, he yanked the zipper open and pulled out stacks of green bills. They had an unfamiliar face on the front, and his breath caught when he saw they were thousand-dollar bills. They seemed to be bundled in stacks of fifty bills each, and there were ten stacks.

Droplets erupted on his forehead as he did the math, and his eyes darted around the room while he weighed his options. He only needed two stacks to pay Romer his deposit, but four more would be enough to pay for Joanna, too. He threw six stacks of bills into his overnight bag, hesitated, then grabbed the remaining four stacks, as well.

He shoved the bag under his bed and ran back to Joanna's room with the empty purse, tucked it back in the safe, shut it, spun the dial and pushed the aerial photo of the Raceway back in place. He was ready to breathe a sigh of relief when he noticed the slip of paper with the combination still clutched between his fingers.

Beads of sweat came to his lip as he ran across the plush carpeting to the dresser, nearly stumbling over a wastebasket, and pulled open the drawer again. He plunged his hand to the bottom of the satin and silk underthings, dropped the slip of paper in the corner. A long breath escaped his lips; he'd made it. He started closing the drawer when he noticed the body stocking again; he'd always had a thing for fishnet. He tugged at its collar and pulled it out. Where had she gotten it, and why hadn't he seen it before? It had the whiff of her perfume; he put it to his nose and breathed in.

Only then did he notice the silence. The shower had stopped. He turned in alarm, and she stood there quietly in all her naked glory, save for a towel wrapped like a turban around her hair.

"You want me to model it for you?" Joanna asked softly. "Or do you just want to inhale it?"

He found himself staring, jaw slack. Her nipples stared back like big, brown eyes; it was the first time he'd seen her fully nude, and he found himself getting aroused. Out of the corner of his eye he noticed the photo over the wall safe, and his heart stopped: he must have slammed it too hard, and it had bounced slightly open. He had to get to it before she saw it, or it was all over.

Joanna took a step toward him and knelt on the shag orange carpeting. "I'm going to let him out before he suffocates."

Nick gulped, shifted his weight to the other foot and decided to let her.

. . .

They'd rung the doorbell, knocked on the doors, peered in through the windows, and still hadn't seen anything. Barbie tugged at Nolin's hand, tried again to pull him away.

"We really shouldn't be doing this," she whispered loudly as Nolin pried at the side window with a screwdriver.

"Nothing's going to happen," he whispered back.

"Either we're going to get arrested or he's going to shoot us. That's what's going to happen."

Before she could say another word, he'd jimmied the window open and was pulling his gangly frame through. She heard a muffled crash, then a curse, then saw his face reappear. "Damn surfboards weren't stacked very securely."

She handed him the flashlight. "Yeah. Doesn't he realize burglars might get hurt breaking in?"

"Funny. Go around front and I'll let you in."

She scampered through the grasses and waited for the front door to crack open, then, with a quick glance up and down the road, silently slipped in.

"I can't believe I'm doing this," she said, following him down a dimly lit corridor. "Why are we doing this again?"

They came to the source of the light: a fluorescent tube shining on a long, thin aquarium that rocked back and forth, sending a viscous wave to and fro.

"These things are so cool. I can stare at 'em for hours," he said.

"If we leave right now, I'll *buy* you one for Christmas, and you can stare to your heart's content," she said hoarsely.

Nolin played the flashlight around, saw the unmade mattress on the floor. "Christmas isn't for ten months."

"For your birthday, then. *Please*, Pedro, I mean Doug, let's get out of here, okay?"

"Aha!" He stepped across the mattress to a small bookshelf, pulled out a photo album, squatted on the floor to examine it.

With an exasperated sigh, she stepped between mattress and piles of rumpled work clothes to squat beside him. "What?"

Nolin flipped to the start of the album, where the first few pages featured snapshots of Romer accepting a plaque from the governor, sitting on a rock by a lake with a beautiful woman, standing in ski gear before a panorama of snow-covered mountains, toasting his staff at an office Christmas party. "Pretty normal stuff, right?" He flipped pages. "Until about here."

Barbie's heart hammered inside her chest. The photos of vacations and work, wife and colleagues ended, and were instead replaced with underwater shots of a giant gray shark with sharp white teeth, a huge black eye and a peculiar jagged notch on its dorsal fin. Nolan flipped through the pages, came to a horrific one of the shark snapping into a bloody piece of meat.

He turned the page and they both gasped: It was a newspaper clipping of a blurry photo transferred from a videotape of the Jet Ski race, and clearly showed a wet-suited body being dragged underwater by a shark with a notch on its dorsal fin.

"Who *is* this guy?" Barbie whispered.

Amee fidgeted in the vacant lot, still astride her bike, impatiently scanning the highway in front of the house. Still no sign of Mrs. Van Horne, although, somehow, her car was already in her driveway. That was curious: How had she gotten to the store?

She must have gotten a ride, or used another car, they had decided. Amee had dropped Jamie off nearly two hours earlier, and the VW had already been there. Jamie had snooped around, finally ringing the front doorbell to make sure she hadn't taken a day off work or something. It would have screwed up their plan if she were home, but no one had answered the door, and they'd gone ahead.

She looked over her shoulder again where the Harley was stashed in some bushes and nervously watched awhile. She didn't have time to get mauled by some dope-crazed biker right now, but she didn't have any way of stopping one, either. *Damn* the moron for dropping the gun in the hospital room. It would have taken care of any biker, and would have made short work of Barbie Van Horne, too.

Instead, they had only the pipe wrench, meaning there would be a lot of screaming and blood. She shook her head sadly and wondered again what to do with the moron after it was over. The smart thing would be to kill him, and use somebody else to kill Nick after they were married. After all, that could take months, and she didn't know if she could manage Jamie on the side for that long. On the other hand, he *was* kind of cute, and him and that roommate of his, Monica, were something else in the sack. She wondered if Monica would sleep with her once Jamie was gone.

She stopped daydreaming and scanned the road again. She had to pay attention. The moron was likely to foul up somehow, and she had to be ready to pull things out of the fire. Plus she had to wrap everything up by midnight, when Nick was supposed to come over to her place, expecting a threesome with her and Lori. The thought made her cringe. She'd lost interest in Lori since Monica came along, and Lori and Nick together would make her stomach turn.

Maybe Monica wouldn't mind a fat slob like Nick, just once, for business. She'd have to run it by her and see. Maybe after the Barbie thing was finished she'd run by the pool hall on her way home and ask her.

Amee rubbed her bare arms and wished she'd brought a windbreaker to wear over her T-shirt. She *really* wished she'd brought a pair of shorts to wear over her thong bottom. It had been such a nice day earlier, but now her buns were freezing. She saw headlights approaching from the north, and she peered out at them.

Her heart sped as the car slowed, left blinker flashing, and finally turned into the driveway. Amee stepped off her bike, dropped it into the grass and crouched low. Across the street, the driver's door on the old Pontiac opened and a woman stepped out, walked hurriedly to the front door, reached for the knob and quickly disappeared inside.

Amee stood slowly, moved to the edge of the clearing and began counting backward from one hundred.

He couldn't get out. He had stayed too long, and now he was too big, and he would never get out. He couldn't even move anymore. His knees were up against his face and he couldn't move a muscle. He thought to scream for help, but no one would hear him. He was all by himself. He had overslept, and now he would never be born. He began to sob to himself as outside, the doctors chastised him: "Who are you? Who the fuck are you, then?" He sobbed even harder. What kind of doctors were they, talking like that to a helpless baby?

He awoke with a start, bashing his forehead against the disposal in front of him, then the back of his head against the cabinet behind him. Tears came to his eyes as he tried to wince the pain away, momentarily forgetting his throbbing hand.

Outside the shouts changed to thuds. It was Cherry, he realized suddenly. She had come, right on schedule, and now was tussling with Mrs. Van Horne! She needed his help; he had to get out. With a lurch he pushed open the cabinet with an elbow and fell onto the linoleum. He uncricked his back and neck and stood, immediately fell. His ankle had swollen to the size of a small grapefruit during his time under the sink. He cursed, reached for the countertop to pull himself up, favoring his good ankle, took a deep breath and began limping toward the sounds of the struggle.

She'd kicked him. The bitch had kicked him right in his busted knee. He'd dropped the gun, but it was around somewhere, not far. He squinted in the gloom and there it was, just a foot from his face. He turned his head to where she sat against the wall, glaring at him, her hands and feet finally, and at great personal sacrifice, tied.

Crawdad examined the casts on his arms. Each had a visible crack down its length. "You have no idea how pissed off I am right now," he told her softly. "Now I'm gonna have to get both of these reset. You got any idea how much that costs?"

Madame Rosa glared at him hatefully. He'd yanked her in as she turned the doorknob, thrown her to the ground and tied her hands behind her before she even realized what was happening. Her long black hair lay in a ball on the floor, revealing the short blond mop beneath.

"Mrs. Van Horne's expecting me," she lied. "She'll be here any minute."

"Good," Crawdad grunted. "I was figurin' I'd get forty, fifty grand for her. I might be able to get five for you. Only 'cause you're blond. You'd be worth a lot more if you weren't so goddamn fat."

Madame Rosa skipped over the implications of his estimate to defend her weight. "It's not something you can help, you know. It's in the genes. If it's your destiny to be full-figured, then you're full-figured. Besides"—she nodded at his generous beer belly—"you're one to talk."

"Yeah. You're a great talker. A big fat talker. I guess you're gonna need a gag." He pulled a soiled blue neckerchief out of a back pocket and wiggled across the floor, his arm casts stretched out before him. "I don't think I could take a five-hour drive listening—"

Without warning, Madame Rosa kicked her feet out in unison, the leather heels on her sandals smashing into Crawdad's knees with a loud crack. Crawdad howled in agony and the entryway light flicked on in the same instant.

Jamie stared at the scene before him in bewilderment, his bloody hand tucked against his belly, his good hand wielding the pipe wrench above his head.

"Grab the gun!" Madame Rosa screamed.

Jamie saw the pistol lying on the floor against the wall. He began limping toward it when he noticed how familiar it looked. The hairy man on the floor slowly lifted a screwed-up face at Jamie, and Jamie stopped dead in his tracks and yelped.

"You again!" Crawdad growled. "I'm gonna rip your scrawny little head off, you son of a—"

"Please don't kill me, sir," Jamie begged, falling to his knees. "I can explain the accident. I really didn't mean—"

"Get the gun, you fucking moron!" Madame Rosa screamed again.

Crawdad crawled on one leg across the hall and retrieved the gun, pushing the safety to the off position. "Shut up, the both of you!" he shouted, and pointed the gun at the door, which suddenly pushed open.

Amee surveyed the scene, fixated on the gun pointed at her head and the large hairy head behind it. "Oops, wrong house," she said.

"Cherry?" Jamie asked. "Who are these people?"

"That's a real good question." Four pairs of bewildered eyes turned to Romer, who had appeared from nowhere and stood in bare feet and a black wetsuit behind Crawdad, the point of his spear gun just grazing the biker's neck. "Sir, why don't you drop the gun, and then we can sort all this out."

Nick mingled through the crowd of sycophants and clingers a mile above his black Italian loafers. Tonight, he *was* Double-Oh-Seven, and everyone there knew it. The Raceway groupies in their too-short party dresses, the society wives with their expensive faces, even the bartender, who didn't bat an eye when Nick asked for a martini "shaken, not stirred," all of them knew there was something different about him, something to be reckoned with.

Because tonight, he would have it all. Tonight he would become sole ruler of the NASCAR empire, and all the petty serfs and peasants knew this from his bearing, his stride, the cut of his tux, the way he idly played with a cuff link while he listened patiently to their pathetic little stories, that it was *his* ring they would have to kiss from now on, not Joanna's. Sure, the drivers held some celebrity cachet among the circle of fawning admirers who listened to them explain how their cars done run real good, how the "tahrs" had been runnin' hot, but how the drivers through their expertise were able to keep 'em from blowin'. But the movers and shakers noticed when Nick moved among the tinkling of glass and the soft plunking of the baby grand.

Yes, because Nick had finally become his hero. For who other than James Bond would be able to sleep with the beautiful villainess, indeed, get a *blowjob* from the beautiful villainess, just before killing her? He would pay Romer his money, and he would carelessly offer an extra hundred grand to take care of his nemesis before morning. True, he wouldn't be able to dispatch Joanna with a laser in his belt buckle or a garrote in the winding stem of his watch, but allowances had to be made.

He nodded sympathetically at the story told by a young blonde with tanned, round, mineral-enhanced boobs bursting from her dress. But he didn't stare. James Bond never stared. Not until later, when they were in private. He noticed the time, gently touched the young lady's elbow, asked if she would excuse him a moment and would she mind if he called her next week? She tittered and wrote down a phone number on a chewing gum wrapper, which he slid into his pocket as he wandered to the bar to freshen his martini.

It would be important to create the impression that he'd never left the party, in case something were to go amiss. He'd fill his drink glass, and then fill it again right when he returned. He stepped as if toward the bathroom, and once he was in the corridor he kept going, turned, through a door and outside by the side entrance. From the bushes he retrieved the overnight bag he had dropped from his bedroom window and walked briskly to his car. He threw the bag in the backseat, opened the driver's door and started at the touch on his shoulder.

"Going somewhere?" It was Joanna, in her long, white, spaghetti-strap evening gown that clung to her curves and told everyone who saw her that, as hostess of the biggest winter party in Daytona Beach, she was bold enough to wear nothing underneath. "I was following you to the bathroom, in case you wanted a quickie."

She lifted her dress to her waist, showing him there was nothing physically in the way of such an event, not on her part anyway. She stepped closer, moved her lips to his ear. "I want you so bad," she whispered. "You make me so hot."

The shock and alarm faded, and Nick resumed thinking through his adopted persona: What would *Bond* do in this situation? Probably pat her on the rear, tell her he had man's work to do and leave. Or maybe, he thought with building excitement, he'd ad lib and take advantage of the situation. He'd have her again in the backseat, then put her in the trunk and blow up the car. Or push it off a high cliff. Nick scowled: He had handy neither bomb nor cliff. But he *did* have a sociopathic former prosecutor with a pet shark . . .

"I'm meeting someone who's doing some business for me. For us, really."

Joanna's eyes began to glow. "You mean about Barbie?" she breathed.

He casually checked his watch. "By now, she's no longer a problem."

"Dear, that's fantastic. Since *my* friend who was supposed to take care of it seems to have disappeared off the face of the Earth."

Nick swallowed uneasily, recalling the dark shape that flew out of the water, the silhouette of a man in its jaws. He cleared his throat. "Well, I don't want to be late."

She smiled wickedly. "You mind if I come along?"

He saw her tied to the surfboard, her white dress soaked and transparent, the giant jaws coming to avenge years of domineering and abuse. He flashed her a grin. "Not at all."

Romer slogged through the ankle-deep water and heaved Crawdad from a fireman's carry into the dinghy atop Jamie and Madame Rosa. The biker's knees smashed into the center wooden seat, and Crawdad howled, then let loose a string of graphic threats against Romer, his family and, particularly, his mother.

Jamie wriggled out against one of the inflatable tubes. "I know how it feels," he told Crawdad. "I busted a knee once, too. Never played football again. Could of had a scholarship, too. Listen, about the other night. I'm real sorry. I wasn't trying to cut you off or anything. It was just an accident."

Crawdad turned his attention to Jamie, his eyes narrowing to malignant slits. "If you don't shut up, I swear I'm gonna rip your little nuts off and shove 'em down your throat."

"That's if I don't rip them off first, you stupid moron," Madame Rosa added. "If you'd grabbed that gun when I said, we wouldn't be here right now."

Jamie went pale at the thought of choking on his privates as Romer bent over them. All three were bound at the wrists and ankles, and Romer tied their ankles to each other and also to the dinghy's center seat.

"Why don't the three of you shut up for a while?" Romer suggested. He stood, felt the wind whistle through his hair. "Second thought: Go ahead and shout your heads off. No one's going to hear you. Don't go anywhere. I'll be right back."

He sprinted across the beach, up the wooden dune crossover and in through the glass door. Amee lay similarly bound on the floor. Romer gathered her onto his shoulder, grabbed his spear gun and stepped back through the door, sliding it closed behind him. His hand slid over her bare bottom as he stepped nimbly down the stairs to the beach.

"Sorry," he muttered.

"Oh no," Amee said graciously. "I don't mind. I mean, you don't have to tie me up. A guy as good-looking as you, I'd do anything with."

He said nothing, continued toward the dinghy.

"Listen," Amee offered, "I don't know what you've got going with those three, but let me tell you that I can keep a secret. Let me go, and you can do whatever you want to them. I won't tell."

Romer slowed a bit, looked back over his shoulder at her face. "Lady, *you're* the reason I'm here."

Amee let out a snort. "*Me?* Why?"

He considered the question for a moment. "I guess you have a right to know. Your husband set this up."

"My *husband*?" Amee let out a breath of relief. "Mister, there's been a huge mistake. I'm not even married."

"Well, technically you still are, even though you've been separated for two years."

"I've *never* been married," Amee protested. "You're thinking of that other chick."

Romer slogged through the surf to where he had anchored the dinghy. "I don't think so. Your husband specifically described you as 'beautiful' and 'slut.' With all due respect and no offense intended, compare that other woman's appearance and dress to your own, and I think you'll agree I got the right woman." He dumped her unceremoniously into the dinghy atop the others. "Not that it makes a difference."

He pulled up the anchor and stowed it while his captives tussled with each other. With the dinghy so overloaded, he knew he was close to capsizing. He would have to play it safe, go directly downwind until it got deep enough. With a quick pull, the outboard began purring and

Romer pointed the boat offshore. "Will everyone please settle down. This won't take long. Thank you."

Amee tried to work it so she could stretch her legs, while Crawdad glared silently at Jamie and Madame Rosa. Jamie, having secured a seat against the tube, stuck his bound arms overboard to let his throbbing hand soak in the cold water. He sighed with relief as the pain edged away.

Senses on full alert, he slowly cruised the shallows where the food signal had come from. He still wasn't very hungry, but he was pretty angry. Time after time, he'd come in on the signal, only to find nothing. Time after time after time. He was ready to hit something, anything, and hit it hard.

He turned quickly and headed back in his wake. Every nerve ending on his massive head and back tingled in anticipation. As soon as he sensed it again, he'd have it in his sights in an instant. No more cat-and-mouse.

It was around here somewhere . . .

There! It wasn't the food signal, but something even better: blood. And close by. Finally! The signal had kept its promise!

He whipped his head around, arched his back and swept his mighty tail through the water.

Crawdad stopped stroking his shattered knee long enough to stretch his neck and see the shore lights growing dimmer amid the rising waves.

"Who sent you?" he demanded. "Squid? Walnut?"

Romer stared silently out to sea. The others waited breathlessly to see how he'd react to the biker's tone.

"How much they pay you? Five grand? Ten? I'll give you fifteen not to. You don't even have to do them. I'll take care of them myself. That's just to *not* do me."

Romer kept a firm handle on the throttle and his eyes on the horizon.

Emboldened, Madame Rosa piped up. "May I just ask, sir, where you're taking us? And why?"

Crawdad snorted. "Where does it look like? He's taking us out here to kill us."

Madame Rosa, Jamie and Amee perked up, looked at Romer to hear his soothing voice reassure them and contradict the ill-mannered biker. Instead, Romer kept his eyes focused where the waves leapt angrily at the sky.

Crawdad laughed aloud. "What the fuck y'all think he was gonna do? Take us on a dinner cruise? He's gonna get into deep water, then put spears through our heads and toss us overboard!"

The others looked pleadingly at Romer. Finally he sighed and pushed the kill switch on the outboard. He pulled out the pistol he'd taken from Crawdad and dropped it overboard. "I want to apologize to all of you for what's about to happen. I mean that sincerely. I don't think of myself as this kind of man, but actions speak louder than words, so I guess I am."

Jamie blinked. "What?"

Madame Rosa elbowed him in the ribs. "He's gonna kill us, moron."

"Just think of today as an unlucky day," Romer continued. "It could happen to any of us. We wake up, everything's fine, and we get hit by a truck. Boom. It's all gone. Think of this as getting hit by a truck, being at the wrong place at the wrong time. An accident. Nothing personal. Although from what I saw in the house, none of you is exactly an innocent babe in the woods. You were all up to no good. What exactly, I can't say, and I guess it's none of my business."

"Come on!" Crawdad urged. "We can take him! The four of us, we can take him!"

Madame Rosa glared at him. "You want *me* to help *you*? You were gonna sell me into slavery, you asshole!"

Jamie lay stunned by the turn of events, his arms still soaking in the water, while Amee thrust her chest out as seductively as she could with her arms and legs tied. "You really aren't going to kill *me*, are you? I mean, I can think of a lot better things to do with me than kill me, can't you?"

Romer pulled a diver's knife from a sheath on his calf. "I have to tell you that I plan to cut your clothes away. Please don't struggle, and I won't cut you. I don't mean to inflict any unnecessary pain. And please don't worry about being naked in front of me. I'm not a sexual predator, and I'm not going to molest you."

Amee pushed herself toward him again. "You don't have to cut *my* clothes away! I'll *take* them off!"

He ignored her and leaned forward to start cutting through Crawdad's leather jacket. So he never saw the mammoth head pop up beside the dinghy, grab Jamie by the arms and pull him overboard.

Madame Rosa and Crawdad shrieked in unison as the cord tying their ankles to Jamie's ankles tightened. Romer felt the dinghy lurch, then go up on its side as the line from his captives' ankles to the center seat also became taut. Amee, Madame Rosa and Crawdad fell in with a splash as Romer used his weight to push the dinghy back on its bottom and his knife to saw through the cord tied to the center seat. If the dinghy flipped, the outboard would be doused and wouldn't start. He'd be as good as dead, with the wind and waves still pushing him out to sea.

Madame Rosa screamed and Romer cursed as he rubbed the knife's blade against the rope, slipping constantly as the nearly sideways boat was buffeted by waves and gusts of wind. With a sudden "pop" that nearly took his head off, the center seat ripped free of its mounts and flew into the darkness.

Immediately the dinghy slapped back into the water. Romer picked himself off the floor and turned just in time to see Bruce circle back from the remnants of Jamie and take a giant chomp out of Madame Rosa, Crawdad and the dinghy seat, all in the same bite, putting an instant end to the screaming.

Amee clung to the dinghy's handhold with tied wrists. Somehow her ankles had come undone, and she threw one foot up over the inflated gunwale. Romer hesitated for a moment, then grabbed her ankle and pulled upward, slowly dragging her inboard. He didn't see Bruce return until his snout jumped back up, swallowing Amee's head, torso, bare buttocks and legs.

He fell back onto the floor of the dinghy in shock, then slowly lifted his eyes above the gunwale, which was now hissing loudly. He ran his hand along the outside and picked out a triangular tooth that had torn through the fabric and into the wooden floorboard. In the water, Bruce was in a classic mako frenzy, darting back and forth between remnants of various limbs, snapping at them and shaking his head vigorously.

Romer stared in awe, finally noticed he had something in his hands. It was a bloody foot, still encircled with a thin gold ankle bracelet. Slowly he pulled the anklet free, shoved it inside the cuff of his wetsuit, then reared his arm back and heaved the foot as far he could.

It landed with a plop. Bruce immediately fixed on it and rushed it, swallowing it whole before returning to the patch of debris he was still tormenting.

Romer waited for the shark to finish cleaning up and settle down a bit before he pulled the start rope on the outboard. It caught on the second pull, and Romer pointed the bow back toward shore, dodging the bigger waves, jumping the small ones and trying as best he could to keep the punctured, port-side tube out of the water.

TWELVE

■ ■ ■

Barbie held the front door open as Nolin played the flashlight beam up and down the shelves one final time. His other arm was already loaded up with three photo albums.

"Come *on!*" She hissed.

"I'm coming," he answered calmly. "Let me get just one last look around. If only there was some actual proof that Romer brought the shark to those races."

"I thought you had videotapes of him at the beach? Isn't that enough?"

"Half the town was at the beach." He pulled open a dresser drawer for the fifth time. "We need something showing that the shark came to the races because Romer was at the races. Like if he was somehow calling it. . . . Wait a minute. You know what I haven't been able to find anywhere in the house?"

Barbie groaned. "Can we *please* leave?"

"Tapes. Cassette tapes. Not anywhere. But in both videos, Romer is wearing a Walkman. In fact, it's just like the Walkman we found at my house. . . . No *wonder* it doesn't play tapes!" Nolin exclaimed. "I bet Romer modified it into some kind of radio transmitter, to call his shark."

He stepped back over the bed and walked toward Barbie. "I left it in the truck back at the park. Let's go."

Barbie started at the sound of tires on gravel, slammed the door just before headlights swung onto the house. "Great! He's home!" she whispered. "Now what?"

"Hide." He pointed the flashlight back along the main corridor. "In the surfboard room."

For just a moment, the new bravado vanished as Nick wondered how he was going to give Romer $300,000 in front of Joanna, when she had only given him $50,000. The worry nagged him until she grabbed his arm and pressed her bosom up against it.

"Are you sure this is the right place?" she whispered as he led her around the side to the back porch.

The nagging fear vanished, and James Bond was back. *Let* her see all her "grease" money, and let her know what was going to happen with it, and he would watch her face as surprise, then anger, and finally fear spread across it. "Be careful of the sandspurs," he warned as they stepped through the grass, and she pressed her breast even tighter.

They got to the patio and Nick stuck his face to the glass door to look inside, while Joanna hugged herself to keep warm in the whistling wind. "I can't believe she's finally gone." She walked up behind Nick and put a pudgy well-manicured hand on his hip. "You know," she whispered, "with her gone, there's nothing to keep us from living like man and wife. Wouldn't that be nice?"

He glanced down at the outline of her curves in the gloom. The thought both excited and repulsed him, and he remembered his date with Amee and her new girlfriend later that night. A tall dark-haired girl, and not a curly hair between them, Amee had promised.

"Yeah, sure," he said gruffly. "I'm kind of busy tonight, though."

"Oh." She pulled her hand back and crossed her arms. "Is it another woman?"

He said nothing and instead moved over to the kitchen window. She idly picked sandspurs off the satin gown.

"You know, it's not fair for you to keep seeing other girls and then come home to me. I thought I meant something to you."

He half wished the mean, domineering Joanna was back. He bit his tongue; she wouldn't be nagging him too much longer. "Okay, Joanna. I'll stop seeing other women," he lied. "I wonder where the hell Romer is?"

"Right here."

Nick turned to find Joanna's neck in the crook of Romer's arm, his spear gun against her back. "Who the hell is this?" Romer demanded.

"That's Joanna," Nick said. "You know. My stepmother."

"Your stepmother?" Romer stared at Nick quizzically. "You *brought* her here?"

Nick's heart raced. Surely he wouldn't kill her right *now*, right before his very eyes. Would he? "Sure," Nick shrugged, and let his breath out when Romer lowered the gun and unwrapped his arm from her throat.

Romer strode to the back door, unlocked it with a key on a chain around his neck and ushered them inside, flicking on a light in the corner of his workshop. "You know, it was a lot more work than we bargained for. There were four of them, and I ruined my inflatable. I expect reasonable compensation."

"*Four* of them?" Nick asked.

"There was her, her boyfriend, a big fat biker with two broken arms and a broken leg, and some gypsy woman. Her name was Rosa. At least that's what her charm bracelet said."

Nick stared at him openmouthed. Crawdad? Madame Rosa? What the hell was going on? They were conspiring with her, that's what was going on. Crawdad must have found out that Nick tried to have him killed, and was plotting something with Barbie. And Madame Rosa . . . Well, it didn't matter. "You killed them all?"

"They were there." Romer shrugged, turned his beady eyes back on Joanna, who had clung to Nick for protection. "A lesson I learned in Laos thirty years ago. There's no complaints about atrocities if there's no one left to complain."

Nick rocked back on his heels, forward again, trying to dispel the chill that had grabbed hold of his spine.

"You brought the money?" Romer asked.

Nick squeezed the handles on the overnight bag. "You're sure about Barbie, right?"

Romer reached inside his wetsuit cuff, pulled out the thin gold chain with the tiny heart-shaped pendant and threw it to Nick. "I figured you'd want proof."

Nick caught the chain. "I wonder when she started wearing an ankle bracelet." Then he recognized it and reeled backward, overcome by a vision of Amee, astride him in full naked splendor except for the trinket he'd just given her. "Oh no."

"What?" Joanna asked, digging her spiked heels into the floor to support his sagging weight.

"Oh no," Nick repeated, turning the chain over in his hand. Finally he raised a stricken look to Romer. "This girl was about five-three, a hundred and twenty pounds, nice ass, big tits? Wearing a red thong?"

Romer nodded. "So?"

"It was a birthday present." Nick fingered the tiny heart. "Are you sure she's dead? Maybe we can still save her?"

"Who *is* she?" Joanna demanded icily.

Romer thought about the job Bruce had done on the girl. "No, I'd definitely say she's beyond saving. What you've got in your hands is the only thing that wasn't returned to the food chain."

Nick rocked again, collapsed on the floor holding the anklet, the James Bond persona now completely vanished. He had *fed* her to his pet shark! Now he'd never get his threesome! Worse, Joanna would likely kill him.

Suddenly she stepped out from behind the heap he made on the floor and glared at Romer, arms crossed. "So, I take it that whoever this little tramp was, she wasn't Barbie. Am I correct?"

Romer's eyes narrowed as the scene in Barbie's house played through his head. "Did you hire that biker to kill her? And that idiot kid? Plus the guy with the rifle who got it last night. How many people did you hire for this?"

Joanna whirled on Nick. "The guy with the rifle? You mean M.J. Weathers? What happened to M.J.?"

Nick sat on the floor helplessly, clutching the overnight bag and the ankle chain. The thought occurred to him that he definitely couldn't let Joanna see how much money was in the bag; she'd know instantly where he'd gotten it.

Joanna turned back to Romer. "Obviously, I'm going to have to take care of this myself."

A crash sounded in the next room; Romer hit the light switch and dove across the floor into a pile of fallen surfboards, coming to his knees with Barbie's ankle in his hands.

"Go!" Barbie screamed. "Get help! Tell them what happened!"

Outside the window Nolin hesitated, one arm holding two thick photo albums, the other still grasping Barbie's hand.

Romer stood, transferred his hold to around her neck and stared at Nolin. "Sure, you'd probably be able to escape. But I doubt you'd be able to get back in time. If you stay, you just might be able to help her. On the other hand, you might not. I'm a trained killer, you know. I could puncture her larynx with this little finger." He waved his pinkie at him.

"Just go!" Barbie repeated. "Tell them what we heard!"

"It's a tough call, I know," Romer said. "You could get killed if you stay. But would you be able to live with yourself if you left and she died? I doubt it."

Nolin swallowed, passed the photo albums back through the window to Romer, then hoisted himself back through the window. Romer whirled Barbie around and studied her head to toe. "Barbie Van Horne, I presume?" He turned to Nick, who had finally managed to pick himself up off the floor. "Why didn't you tell me you were married to the Nipple Girl? I wouldn't have wasted my time killing those others."

Romer waited until they had cleared the stone jetties before he tweaked the twin throttles forward an inch. The *Checkered Flag* surged forward, her turbocharged diesels spewing heavy smoke with the increased load before adjusting to the higher rpm. Nick stood on one side of him on the bridge, his overnight bag gathered to his chest, and Joanna stood on the other, rapping her fingernails on the teak console.

"Can't you go any faster?" she said. "I'm hosting a party I've got to get back to."

Romer stepped back from the wheel. "Be my guest."

"No!" she shouted. "I already told you we don't know how. That's why we have a captain."

Romer slid his hands back onto the stainless steel wheel and steered a hair to the right. The wind had risen to nearly gale force, and the *Checkered Flag* surged ahead of the building waves in the channel. "The Green Number Two buoy out here's got a broken light," Romer muttered. "It would really screw up our night if we hit it."

Finally he saw the dark shape off the starboard bow and slid the throttles forward another two inches. *Checkered Flag* lifted her bow in the air and began planing through the dark night.

"There," he said, flipping a switch on the console to engage the autopilot. "We'll be far enough offshore in just a few minutes."

Joanna leaned forward against the console and grabbed the handrails on the deckhead. "Far enough for what, exactly?"

"Far enough so that, with this wind for the next day or so, anything we throw overboard will be blown into the Gulf Stream. From there, the next stop is Cape Hatteras." He turned to Nick, who looked pale and green even in the dim red lamps of the bridge. "So did you bring all my money, Mr. Bachs? I'll expect an extra harbor pilot's fee, you know."

Nick suppressed an uncomfortable burp and lifted the bag. "All here."

Romer nodded and studied Joanna. She had kicked off her high heels once she realized the floor would be moving, but she couldn't do much about the long evening gown that clung to her as far down as her thighs. She left her post and maneuvered her way next to Nick to get in his face.

"So who was that slut you were so broken up about?" she demanded. "You were buying her jewelry? And what else?"

Nick burped again, struggled to get air. He was starting to sweat, despite the chill. "She was nothing," he muttered.

"Nothing? Well, I have half a mind to cut your allowance. That ought to cut down on gifts to tramp girlfriends." She lowered her voice to a loud whisper. "If you expect to share my bed, you'd best make sure you're not sharing anyone else's. Do I make myself clear?"

Romer watched in amusement, shook his head. "Aren't you his *mother*?"

"Stepmother," Joanna snapped. "And mind your own business."

Barbie leaned her head close to Nolin's ear and shouted: "I'm sorry I got you into this."

Nolin barely heard her over the roar of the diesels. "It's not your fault. It's *their* fault." He tried to jiggle his hands again, but even his fingers were tightly bound. He tried his feet, but there was no play there, either. Romer was clearly not an amateur. "Maybe we can still talk them out of it. I'll tell them about the videotapes in my safe. Maybe that'll change their minds."

"The tapes of the boat races? I thought they were on my living room table."

"I won't tell them *that* part." He lifted his eyes to the little runabout secured on davits above their heads. It had an enormous, seventy-five-horsepower Johnson clamped to its stern, and was held aloft by two cables that ran through the hoists and down to a box on deck. A rotary switch selected between "manual" and "winch," with a lever next to it marked "locked" and "hoist."

He tried wiggling his fingers again, but still couldn't budge them. He could've used his toes, but his tennis shoes were still on and tied. He looked in exasperation around the deck, and settled on Barbie's feet. Bare feet, with long, ungainly, wonderful toes; she had lost her sandals at Romer's house.

"Barbie," he shouted over the engines. "Turn around. See that little dial on that box?"

. . .

Romer eased back on the twin throttles, and the diesels rumbled down to an idle. "This is about far enough."

He pushed the kill switch, and the engines gasped and died. *Checkered Flag* quickly lost her forward way, and soon turned broadside to the wind and began to wallow. Nick's eyes grew wide; he let go of the grabrail to cover his mouth and ran out the cabin door.

"Be sure and puke to leeward," Romer shouted as Nick stumbled over the sill, staggered to the windward side of the boat and vomited into the gusty wind, which promptly deposited much of the stream back on his already damp tuxedo shirt. Five ejections later he collapsed in a putrid heap on the teak deck, the brown leather bag still clutched to his belly.

In his haste, he hadn't noticed Barbie manipulating the hoist-control box with her feet. And in his red-eyed agony, he didn't notice her scramble back into position just as Joanna and Romer walked through the cabin door and out onto the rolling deck. Joanna had picked up Romer's spear gun from the pilot berth in the bridge and carried it, infantry style, across her chest.

Joanna walked over to Nick and prodded his butt with a pedicured, pearl-enameled toe. "Come on. Let's get this over with so we can get back." She sniffed the air and made a face. "You smell awful. You'll have to shower and change. I hope you have another shirt pressed."

She looked down at her own dress, frayed at the hem, stained from spear-gun grease and God only knew what else. "I'll have to change, too, which means people will talk, make snide remarks about us both having showered and changed," she muttered. "Well, let them. To hell with them."

Nolin studied the control box out of the corner of his eye. If he could just step on the lever, they had a chance. A minuscule chance, sure, but it was better than getting skewered and left for shark bait.

Romer nodded to him in greeting. "I just want you to know that it's nothing personal. Think of it as a real unlucky day. As if you were to get hit by a truck while crossing the street. Just bad luck."

"Yeah? Well, I suppose a little stint on Death Row is just a little bad luck, too," Nolin blustered. "Like when the cops get hold of those videotapes from my safe. The ones Van Horne had me hold onto so he could blackmail you into killing Barbie."

Romer smiled. "You mean, by chance, the tapes you left on your girl-friend's living room table? Thanks, I got them. Not that they have enough evidence on them to prosecute anyone. Not without the Walkman, which, by the way, I took the liberty of retrieving from your car, as well."

Joanna snorted in frustration and shoved the spear gun at Nick. "Here. Hurry up and do it."

He studied the unfamiliar weapon with bleary eyes. "Why do *I* have to do it? I thought that's why we brought *him*?"

Joanna turned to Romer. "Well? What do we do now?"

Romer glanced at Nolin and Barbie for a moment, swayed from one leg to the other to counteract the swaying of the deck. He shrugged. "Nothing. We're ten miles from shore. They're bound. They can't swim. When we throw them over, they'll drown." He turned to Nick. "In fact, someone who fell in way out here, even if they *weren't* tied up, they wouldn't make it."

Joanna blinked. "What's *that* supposed to mean?"

"Can I just ask one question?" Barbie blurted. "Why?"

"Oh, shut up," Joanna snapped. "You brought this on yourself. I offered you a lot of money not to marry J.R. in the first place, then I offered a lot more to mind your own business and leave us alone. Well, the time for begging is over."

"Not you." Barbie stared at Romer. "I mean you. Why? The money? I can't believe that."

He considered the question for a moment. "Never take a surfer's waves away from him. The perfect wave is as close to God as we'll ever get in this world. Your damn theme park would have infested everything from Daytona Shores clear down to Ponce Inlet with those asshole Jet Skiers."

"*My* theme park!" Barbie yelled. "That's *Joanna's* idea from start to finish! That's why they're trying to kill me, because I'm suing the county to protect the sea turtle habitat! You should be after her!"

Romer's face darkened, turned toward Nick. "Is this true?"

"I can't believe we're arguing about this!" Joanna shouted. "Throw the two of them overboard right this minute or we're not paying you a dime!"

"Is it true?" Romer insisted.

Nick swallowed, fumbled with the spear gun.

"Kill them now!" Joanna demanded.

"It *is* true, isn't it?" Romer stepped toward Nick. "In light of this information, consider yourself in breach of contract. I'm not going to kill those two. I won't have them on my conscience." He glanced at a wild-eyed Joanna. "But I think I *will* take you up on that offer about Joanna. Did you bring the two hundred grand?"

Joanna turned to Nick. "Two hundred thousand? To kill *me*?" She grabbed the overnight bag from him, yanked open the zipper. Her eyes blazed. "You got this from my safe, didn't you? *That's* why you were in my room, wasn't it?"

Romer kept stepping toward Nick. "Our agreement still stands? I kill Joanna, you pay me two hundred grand. Right?"

Nick swallowed again, lifted the spear gun, looked at it up and down for a safety catch. "She has to die after Barbie. Otherwise Barbie gets some of the money."

Joanna gasped. "You vile piece of shit! And to think I put that disgusting, shriveled little thing in my mouth! You're going to regret this day as long as you live, John Robert Van Horne. You point that gun at that son of a bitch and pull the trigger right now, you understand?"

Romer stopped two paces from Nick. "What's it going to be, Nick? You're the man. You've got the gun. You're empowered. You choose. Point the gun and pull the trigger. Kill me and you live under her thumb the rest of your pathetic days. Kill her and you're a free man. What'll it be?"

Nick's hands quavered. He looked at Romer, then Joanna. Her eyes burned through him. He swallowed again, found the safety and released it.

"Shoot him!" Joanna ordered.

Without warning he felt a tidal wave developing in his stomach, surging upward. He dropped the gun and rose to his knees, his head over the rail, his mouth spewing what little was left in his belly. Romer shook his head as Joanna bent for the gun, aimed it at him. He feinted left, cut right and sprinted for the leeward railing, then dove headfirst at the crest of a wave and cleared the bulwark as the spear whistled by his head.

He parted the waves cleanly as Joanna ran to the rail to search for him in the dark water, hands fumbling with the gun to reload. Behind her Nolin kneeled next to the hoist control, with bound hands pushed down on the chrome lever with all his might. It wouldn't budge. He repositioned himself to get his weight above it, and Barbie crawled over to help, all under Nick's bloodshot gaze.

"Joanna," Nick called feebly.

"Shut up," she shouted. "And come help me find that son of a bitch. He's out there somewhere."

"Joanna . . ." Nick tried again.

And the lever moved with a click, letting the runabout fall the ten feet from its davits down to the water, hitting the surface with a loud splash. Joanna whirled around, the spear gun loaded but not cocked, as Nolin and Barbie struggled to their feet.

"What the—"

And Nolin kicked her legs out from under her, sending them both to the deck. "Go!" he shouted at Barbie, and rose to his knees, then his feet, hopping toward the railing against the pitch and roll of the boat. "Over! Hurry!"

Nolin pushed Barbie over the side, then tipped himself over as Joanna's second missile dug its way into the teak caprail, a howl of anger behind it.

The cold water was shocking, then bracing as he gasped lungfuls of air between waves that broke over his head, bounced off *Checkered Flag*'s hull, then crashed over his head a second time.

"Over here!"

He turned and saw Barbie had made it to the runabout's side and was hanging by a handhold, trying to swing her legs over the side. He dog-paddled over and grabbed the second plastic handhold as the runabout began swinging close to *Checkered Flag*'s transom.

"Look! They're over there!" Nick was at the rail, pointing at the runabout as Joanna tried to load the third arrow in the quiver into the gun.

"I can't swing up like this," Nolin shouted between breaking waves. "We got to get something untied or we're gonna drown!"

Barbie lifted her legs to the surface, putting her feet on his chest. "Put your legs up here!"

A flash of steel whistled past their heads and stuck into the rigid bottom of the runabout, accompanied by a loud "Shit!" He let his legs float to the surface, and she grabbed at the loose ends of the knots with her toes, losing them with the rise of each passing wave, then re-grabbing them in the trough. Her arms strained at the effort as water splashed over her head.

Finally Nolin felt the pressure around his ankles slacken, and began pulling them apart. "Hold still," Barbie ordered. "Almost there . . . Got it!"

Nolin's legs were free. He took a deep breath, pulled up with his arms and swung one leg over the runabout's gunwale, then the other. He stopped to exhale, then turned to hook his bound hands under Barbie's and leaned back until a helpful wave sent her sprawling atop him.

"I'm exhausted," she gasped as above them, Joanna pointed at them and cursed at Nick.

"No rest yet," Nolin said. "She's trying to reel us back in. Quick, get that front cable off."

As they moved to either end of the boat, an electric motor started to hum. The loose cables began to take in their slack.

"They got the winch started!" Nolin shouted. "Quick!"

The cables were attached to the runabout with pelican hooks secured with pins. He fumbled with immobile fingers against the wet metal, scratching and cutting his hands as the slack quickly disappeared.

"Got it!" Barbie shouted triumphantly behind him.

He watched the runabout's bow swing away from *Checkered Flag* as the single cable on the stern continued drawing straight. He swallowed hard; once it was taut, there would be no way he could force the hook open.

He slapped at it with the heel of his hand, opening yet another cut, but he saw that the pin had come free. With bleeding fingers, he pushed the gate off the tip of the hook and bent it open. The cable tightened and pulled the hook out of the metal ring at the stern. The next wave pushed the runabout beneath the swinging cables and away from *Checkered Flag*. They watched for a moment as Joanna waved a fist at them, then cuffed Nick in the ear, pointing at the far railing.

"Now we need to get out of here." Nolin studied the cord binding his fingers. Romer had picked Dacron, so it wouldn't stretch when wet. "And for that we're going to need our hands."

Nick gulped back another burp, wrapped his hands around the shaft of the spear and leaned his considerable bulk backward. Still the shaft refused to budge. He released it, wiped the sweat from his hands onto his tuxedo trousers, fought back another wave of nausea and tried again.

"Hurry it up, you moron!" Joanna screamed.

He cursed her under his breath. If she hadn't missed all three times, she wouldn't be needing him to dig this one out of the railing. He wondered wistfully what he had eaten that had given him such cockiness earlier. Or maybe it was just the sex. Whatever it was, it was gone now, and he knew he wouldn't dare lift a finger against her again.

"I don't believe it!" Joanna stood at the aft railing, the wind whistling through the torn gown that fluttered off to one side. "He's playing with her toes!"

Nick let go of the spear and walked back to the aft rail, squinted out into the dark night. "No. He's getting her to untie his hands. She's got amazing toes." He nodded.

Joanna turned to him in amazement. "The *spear*, you idiot!"

He stumbled back to the rail, leaned over to puke again, then grasped the shaft and threw his weight backward. The fluted rim at the back cut into his palms, but he had felt it move. More confident, he grabbed it again, clamped down tightly and pushed off the bulwark with his feet.

Helped by a wave, he flew backward, falling flat on his back and sliding several feet along the teak deck, the freed spear in his bloody hands and a satisfied smile on his face. "I got it!" But over the whistle of the wind and the slosh of the water, he heard a new sound: the high-pitched whine of an outboard.

Joanna turned toward him, mouth agape. "She untied him with her feet, and now they're leaving."

Nolin stood with knees bent, trying to absorb most of the shock as the little runabout leapt high off a crest and landed with a crash in the trough. He kept one hand on the wheel, the other on the throttle, easing off when the prop was ventilating to keep the engine from burning up, pushing it forward as they fell back in the water.

Barbie stood beside him, hanging onto the console with white knuckles. She let out a cry as they remained airborne for what seemed like a full minute before crashing onto the backside of the wave. "How many of those can we take?" she screamed.

He shook his head. "I have no idea. I've never driven a rigid inflatable before. I'm trying to go around the really big ones, but some of these I can't help. I'm not even going that fast. You're sure Nick doesn't know how to drive that thing, right?"

"Positive. He's afraid to be out on a flat day, let alone in weather like this."

Her ears picked up a new sound, though, a deeper rumble over their own whine, and she turned around to see the red-and-green lights of *Checkered Flag* directly behind them, illuminating the spray kicking off the bow beneath as the trawler charged through and above the waves.

She tugged at Nolin's shirt and leaned toward his ear. "I take that back. Go *faster!*"

Romer squinted his eyes against the stinging spray, trying to catch a breath in each trough before the bow hit the next crest. His bare feet gripped *Checkered Flag*'s rubrail, and his fingers clawed the bronze lip of a porthole.

He had been creeping forward along the hull when the big diesels roared to life and the mighty trawler pointed her nose into the wind and waves. Somehow the girl and her boyfriend had managed to get the runabout in the water, climb in, untie each other and head back for home. He shook his head in amazement. Well, good luck to them. If they made it back, they certainly deserved it.

He held his grip while trying to relax his other muscles. He would need them for what he still had to do. He couldn't make any progress in these seas, but the waves would diminish as they closed land. Then he'd be able to work his way forward and climb the rest of the hull using the anchor hawse pipe by the bowsprit. Then he would take care of the Van Hornes once and for all.

Without warning the trawler hit an exceptionally large wave, washing his feet off the rubrail and leaving him hanging by his fingertips. Calmly he found the rail with his toes and reestablished his grip. Just a few more minutes . . .

Nick balanced against the slight roll by shifting his weight from leg to leg, focusing on the tiny boat still a hundred yards ahead. His nausea had disappeared, now that *Checkered Flag* was planing again, and he decided he rather liked driving her. In the future he would avail himself of the opportunity frequently. The society girls would love to go out on a big luxury yacht like this. In fact, he bet a lot of those stuck-up little prissies who were too high and mighty to wear a bikini on the public beach would probably go topless, or even better, if they were alone with Captain Nick.

"You know what? I kinda like this. I'm gonna do this more often."

He glanced at his stepmother, now falling out of her ragged dress. She stood with both hands on the console, her toes curled against the varnished teak sole. A larger-than-average wave made the cockpit lurch, and a spaghetti strap slipped off her shoulder to reveal a pale white breast that jiggled with the engine's vibration. She covered herself hastily.

"You know, you have really nice tits for a woman your age," Nick said expansively.

She glared at him with burning eyes. "Shut up and drive, idiot. You couldn't even figure out how to start the engines, remember? And don't think I've forgotten about your little deal with Randy Romer. You just wait till we get home. You think you have a tiny allowance *now*? Wait till I get done with it."

Nick's chest deflated and his shoulders sank. She was going to make his life a living hell. If only he'd turned the spear gun on her when he had the chance. Now it was too late.

"Speed up, or we're never going to catch them!" She slapped his cheek with a quick backhand. "You want 'em to get to the beach and go running to the cops?"

Meekly he lifted a hand to the throttles and slid them forward another inch. *Checkered Flag*'s bow lifted completely out of the water. He snuck a sideways glance before turning his eyes quickly back to the runabout's wake in front of him.

Well, maybe after they'd run down Barbie and her boyfriend, she'd calm down a little.

It wasn't the food signal, but it was familiar . . . Two separate high-pitched noises, moving quickly from left to right.

Yes, now he remembered. It was just a few days ago. The high-pitched noises, then a loud crack, and the noises stopped, and then: food! Lots of it! Just floating on the surface, waiting to be plucked down. He wasn't particularly hungry, but food was food. He would need to investigate.

Somewhere in the folds of his brain, an intercept course was plotted and with a swish of his tail, he was off.

Barbie looked back over her shoulder, snapped her head forward. "They're gaining!"

Nick snuck a peek, saw the red-and-green running lights were now flying high above the water and closing fast. He ground his teeth, turned back to the mangled seascape ahead. Over the largest waves he could see the occasional blink of light from the beach. They weren't far now . . .

He would have to risk it. Slowly, waiting for a trough, he pushed the throttle right to the forward stop and grabbed the wheel in both hands as the runabout flew off wavetops, bounced off the backs and instantly took off again.

His palms bled from where his nails wrapped around the wheel and dug in; only a couple more miles . . .

Romer felt more than saw the lessening of the seas. He turned his head into the spray and opened an eye. Sure enough, Ponce Inlet Lighthouse was maybe a mile and a half off and closing fast.

He took a deep breath and started inching along the skinny rubrail, reaching from porthole to porthole for fingerholds. Slowly he made his way forward until he was at the anchor hawse hole. There he waited a few moments, and the waves shrank noticeably.

With another deep breath, he leapt the few inches to the hawse pipe and swung his legs up to the bowsprit.

Nick steered sullenly, occasionally glancing at Joanna. It wasn't fair. None of it. Why couldn't *he* have a good life, too? He deserved it. After all, it was *his* granddad who started the track, not Joanna's and certainly not Barbie's. He could see her now, clinging to the console of the little boat, shoulder to shoulder with that lawyer. *His* lawyer, no less, the traitor. Probably was seeing him even before she moved out, the slut.

If only she'd been a better wife, none of this would have happened. Even if she'd just stayed out of his business, none of this would have happened, and Joanna wouldn't be cutting off his allowance. And Cherry would still be alive, dancing around in her bright red thong. Yup, it was all Barbie's doing. All of it. Come to think of it, Joanna had a point. He *would* be better off with her gone.

So when Joanna shouted, "Faster, idiot!" again, he was only too happy to jam the throttle knobs all the way forward. The bow lifted before him, blotting out the runabout, the wake, even the horizon.

· · ·

Barbie watched, heart in her throat, as the big white bow loomed up behind. There were barely two boat lengths between them.

"They're almost on top of us!" she shouted, turned back forward and screamed aloud. "Pedro!"

He nodded, leaning to move their weight as far forward as possible and help the propeller take a deeper bite. "I see it. I'm just hoping they don't."

Not two hundred yards ahead was the silhouette of the unlit buoy, looming ever taller, a growing shadow on the horizon. Nolin tightened his grip on the wheel, preparing to jerk it starboard. He wondered idly if the hull would keep its hold on the surface or if they would flip over. Well, they would soon find out.

"Hold on tight, and get ready to lean left!" he shouted into the stinging spray. "Just another few seconds . . ."

Nick clenched his jaw; any moment now he would hear the satisfying crunch that would tell him he'd caught Barbie and her shyster boyfriend. He cocked his ears, listening carefully, waiting for any telltale noise. Any noise at all.

So that when Romer swung up and over the bowsprit not ten feet in front of him, the shock for a moment froze him, then drew a terrible scream from his lungs as Romer stood on the bowsprit, then like magic, like he had wings, suddenly took off and flew forward into the night.

And then the crash split his eardrums and his stomach in a sickening, soggy crumple of fiberglass on steel. *Checkered Flag* went airborne for a second, landed with a surprisingly soft plop as Nick bounced off the instrument console, then tumbled against the bridge's aft wall. His legs tangled with Joanna's, his hands caught in her hair, in the spaghetti straps of her torn dress. And suddenly they were up to their waists in water, the cabin sole sinking beneath them.

He stood, slogged through the open door toward the bulwarks, stared in bewilderment at the shattered bowsprit, at the buckled teak deck, then a hundred feet behind him at the solid, green, unblinking metal buoy. So *that* was the culprit . . .

"The bag, you idiot!"

It was Joanna, treading water just beyond the fast-disappearing bulwarks, pointing at the leather overnight bag bobbing in the water a few feet away. He began treading water himself as *Checkered Flag*'s deck sank beneath the reach of his feet.

"Go get it!" Joanna demanded. "It's *my* goddamned money."

He began stroking water toward the bag, watching the buoy the whole time. How the hell had *that* gotten there? How come he hadn't seen it? And finally he noticed the big gray fin, just a few feet away. He stopped moving, tried not to breathe as it circled him, edged toward the bag. His heart pounded. Surely it would hear him . . .

"What's the matter with you? Get the *bag*!" Joanna shouted, all the louder now without the rumble of the giant turbo diesels. "Oh, the hell with it. I'll get it."

She took three powerful strokes toward the bag. Nick gently pushed himself away as the fin circled the bag, bumped the bag; Joanna splashed ahead, heedless, reached for the bag, grabbed the bag. And the mighty tail swished once, the back arched, and enormous jaws spread and crashed down on the bag and an attached arm.

She screamed, grabbed at the bag with her other arm. "You son of a bitch, give that *back*!"

And the jaws snapped and the head shook, and the frenzy began. Wads of chewed thousand-dollar bills flew past Nick, along with bits and pieces of Joanna's arms, torso, and legs, still clad in skin-tight gown. Nick turned and began slapping toward shore, kicking his tuxedo-trousered legs as best he could. He felt the bump against his knees and kicked even harder, except he wasn't moving anymore. And then he saw the shark turn a few yards away, his tuxedo-trousered legs in its jaws.

And his vision darkened suddenly as he passed out.

Nolin leaned over the runabout's gunwale and picked out the scrap of pearl-colored gown. Tears and three ragged puncture marks marred the once lustrous fabric. He scanned the black surface for any more remains, but there were none. The shark had been thorough. Again he examined the piece of satin. Two seams joined at a point to give the fabric some fullness, and the remnant of a spaghetti strap was sewn to the edge. Part of the bust, he decided.

He sighed, wrapped his arms around Barbie and pulled her close. "I guess this resolves the moral dilemma of whether to pick them up."

Barbie turned her head from his chest to study the wind-rippled surface near the buoy. "It ate them *both*?"

"Every last bit. Except for this." He held up the scrap of Joanna's dress. By the time they had caught their breath and returned to the buoy, the shark was finishing his frenzy, snapping at empty water before finally submerging. "I guess he was hungry."

Barbie shook her head sadly. "Now what?"

Nolin shrugged. "Well, for starters, it looks like you win your lawsuit. The county attorney will drop his objections when I tell him what happened tonight. With the Van Hornes and their goons gone, it looks like the beaches will be safe for turtles after all. You did it, baby. You beat them."

Barbie sighed again, snuggled next to him to get out of the wind. "I can't believe Madame Rosa was in on it."

He nodded. "I guess you need a new spiritual adviser."

"Yeah. Serves me right for going with a crystal-ball psychic. They're all frauds." She looked up with the beginnings of a smile. "I'll go with tarot cards next time."

He laughed, pulled himself free to step back to the outboard. "I guess we better head in before the wind pushes us back out there." He pulled the starter rope and the big Johnson purred on the first try.

She looked over the runabout from stern to bow. "What should we do with this?"

He stepped to the console. "Whatever you want. It's yours, now. As well as the Van Horne house, all their bank accounts. Oh yeah: and three major stock car tracks in the Southeast."

"I guess I hadn't thought of that." Her eyes widened as an idea flashed through her head. "Can I do *anything* I want with them? Can I close them? Maybe turn them into marine biology research centers?"

Nolin nodded slowly. "You could, but as your attorney, I'd advise against that, unless you want three million pissed-off bubbas to come down here with their pickups and their shotguns. On the other hand, if you *sold* them, you'd probably net, oh, four hundred, five hundred million. You could open a dozen marine biology labs all over Florida. All over the world, for that matter. Shoot, you could *buy* Woods Hole, if you wanted."

She thought it over in stunned silence. "Yeah. I guess I could."

He slid the throttle forward until it engaged into gear. "Where to?"

With a heavy sigh, she moved to his side and pulled his free arm around her. "Home."

Romer listened carefully as he lay face up, his ears submerged in the cold water. Nothing. Finally they were gone.

He turned onto his belly and began a slow, rhythmic stroke toward the beach, careful to avoid splashes or irregular movements. Bruce had gorged himself and calmed down, but it wouldn't take much to rile him back up. Romer stroked evenly, calmly. He could have stroked the twenty-five miles up to Flagler, if he wanted. But he could still walk faster than he could swim, and it had already been a long night.

As soon as he got home, he'd have to pack his things and leave, of course. The surfboards would have to stay behind. As would the wave tank. But he could make more surfboards, and buy another wave tank. He might even be able to hook up with Bruce again, someday.

He cleared his mind and concentrated on his stroke: left, right, left, breathe; left, right, left, breathe. Soon he could touch bottom, and then he was through the surf. He zipped up his wetsuit as high as he could, and began the long, cold walk home.

THIRTEEN

■■■

Circuit Court Judge Anthony Antoon stared down over his spectacles, his mouth slightly open, his pen lightly rapping his notebook.

"And that's how it stands, Your Honor," Nolin finished.

For a minute Antoon sat brooding, staring alternately at Nolin, then the county attorney. Nolin had asked for a sidebar conference at nine-thirty. It was now ten. Fifty prospective jurors sat on the opposite side of the railing, wearing big yellow "Juror" buttons and bored expressions.

"So I understand correctly," Antoon murmured, his voice low. "You suggest that if this case proceeds to trial, this entire story will come out, including the Van Hornes' employment of the former state attorney of this county and his . . . *trained* shark to murder your client in order to stop her lawsuit?"

"That's correct, Your Honor. We haven't gone to the police, because my client is satisfied the threat to her life is ended, and she has no desire for any publicity in this matter. However, if my client takes the stand, she will naturally testify to the measures that some in this community took to stop her." Nolin gathered his thoughts. This would be a tricky moment.

"Testimony like that is sure to attract national press attention, including the tabloid television that I know everyone in this town is so tired of."

Nolin let that settle, hoping the threat had been subtle enough not to piss him off yet strong enough to convey the message.

Antoon turned toward the county attorney. "And the county's position, counselor?"

The county attorney cleared his throat, leaned closer to the judge. "Your Honor, I must again stress that my office had absolutely *no* knowledge of anything the Van Horne family may have done. None. But given the circumstances, we believe it's in the county's interest to avoid the type of publicity a public airing of these charges might bring."

Antoon rapped his pencil faster. "So you're saying . . . ?"

The county attorney grimaced painfully. "That we concede, Your Honor. From State Road 40 northward, and U.S. 92 southward, including all of the beach south of Ponce Inlet, vehicle traffic shall be excluded within thirty days. And traffic will be excluded from the remaining six miles as off-beach parking is added, no later than two years from the date of your order."

Antoon shook his head. "I guess, Mr. Nolin, that your client has managed the impossible. Write me an order, and I'll sign it this afternoon."

Nolin walked back toward his table, beaming at Barbie. She smiled back, gave his hand a quick squeeze but dropped it when she caught a stern look from Judge Antoon.

Antoon lifted his gaze to the prospective jurors. "Ladies and gentlemen, thank you for your attendance and your patience. However, the parties have agreed on a settlement, and your services will not be required. Please hand your juror buttons back to the clerk downstairs, and both I and the parties thank you for your time. You are dismissed. Court adjourned."

The judge ducked out the back way, the jurors filed out, the county attorney shut the snaps on his case and left.

Barbie and Nolin slowly gathered his papers and walked up the aisle, arm in arm.